ARCFIRE
OF
ANTIQUITY

THE INCURSION CHRONICLES

ARCFIRE OF ANTIQUITY

ERIC N. LARD

4 Horsemen
Publications, Inc.

DEDICATION

My wife, who inspires me to be a better father. My boys, who inspire me to be a better person. My parents, the four of them, who still speak wisdom into my life. My beta readers, Bill, Taylor, and James, all who share my last name, as well as Sue McKern, Tim Marquitz, SK Marre (pen name), and Rachel Csabi, whom I name here because their input and encouragement helped craft the words that follow. God, because he cared to know me first.

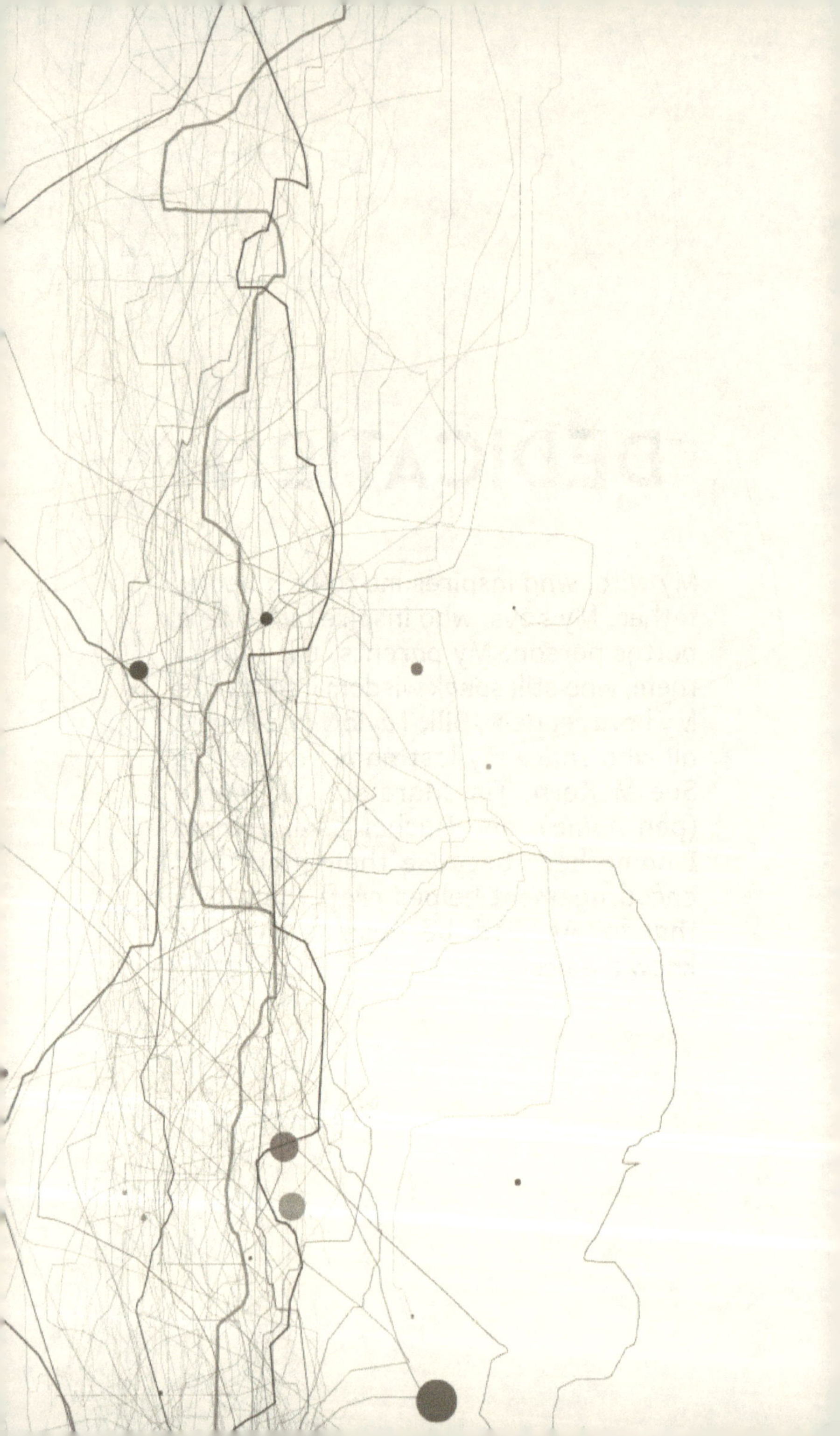

TABLE OF CONTENTS

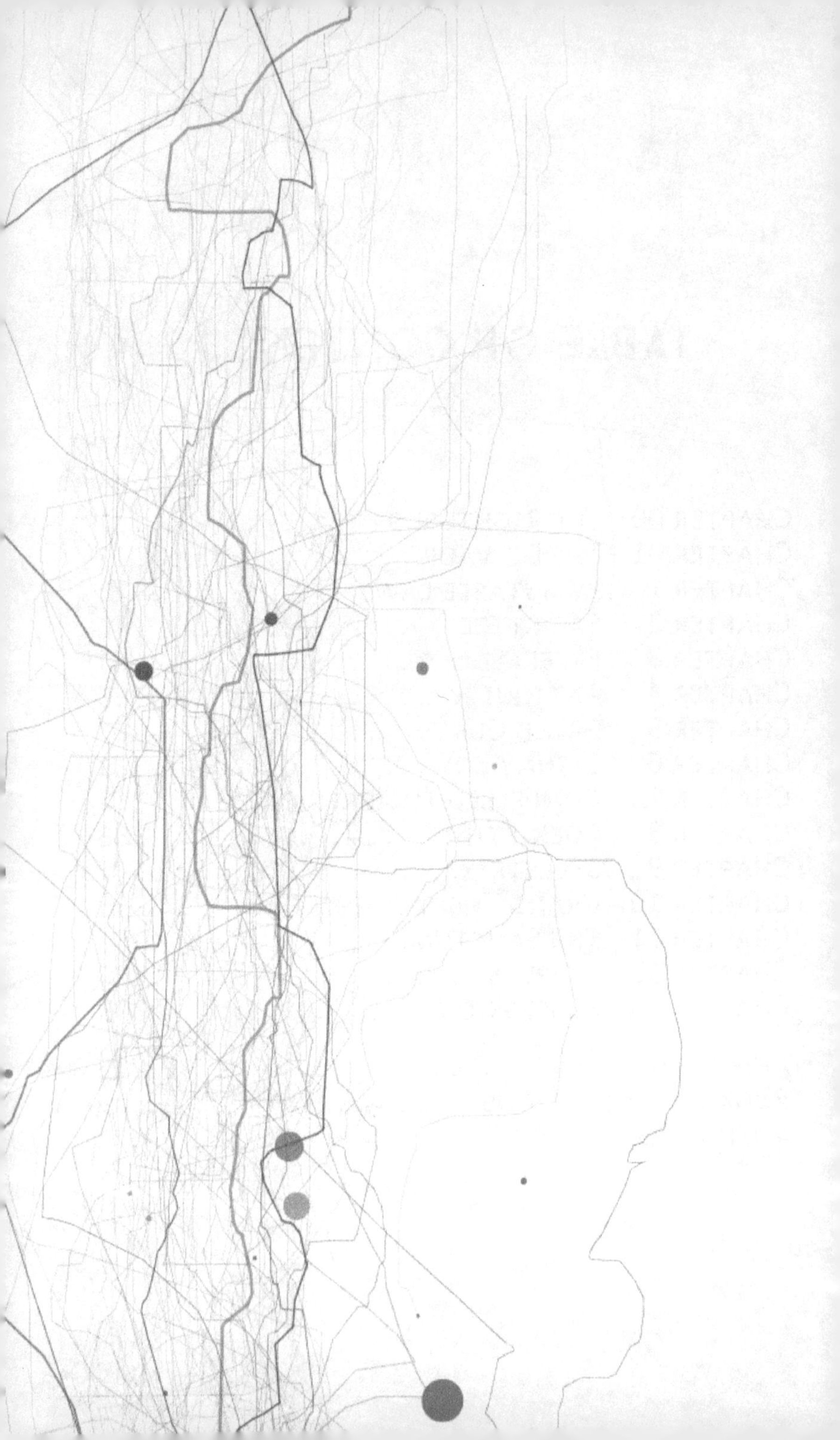

CHAPTER 00

THE RIGHTEOUS FURY

In hindsight, there was no reasonable indication of how terribly things were about to go down. No chilling wind from the south. No accompanying sense of impending doom. There should have been, but there wasn't. To Cadian Galas's nine-year-old mind, the night was perfect.

She loved summertime in her village of Kozst. It lay in the path of a breeze that welled up from the red rock canyon, carrying the leftover warmth of the day. The breeze held the alpine chill at bay, allowing her to watch the stars for a time before a late supper.

It was especially pleasant when the bright white moon of Skleetrix hid behind its larger, gray-blue sister, Cyclopedae. Cadian could really see the stars under those conditions. They became bright, intimate, and, in a way, inviting.

She shoved her hands in her pockets as she thought for a moment about the other planets of the Epriot system. Not long ago, humanity had lived among them. She would have loved to have visited Guisse IV with its endless waterfalls and more kinds of clouds than they could even count. Maybe someday, if the invaders ever went away. *Why couldn't the Delvadr keep to themselves?*

Tumenum trees peeked from between buildings while Cadian quick-walked, sometimes covertly skipping, toward the grove. She was allowed outside after dark so long as she stayed in the village and within earshot of home. She fancied herself as having keen ears so what that meant to her was the smooth, warm, block-like boulders at the village center. They rested at the spot where the narrow streets and buildings bent like a boomerang around the grove. The majestic tumenum had thick gray bodies like castle towers, with twisty spires for branches, and little messy tangles of yellow, orange, and pink foliage.

In the early dark, she saw the erratic curlicues of glow bugs as they swooped and swooshed in slow motion between the massive trunks. The forest was filled with a low, wavering cthixi bug choir.

She had no reference for such things, but to her, this was the best childhood anyone could have. Who would want to live in the big cities when, on nights like this, it was as if her very soul hummed in harmony with the world around her and the stars dotting the inky sky above?

The warm canyon breeze rose, erasing the goosebumps from her arms. Cadian closed her eyes and breathed in the smoky-sweet scent of lalish rushes mingled with the old-book smell of the tumenum. She stifled a giggle, self-consciously looking around to make sure no one was watching and wondering what the odd, skinny, redheaded girl was laughing about all by herself.

Was it foolish that such a simple thing could make her so happy? Some of the girls in her class thought so, always brooding, chirping away at each other, and sniggering when she walked by. Oh well, they could worry about their cliques. Cadian had the stars.

She craned her neck to look up into the sky. Meandering lights like those she'd seen in the woods greeted her.

"That's odd," she mumbled to herself, her mind suspended in that space between confusion and a creeping sort of concern.

The lights floated in the night sky as if suspended in liquid. But then they formed into pairs and then, after a moment, gathered into groups of four. She couldn't tell what they were, but glow bugs didn't make patterns like that. Ever. She squinted to see them more clearly as more and more of the pinpoint lights appeared, swooping erratically, and then pairing and grouping and moving with more deliberate purpose.

She searched the sky, but they were only congregated in the space above her. And yet, where at first there had been dozens, now there were hundreds, and some of the early ones were larger, she was sure of it. Then, among them, she saw tiny poofs of light. Her skin prickled as she realized that up in the great expanse of stars above, there was a hole in the sky. Or not a hole, but a vast area where the stars were missing, covered up—by a ship.

Cadian's goosebumps returned in force as concerned thoughts rose into alarm. The lights flew around the dark expanse of space, and the tiny blips were explosions.

Voices broke the silence of the scene, and she realized there were more people in the street than a few minutes before. All of them were looking up and murmuring to one another.

Parle Fritch stood pointing at the sky, and comparing thoughts with his twin brother Toryn, whose eyes were saucer-round at the spectacle above. The two were a year older than Cadian, though she played tag-rag-seek as well as either of them. Their father, like hers, was a mech commander in the terrestrial force. Only, her father's mech, the *Hillal*, was one of the biggest. It had a crew of eight and would stride waist-high through a tumenum grove.

Cadian returned her attention to the display above when a sharp light burned away the shadows, forcing her to shield her eyes. When she looked back up, a ripple of light streaked from one end of the dark shape to the other. It appeared to take up a third of the sky.

Her breath caught. The ship was much lower than she'd thought or had ever even seen before. She couldn't see the ships that protected Epriot Prime in the daytime. They had to be right at the edge of inner orbit, the sky clear and the sun at just the right angle. But this wasn't close; this was ... wrong. Everyone knew that the big ships never went planet-side.

Orange-white blooms grew in geometric patterns across the great ship's belly. The glow bugs, which weren't glow bugs after all, kept after it, forming up in diamond patterns and swooping at it like bale dogs at a herd of kheen-oxen.

These smaller packs of lights were brighter now, too, and moving faster. *How long have I been standing out here now, watching this unfold?*

A cool hand gripped hers, and she glanced up to see her mom. The lights danced across her eyes, the larger explosions occasionally casting her pale skin in deep contrast to her tightly bound, dark auburn hair. She was scared. Cadian could see it.

A low rumble, very much like distant thunder, reached her ears, and she saw her mother's shoulders tense and then slump.

Cadian watched her mom take in the event. Her mother's hand rose to her mouth, and she inhaled sharply. Cadian instinctively turned and saw what her mother saw. The ship was drawing much closer to the horizon now, scribing a massive half-circle through the sky in ultra-slow motion. And, unless something happened, it was going to be heading back in their direction.

Cadian was a good judge of things like this, distance and speed and angles. Her father said she would make a great mech pilot someday, but hoped she'd never have to. A knot settled in her stomach. She licked her lips as she tried to swallow with a dry mouth. Cadian gripped her mother's arm tightly and leaned in close.

"Mama..." she whispered. "Mom," Cadian said more urgently, looking into her mother's wide eyes as the woman slowly shook her head in disbelief.

"*The Righteous Fury*..." her mother exclaimed in a breathless, stunned whisper.

"Mom?"

Cadian's mother spun and stooped to look directly into her daughter's eyes. "Cadian. Go get your things. Get your travel bag like you're going to visit father on the *Hillal*, only ... grab water ... and meal bars, too." Her mother glanced back, scanning the village and their neighbors, looking for... Cadian didn't know what. "Do it quick. Ten minutes. Run!" her mother whispered urgently, pushing her in the direction of their two-story shop apartment.

"Mama?!?"

"Cadian Frey Galas. Go now and meet me back here. You have nine minutes now," she said and turned back to the sky and the terror spreading across it. "Make that five..." she said, trailing off.

Cadian gulped and ran off down the street, moisture brimming in her eyes, turning torchier light and shop windows into smeary streaks. She wiped away the tears, looking over her shoulder only briefly. The sky was a fire in the distance, hidden by a thunderhead that appeared to push from the heavens down toward the ground. Within it, the glowing hulk of an impossibly massive ship.

The glowing lights she had mistaken for bugs fell like meteors now. Some drew closer and materialized into fighters streaking overhead in a terrifying screech as they transitioned from thrusters to atmospheric engines. They were headed somewhere other than Kozst, thankfully.

Others were drop pods plummeting to the planet's surface, loaded with soldiers, most likely, and jump marines. Her father had told her about the deadly Delvadr jump marines in particular.

Suddenly, it clicked in Cadian's mind what her mom was saying. *Righteous Fury*... The *Righteous Fury*, Epriot's great defender, was crashing into the planet. She thought about what that meant. It would take out half of the archipelago continent. She understood a lot of things for her age, but this she couldn't begin to comprehend.

Cadian rounded the corner, raced up the steps, and smashed into the door a couple of times before finally managing the handle and tumbling inside. She scrambled to her feet and rushed to her room, where her backpack, boots, and parka were. Terrified, she thought about grabbing Ma'tild but already knew the doll wouldn't fit with extra waters and food.

"Sorry, Mattie," she said breathlessly, shaking. "I'll come back for you," she said over her shoulder to the doll she'd favored all through childhood. Instead, she reached for underwear—two pairs. Just in case they were gone for a while. And a knife. And a flashlight. Being the daughter of an officer, she had her own, of course. Always prepared. Always with a plan. *Of course, there is no plan for this,* she thought ironically, shaking her head, but keeping her hands busy with the task.

A distant boom shook the two-story house, causing it to buck violently on its foundation. Window coverings, displays, and cookware crashed to the floor right before the lights went out. In the darkness, the groaning structure, crackling fire, and rumble of impacting debris were amplified.

She grabbed her pack and made her way by rote out the front door. Through the opening, she watched in horror as a flaming, tumbling chunk of ceramo-metal the size of a house cartwheeled across Darnul's Field south of town. It splintered an equipment barn before embedding itself in a grain silo. Then, after a moment, the silo collapsed on top of it with a cavernous huff.

Cadian stared, mouth hanging open as another piece of debris, this one the size of medium transport, cleaved the village in half. The sound was deafening—a cacophony of destruction, twisted metal, and gouts of upended earth. With them, buildings and streets.

She grabbed the door frame as the ground jerked and rolled beneath her. She couldn't pull her eyes away from the towering wave of dust and smoke and fire plowing past.

At the last second, she threw herself back indoors as wreckage and chunks of buildings and rock hailed down on the building. Windows that were still intact shattered as debris punched holes in the walls. She thought it was over, and then something crashed through the ceiling and ripped off the back half of the building.

When the wave of debris passed, Cadian lay in a curled bunch on the floor, covered in dust and grit and chunks of plaster. The back of her apartment was open to the night air, and the floor and ceiling hung dangerously, looking like they would fall at any moment.

Her thoughts went to her mom. Had she been in the path of the wreckage? Was the village there anymore? She patted at her wrist communicator, but the screen just showed a circle with dust flowing in through the top and out the bottom.

Out of service, or trying to find service. She didn't know or care if there was a difference. She'd seen the symbol only once before while spelunking with her father. All it meant to her right now was that she had to go. Go find her mom. Cadian hoped she'd headed for the house too. *If she did, wouldn't she be here by now?*

More booms thudded in the distance, farther away. Then an ultra-low hum followed. It was so loud it rattled in her body and she heard the rubble pattering throughout her kitchen and what was left of the sitting room. *Is it safe to go outside?* It didn't matter. Worry had grown into a desperate need to see her. To hear her comforting voice and to have her make sense of this madness.

Cadian stepped through the front door. The scene was a panorama of fire, dust, and roiling black smoke. Flames reached for the skies in the fields to the south. Fires engulfed the buildings that were still standing. Overhead, what looked like a city, itself ablaze, scrolled across the sky. Village-sized chunks of metal, glass, and ceramo-composite still fell from it, smashing into the planet's surface with deafening booms.

Something else happened as well. As the massive ship passed overhead, she could see it collapsing and contorting. She realized its failing gravitic systems were competing with planetary forces they were never intended to experience. The fact that it was still somehow aloft was a mystery.

She watched, unable to peel her eyes from the carnage still raining down around her. What if she left at the wrong moment? There was no evading some of that debris.

A huge plume of fire exploded into the sky a mile or so away, and her thoughts ripped back to her mom.

Cadian flew down the steps into the street, her eyes darting from pile to pile of debris. The village she knew looked completely foreign. She stumbled over collapsed walls and broken pavement—numb, tears in her eyes and on her cheeks. The dust and smoke choked her, but she kept pushing forward, putting one foot in front of the other, back toward the village center where she'd last seen her mom.

She saw dust-covered bodies everywhere, but none were her. Then she saw one mostly covered by a collapsed awning. The person was about her mother's size. Luckily, she could see their left hand, and it didn't have the fine-line flower tattoo her mom had had for as long as Cadian could remember.

Cadian was glad for that tattoo. She didn't think she'd have had the stomach to look at the woman's face. She knew she had a name. Was sure she knew her. It was Kozst... of course, she knew her. Still, Cadian would find the resolve if it came down to it. She'd do whatever she had to.

Cadian clenched her teeth and continued past what buildings still stood and into the ones that hadn't been so lucky. Then she saw it. The grove, too, was on fire. Her eyes followed the line of billowing tree-tops to an area of darkness beyond the smoke and lingering dust.

Before she realized it, she was running past building after flattened building to where the village center had been. It was a canyon of tilted earth. It was gone. The village center and as much of the west end as she could see through the haze were gone—destroyed by the very thing that was supposed to protect them.

CHAPTER 01

THE DELVADR

Cadian's thoughts drifted back to her mom. She wondered how anyone could have survived. Still, her eyes tracked from object to object in the carnage below, struggling to make sense of it. Shorn metal, rock, dirt, smoldering piles, smoke, and then something stood out. Something black but vaguely human-shaped. She could just make out an arm or a leg exposed between the chunks of rubble. Cadian burst forward and skidded to a stop at the edge of the buckled street.

A toppled slab of pavement to her left provided a ramp to another chunk that she navigated to yet another and then bounded to a boulder farther on. As she slid over the edge of it, things became clearer. There were vast portions of what must have been the ship mixed in with wood and stone from the village. And there were more bodies.

These were her people. And maybe some others. None moved. And then she heard a voice. Someone calling for help but farther away. Up the far slope.

Cadian's heart jumped. She picked her way through the rocks and dirt and scattered fires. The person whose voice she'd heard wasn't readily visible as smoke was thickest toward the middle of the chasm, where larger chunks of the ship and buildings burned more intensely. She navigated through an arch of crumpled metal. The heat of the fire burned her exposed arms and neck. She scampered through, worried it might collapse at any moment.

The voice cut through the crackle of fire. Small and uncertain, and there was terror in it. It didn't sound like a woman's voice anymore, but Cadian couldn't ignore it. Besides, maybe they could help find her mom. And others, there were so many she was sure were dead. But maybe there were other survivors?

This was what she had to do. Find everyone she could so that all of those people could help find the rest. That was her mom's best chance of survival. Cadian couldn't search the whole town on her own. It would take days. And she wasn't strong enough to move all the rubble. She breathed a deep breath and let it out while wiping away tears from her face. Okay, she was ready to go.

Cadian began to wonder if the person she was hearing was in shock. She'd heard of that. In really bad situations, people got confused and didn't make any sense. She worried for a minute that maybe she was in shock, too. Maybe making bad decisions that could get her or someone else hurt as well. She certainly was scared. And then she thought again about her mother and just pressed forward, regardless.

Her backpack slid around awkwardly as she crawled around and over the debris. She twisted the adjustment knobs on the straps until they were snug and the weight of the pack was closer to her body. It made an instant difference and her pace quickened.

She returned to her search. Her foot slipped, and her shin slid into a jagged chunk of still-hot metal that punctured and seared her leg. She yelped, and the other voice yelled again in response.

"I hear you," Cadian yelled back. "I'm coming your way." She stumbled forward, but more carefully now. Blood ran down into the top of her sock, but not a lot. She'd had worse.

"Who's there? Parle?" the voice asked. Cadian searched the hillside as she drew closer, climbing now with hands and feet, up the crumbling slope.

"No, it's Cadian. Who is that? Toryn?"

The voice replied something, but Cadian couldn't make it out as the roar of more jets rumbled overhead. She stopped to look, her eyes searching skies that glowed with smoke and dust reflecting the fires below. She remembered why the ship crashed in the first place—the Delvadr. Then, in the wake of the jet noise, she heard a resonating growl, something like a not-too-distant waterfall. Her heart sank into her stomach as the stories from her father burst into her mind.

"Toryn?!? Toryn, if that's you, be quiet now. I'm coming to you, but I think the Delvadr are close."

"Wha-what?"

"I'm coming. Be quiet," she urged as loudly as she dared as she angled, scrambling toward the voice she thought was Toryn, Parle Fritsch's twin brother.

She peeked over her shoulder and realized she was halfway up the slope now. The rumbling growl in the distance had changed into an emphatic whirr, but not from just one direction. *They're all over the west end.* Her mind returned to those stories of the Delvadr Jump Marines—elite soldiers in power armor with jump packs. They could leap right into the thick of the action from fast-moving shuttles. And, in packs, they could take down even the mighty terrestrial mechs like her father's Hillal.

Concerned thoughts of him fighting them crowded her mind. She hoped he was on his way here, but knew that was unlikely. Even though he was a commander, he couldn't choose where to fight. He had orders, and they were probably to protect Command Base Noam where he was stationed on the north island.

Something heavy heaved onto the ground above, and she heard Toryn squeak. He was only about ten meters farther upslope. Cadian, sensing danger, veered into a big ceramo-metal box about the size of her apartment common room and worked her way deep into the shadows. The metal was hot, but thankfully not so much that it burned her skin. She maneuvered through the wreckage, around twisted stairs to a spot that opened back to the hillside. It gave her a view of where she thought Toryn was and a partial view of the lip of the freshly carved canyon.

That's when she saw the silhouette of a massive figure. Half again as tall as any of the men from the village and broader by double. She could see the side-by-side rectangular vents of a jump pack on the figure's back, the upper edges wavering with heat still emanating from within. The jump marine carried a huge gun mounted on swivels at his hip and shoulder.

He scanned the wreckage, his visor pointed exactly in her direction for an uncomfortably long moment before casting farther up the gorge. Suddenly, he stopped and brought up his weapon. Brilliant plasma burst from it. On the far slope near the still-burning grove, dirt and metal exploded into the air. The air rumbled as the soldier launched into the air, heading in that direction.

Cadian realized that this was her chance to get to Toryn. She scrambled out of cover and started to charge up the hill, but something yanked her back. Her heart leaped into her throat, but then she realized her backpack had caught metal from the structure she'd been hiding in. She dropped low and worked her way on all fours before regaining her feet and charging upslope. She hoped against hope that her mistake hadn't cost her and Toryn their lives.

Further bursts of light cast the gorge in stark contrast. The soldier had found something or someone. Cadian's heart sank as she worried again about her mom. But then she made it to the twisted chunk of building structure where Toryn was hiding and saw now why he'd stayed put. Only his upper half was visible. The rest of him was pinned by a section of a beam and the shattered floor. His hands were dirty and bloody from where he'd been digging at the dirt and rock to get himself free.

"How'd this happen?" she asked in a hushed whisper.

Toryn's eyes shot from where the soldier had disappeared over the structure to Cadian. His eyes were full of terror, and his dirt-smeared face was streaked from tears. He quickly scrubbed at his cheeks, probably realizing how he must look to her.

"Cadie. I'm so glad someone's alive. I'm stuck. I was trying to figure out a way down when the building broke away. It slid down the hill and I couldn't get away from the rocks and the dirt. Then when it all stopped..." He looked down and shrugged, grimacing. "Got real lucky, I guess."

Cadian nodded dumbly, not sure what to say about luck given their current situation. "Does it hurt?" she asked, looking at his side at the blood soaking through his shirt.

Then the whirring of jump packs began to grow loud again. More marines were coming. She couldn't see the first one anymore, but that meant he probably couldn't see them either.

"It doesn't hurt too bad," he said and then arched his neck toward the edge above. "Are there more? Sounds like there's more. They're going to find us, Cade." His look was feral. "My dad says Delvadr never take prisoners. Not even kids."

Cadian stared at him and nodded. She dropped down to help clear away the rocks and debris. The rumbling above became distinguishable, and she guessed one of them was close to their position, maybe even nearing the edge above. She frantically searched the rubble and broken building for something to hide under. If the next soldier stood a little farther left from where the first one had, they would be spotted.

She saw a sheet of corrugated roofing material, ran over to it, and pulled it back to where Toryn was. The rumbling was very loud now, and then came the *thud* of heavy armor just beyond the lip. She slid down next to Toryn and yanked the sheet over their heads.

Their eyes met in the semi-darkness. She brought one finger to her lips. He nodded his understanding. She couldn't see them, but now there were two of the jump marines in their vicinity. Flashing lights lit up the ground visible to either side of their cover, and the other soldier's weapon crackled away at something.

Rumbling turned into a heavy whine as some other, unseen soldier accelerated through the sky overhead, bypassing the gorge entirely and moving toward the part of the town that she had come from.

More lights and the sound of gunfire told her he was tracking someone. She worried for a minute she might throw up. There were very few people in the village she didn't know by name. Whoever he was hunting, she knew them. These were her people, she thought as her gut churned. She didn't have a frame of reference for the hollowness inside her. The deep emptiness was only crowded out by the intensity of the fear gripping her.

Bright white light exploded all around them, making her jump, but then she realized it was a searchlight, not the energy weapon. Still, what was he looking at? The light shifted but never veered far from where they huddled between the dirt and the thin metallic sheet. Her heart pounded in her chest. She could hear it in her ears. When she swallowed, she heard every *pop* and *click* of saliva. She was sure it echoed throughout the whole area. Cadian breathed in a slow, shuddering breath, struggling to calm her growing terror.

Then a quick roar of jump engines preceded a crashing *thud* as the fractured building they were huddled against shook, and then tilted away ever so slightly.

She expected any second now to have her flimsy cover ripped away and that blinding light to be the last thing she would see. But it didn't happen. The Delvadr marine must have wanted a better vantage point and used their building as his next perch.

She looked at Toryn. His eyes darted to his lower torso and to the darkness that was now visible below. There was a gap underneath the beam. The soldier moved around, and the building swayed even more, revealing Toryn's bloody legs. It was either pull him out and risk being seen or slide deeper into the shattered building and risk being squashed when the marine leaped away. The second was the quieter option.

She knew they were running out of time to choose, so she decided for them both. She pointed for Toryn to slide farther in. His eyes widened, but she quickly mouthed the words, "No time," and pushed him down, following head first behind him.

The two wiggled their way deeper inside and hoped for an opening. Toryn slipped out of view. She followed and as she dropped to the floor behind him, a roar of jump engines shook the building and it dropped back into place.

She couldn't see him very well in the darkness, but then their eyes met. Toryn reached for his side to check it, but then the earth fell away beneath them as they started sliding. There was a quick rush of weightlessness before it jarred to a stop. She and Toryn catapulted into the wall below them, knocking the wind out of them both.

The two lay there for a long time. Hours, she was certain. He explained how, at some point, he and Parle had moved into the grove to climb one of the tumenum trees and get a better view of the impacting wreckage. Then the first chunks started hitting the village.

They both lost their footing and tumbled into the thick foliage of the hillside below and had gotten separated. Then the fires broke out.

He was adamant Parle was out there somewhere but held little hope for anyone near the village center. Galas remained quiet. She understood he didn't know that her mom was there in the village center. She thought she should be mad, but there was nothing in her but a big emptiness.

After a while, the roar of jump engines and plasma rifles faded. They sheltered in place until the first rays of sunlight peeked through gaps in the shattered walls. Then they climbed out and began the search for other survivors. There were few. None of them were Parle or Cadian's mom.

CHAPTER 1

IMMUTABLE LAWS

C apt. Cadian Galas scanned the expanse of water. Her pupils glowed gold with the digital information of the SortieNet displayed through her corneal implants. She sat cross-legged, hands steepled in her lap, on top of the broad ceramo-metallic shoulders of a forty-ton battle mech. The machine, known as Betsy, plowed relentlessly through the briny waters of the inner coastal channel.

Galas soaked it in. The sun on her face, the salt on her tongue. It was like yachting, but her boat was a robot that was part tank, part fighter jet, and a hundred percent badass. She patted Betsy's cyberpunk-painted exterior with pride. People didn't mess with mechs. And, by extension, people didn't mess with Galas. Which was how she liked it.

The ocean breeze tugged playfully at her long auburn bangs while water piled up and spilled to the sides of the machine's chest armor. It left a foamy, churned-up trail in its wake that threaded off in the distance behind them.

For Galas, this was not warfare as usual. But she'd spent weeks confined to the interior of the cramped machine. Tired of her own aroma and the cocktail of ozone and disinfectant pouring from the air vents, she'd climbed topside at the first glimpse of sunlight since accepting this idiotic mission.

"There is just nothing out here," she mused aloud, the marine breeze and dull rush of water nearly drowning out her words.

She knew it'd be solitary but was stunned at how desolate the southern continent had become over the last three decades. Yesterday she'd glimpsed the jagged, crumbling towers of Nadas Barrn as she'd steamed by under repulsor power. The once-glimmering resort town with stunning peaks in the background and pink sand beaches looked sullen and haunted. Empty windows, like skeletal eye sockets, stared out onto an oceanic playground reclaimed by its original inhabitants.

Taking to the ocean was slower, but she'd chosen to stay far off-coast for this section of the journey rather than attract undue attention by taking an overland route along the hundreds of kilometers of shoreline.

There may be some remaining locals scattered amongst the ruined towns, but it was impossible to tell from here. The breakdown of society since the Delvadr invaders had re-entered the system—at least in this corner of the world—appeared to be more than complete.

There had been other towns, huddled against the near-vertical chain of peaks that lined the coast. All appeared similarly vacant if not fully engulfed by the surrounding jungle.

Galas's eyes locked on a flock of white sea birds as they took to the air in the distance, startled by a massive breaching ray. "Wow. Big boy," she gasped in awe. She'd never seen anything even close to that size.

Fully as wide as the mech's shoulder decks, its dark gray back was splotched with vibrant fuchsia polka-dots that were thickest down the ridge of its back. She saved the video file to the SortieNet with a thought. *Maybe a new species...a Galas Ray.* She liked the sound of that. Then she noticed some sort of disturbance in the water. She zoomed in. The cresting manta ray had crashed down on handfuls of the birds and now a pod of baby mantas was frolicking in the resulting carnage.

"Eewww."

Galas edited that last entry to remove her name from the title.

The SortieNet was the main tool for managing the myriad functions of the battle machine she piloted up the channel. It was also connected to a network of drones that operated tirelessly—some in the air overhead, some scanning the ocean around her, and yet others deployed to connect to the mech or other machinery.

In that support function, they could act to augment or sabotage as she saw fit. This made the drones more like minions, and they were a major component of the arsenal that was the Dragoon; a Cutlass class, medium battle mech, of which Captain Cadian Galas was commander, pilot, part-time cook, and full-time dictator. That last according to previous members of the crew, most of which were now deceased. So, there was that...

A *ding* issued from the open hatch, and Galas jumped to her feet and slipped below. She re-emerged onto the deck, feeling the thick salty air flowing over the broad shoulder deck of the mildly undulating machine. She shoveled steaming spoonfuls of a yellow-orange, chunky substance from a thin and well-used metal bowl. Occasionally, she paused while the machine maneuvered beneath her—guiding operations with her thoughts—and then resumed eating once more.

The terrain beneath the inner channel was more uniform than farther south along the exposed coastline, but there were still obstacles to navigate. She paused again from her meal as a monkey-like creature with a fox face and bat wings exited the hatch and stood blinking in the sunlight. It had manipulated the pigment of some of its lightly furred scales to resemble a tropical print shirt. Sans pants, she noted.

"Nice look. We're almost to the river mouth," she told her co-pilot around a mouthful of the steaming orange chunks, something called Nohmii. It was a spore-based material popularized by the once prolific orbital colonies on account of how easy it was to grow and fabricate. That fact made it a staple for mech-based operations as well.

Galas cursed around a mouthful and sucked air through her teeth to cool a bite she'd shoveled in too quickly.

Her companion smiled at what he assumed was a compliment and then leaked a yellow substance onto the deck.

She swallowed. "Ugh, you're disgusting." She immediately had to work around a gag reflex before moving upwind and tipping her bowl over the side. The alien creature shrugged, dropped to all fours, and slurped up the liquid from the deck with a long purple tongue that functioned like a straw.

Cycarians' digestive systems, after initial consumption, require the addition of oxygen to complete the process of converting food to nutrients. As a result, their homeworld was very fertile. Living with one in a confined space, however, was highly undesirable. Luckily for Galas, Jinnbo was much more sanitary below decks and had his own quarters, thankfully *below* Galas's own.

"I am so excited at the opportunity to meet the esteemed Professor Goodfall that I can barely contain myself," Jinnbo said between slurps, lisping slightly due to the substance still coating his retracted tongue straw.

Galas stared at him coolly, still feeling slightly green.

The stealth-scaled, monkey-bat thing that was her co-pilot looked the tiniest bit sheepish but offered no apology, his tongue instead flicking out to clean his snout from the remains of breakfast 2.0.

Looking up at the partial lunar-lunar eclipse hanging a third of the way up from the horizon, he commented, "Cyclopedae is in transit. Only fifteen cycles before Skleetrix is fully dark. Do you think we'll make it in time? Is eight days enough to find Goodfall and the artifact before the Delvadr return?" He peppered her with questions.

Galas considered this. Her auburn hair flashed gold in the sunlight as she smoothed her bangs back, tucking them under a beat-up billed cap she had folded in her back pocket. She stood there without speaking for a moment. Galas stared out at the back-drop of dense green vegetation stacked in folds like a crumpled rug. Over the course of only thirty kilometers, that rolling terrain made its ascent up to a snow-capped peak that dominated the scenery.

She turned to her copilot as his coat of scales washed a vibrant green from head to toe and settled on a purple-infused, tawny-brown color that was his default pigmentation. *Probably because it complements his yellow eyes,* she thought randomly while simultaneously evaluating volumes of information flashing through the SortieNet's dashboard. This was just how her brain worked. Everything, all at once.

"Sorry...the Deathhounds. They're gaining on us," she stated quizzically while still parsing the flood of warnings and drone feeds. Then she spun to get her own eyes on the situation.

Far in the distance behind them, there was a mass of dark gray and black specks low on the horizon. She used the digital zoom feature of her implants to bring them into better focus. The vague swirl of activity resolved into hundreds of seabirds, circling and then plunging into the water below. Presumably to feed off the detritus left in the wake of the company of Deathhound mechs that were stalking her. And by default, Jinnbo.

She hadn't been able to see that before. The Deathhounds *were* gaining on them. "That's impossible," she whispered, fear and awe battling for dominance in her mind.

It should have been impossible. Her Dragoon was faster and operating at near full capacity.

Her fear was justified. Staying ahead of them was still just a temporary stay of execution. Once a Deathhound had your scent, there was no stopping the inevitable.

She spun again toward the notch between the towering peaks north and south of her. She could only hope to reach Professor Goodfall before they caught up with her.

"Jinnbo, call in the drones. Augment Betsy's reactors."

"Coming in hot and blind," she said to herself. "What's new?"

Galas ducked through the open top hatch and slipped into the blunt, bullet-shaped cockpit that protruded from Betsy's broad chest armor. Leaving the inner coastal channel behind, murky red-brown water parted to either side of the partially submerged metal and plasteel canopy as the machine continued its journey upriver.

She truly was running blind, now that the drones were pulled in to augment the reactors. The trade-off provided a much-needed boost in speed. Hopefully, it'd be enough to at least temporarily outrun the gang of Aardwolf, Chacma, and Shrike mechs that made up the pack of Deathhounds. Over the course of the last three weeks, they'd been steadily growing in numbers. At first, it was two or three. They'd been discreet, keeping their distance. Now they were fifteen strong. Galas was somewhat of a phenom, but those odds were impossible.

And now, this sudden burst of speed? It didn't make sense. It defied everything she knew about interdimensional physics, which, admittedly, wasn't much. But what she did know was that it didn't bode well for her mission.

Ordinarily, the Deathhounds' filthy, quasi-trans-dimensional tech had limitations. It was strange and shrouded in mystery. Its most identifiable trait was the trail of corruption that it left in its wake. Which was why a cloud of scavengers was a fixture above the pack that followed them.

She scanned the prior video feed while she navigated.

"What is that? A Helminth Kurt?!?" Galas wondered aloud. The small, five-ton mech burst out of the pack, momentarily airborne on shitty hover buckets. It looked like a less aerodynamic version of a pot-belly stove, with armaments bolted on as an afterthought. She shook her head in disgust and ran her hands through her hair before replacing her cap. She knew that there were more formidable mechs in the pack, but still. This was how she was going to die? Oh, the humiliation.

Galas got up, clasped her hands behind her back, and stretched them as high as they would go before jumping up onto the ceiling-mounted bar behind the captain's chair. She pumped out pull-ups with her legs piked out in front of her while chewing on the dilemma.

In her days upon days confined to Betsy's interior, she had put considerable thought into the peculiar timing of the Deathhound's appearance. They'd started showing up right after her assignment had come down from EDC high command—an oxymoron if she'd ever heard one. The state of humanity's only hope, the Epriot Defenciary Collaborative, was an unfunny joke. When this last battle finally went hot, it would break down to an under-supplied army of survivors operating antiquated equipment. With the enemy having a seemingly infinite number of reinforcements, they were losing a battle of attrition.

That was the kernel of it. Humanity was doomed. Worn down to a pathetic nub by an unrelenting force over decades. As it was, they were living on borrowed time, and the clock was, quite literally, ticking away.

Eight days. She shook her head and breathed out a deep sigh. And now this: Deathhounds of all things. It was oddly coincidental, to say the least. But there was nothing that could be done about it. She had to complete her mission before the inevitable confrontation. The odds of a positive outcome, given the numbers involved, were less than heartening.

Great. Save the world and die, anyway. Well, best to focus on one thing at a time.

She switched to an underhand grip, pulled up, and let go with her left hand. In this way, she managed the descent as best she could with one arm. She pulled up again, letting go with the right this time, and repeated the process until failure. Her arms were noodles, and she wore a sheen of sweat on her brow. She needed that. Being cooped up in her mech was grating on her.

She caught a whiff of something pungent and sniffed at an armpit. "Gracious Maker!" She smelled of onions and nohmii. She pawed at her nose and tried to get away from her own stench, but now that she was tuned into it, it was impossible.

Could she shower and pilot the mech at the same time? Maybe if she had her drones. Which wasn't an option.

"I hate this mission," she grumbled.

Galas returned to the captain's chair and turned her thoughts to the mission at hand and to navigating against the river flow without the aid of her drones.

In the distance, tree-lined banks, originally far to the north and south, were drawing slowly together as the broad delta gave way to the river proper.

They were making headway. The mission, as her briefing packet had described, was to track down the source of a cryptic transmission originating from uncharted and largely uninhabitable mountain terrain.

What was peculiar was not the destination or even the signal itself, but the fact that it bore the digital signature of one Professor Goodfall. He had been an Epriot Alliance scientist researching ruins of the planet's previous inhabitants and—more importantly for Galas and the remnant of humanity—what promised to be vastly superior tech than they were currently capable of.

Understanding that tech could allow them to activate what some theorized were long-dormant planetary defenses. Such a weapon could turn the tide on the Delvadr invasion and possibly keep them out of the solar system for good.

The war against the invaders had been, thus far, nothing more than a fighting retreat. They had been forced to give up, first, the outer ring planets and, more recently, not one, but two of the inner triad, leaving the Epriots nowhere else to go.

So, Galas's mission was one fat string of could's, might's, and possibly's punctuated by one more stellar fat: the thing that was most peculiar about Professor Goodfall's message was that he disappeared nearly twenty-five years ago. While not impossible that he was still alive, he was no young man when he'd undertaken the expedition to discover the origins of the prior civilization. And he hadn't been heard from since.

It was a colossal boondoggle. A snipe hunt on the eve of humanity's destruction. Still, if there was the faintest sliver of hope, she had to take it.

Galas's attention was drawn to what appeared to be a frog stuck to the inside glass of the cockpit. *Good,* she thought. Maybe it'd clear out a few of the bugs that had found their way inside while she had the top hatch open. As if on cue, a mosquito bobbed and buzzed on by and was snatched out of the air.

She studied the frog, suddenly concerned that maybe it was an unsafe companion to have in the cockpit with her. What if there was a mosquito near her face while she was negotiating a particularly tricky section of river?

Then she noticed there were two frogs. And then a creaking noise, like a rusty gate, emitted from behind her ear on the pilot's chair. She leaped up, turning to see another of the pale green, smooth-skinned amphibians just inches from where her head had been.

"Jinnbo!" she yelled. "Get in here quick. I think we have a problem."

Jinnbo materialized at the doorframe, leaning against the bulkhead with a frog skewered on a short gig. He took a bite with his foxlike snout, and a drop of inner goo fell to the metal floor, sizzling softly.

"Kind of spicy," he said, letting out a discrete burp.

"They're made of...acid?!?" Galas gasped, stepping farther away from the pilot's chair and hearing a squishing sound coming from under her boot. The squish noise preceded a more pronounced *pop* and *sizzle* as both the floor and her boot caught on fire.

"What the...?" She jumped back and whipped off the boot while Jinnbo gleefully ran around gigging frogs and chomping them down. Galas's pupils flashed gold as she mentally ran through a handful of actions within the SortieNet while continuing to guide Betsy unconsciously. Within seconds, the machine slowed noticeably, and the air vents began whirring emphatically—frigid air blustering out.

In the meantime, she had pried the closest fire extinguisher from its cubby and doused the flaming deck, and her fully engulfed boot. She was almost done when she heard a different whir. This she recognized as the warm-up cycle of a plasma pistol. Her head snapped in the direction of the noise as the extinguisher fell clattering to the floor.

"Jinnbo!" she yelled as she bolted through the cockpit bulkhead to the core vestibule, a three-by-three-meter connector between the galley, armory, storage, maintenance, crew quarters, and access hatches. Hanging halfway up the ladder to the top hatch was Jinnbo, eyes swimming dazedly while he attempted, in drunken fashion, to aim at a frog on the opposite wall that was nowhere to be seen.

"Give me that!" she cried, frantically swiping at the pistol and gaining control of it just in time to keep the crazed Cycarian from blowing a hole in Betsy's side. They had enough to worry about without having to undergo major repairs while forging upstream into uncharted waters. Luckily, the mech's atmospheric conditioners were functioning better than her co-pilot was. Frogs began dropping to the floor surreptitiously as they froze. Galas ran around bundled in a thick woolen blanket, scooping them up into a metal bucket normally reserved for the Cycarian's meals before second consumption. Luckily, it was empty.

Five bucketfuls later, Galas held Jinnbo's ears back as he retched up the last of the acid frogs over the side of Betsy's top deck. An oily residue coated the foaming water trailing behind. Off in the distance, the cloud of scavenger birds hung over the Deathhound pack like a solitary thunderhead. It was no nearer, but no farther than it had been before. Galas grimaced before turning her attention back to her queazy crewmate.

"Are you going to be okay?" she asked Jinnbo, who nodded weakly, his eyes goopy and half-closed as he rested, shaking on his skinny, webbed arms. He looked somehow more alien than usual in his current state.

"Okay, I'm going to go down and scan one more time for any leftover frogs before turning the heat back up. Don't bother coming down until I give the all clear, got it?" she asked, and he nodded again.

Galas once again popped below, instantly regretting it as her bare foot touched down on the frozen floor of the vestibule. She rested her frigid toes on her other boot while scanning for something to use to protect it from the cold. No luck.

She hopped one-legged the few feet to her quarters and then plopped down in the recessed bunk. A cold lump told her she was sitting on yet another of the frozen interlopers. She jumped up, hitting her head on the overhead cabinet, which caused her to put her foot down on the frozen floor. Galas yelped, growled obscenities, and then flicked the amphibian into the vestibule with her boot knife to be taken care of after she found her other boots.

The cabin was freezing. She could see the vapor of her own breath, but then the air grew even colder. Her breath came out in a thick fog. She shook her head, shoulders sagging in resignation.

"Not now," she implored weakly.

Betsy's insides rattled and clattered together. Galas's boots, which were still unaccounted for, shot out from under her bunk, banging uselessly off the bulkhead separating her quarters from the cockpit. A notepad flew from her desk, whipping through the air past her face and into the vestibule. The lights dimmed, threatening to go out before going over bright until one of them popped somewhere beyond the core vestibule. She couldn't quite be certain where.

And then the coldness was gone. She rubbed her face with her hands. Too much. Too much shit to deal with. Even with her perfectly divergent mech pilot brain, it was too much — Deathhounds. An impending invasion. An impossible mission to find a dead scientist's beacon signal in the hopes that he left detailed instructions on how to kick-start a mythical super-weapon. Acid frogs. A hallucinogenic co-pilot. And now this; her ex-boyfriend and blademate, Drakas, was acting up again.

Galas grumbled expletives under her breath as she snatched her boots and put on the new pair.

"Thanks for finding my boots," she muttered to the empty cabin.

Drakas, the ghost of the mech—her years-dead partner and lover—had not been vengeful in life. But, since passing, he was fixated on one thing and would occasionally vent his ire. Usually at the least opportune times.

Blademates were not meant to die alone. Part of the strength of their bond was knowing the other would risk their very life to protect them since their blood pact required that if one died, the other must either go out in a blaze of glory or commit ritual suicide.

Galas had not quite gotten to that part of the deal. She'd tried the blazing guns thing, but it turned out she was too good at it. Drakas, in petulant poltergeist form, was likely to help her get it right.

She strode over, bent down, retrieved the notepad that had gone flying in a spectral fit, and placed it back on her desk. As she did so, she bumped a picture frame with three images. One was her and Drakas on leave in some obscure, exotic port. Probably Tachi Bunga by the endless beach behind them and turquoise-green waters. Wherever they were, they were wearing little to nothing, sporting great tans and mildly inebriated smiles. A good-looking couple. Even through the broken plasteel. That was new. Nice touch.

The other two images were her mother—a simple beauty with kind, deeply intelligent eyes—and the last was Seraf, her baby girl. Only eight months old when this was taken. Galas choked down the lump in her throat.

All had been stolen from her. Her father as well. She cursed this stupid mission that sent her off into the jungle on a fool's errand instead of giving her the opportunity to die with dignity, fighting the enemy that had taken everything from her.

She wanted to sulk, but the optimist in her couldn't be squashed so easily. Who knew? Maybe this mission wasn't a complete waste of time. If the prior race tech that the professor was hunting for actually existed, maybe there was a chance.

Still, the longing to exact vengeance face-to-face was a temptation she could barely keep in check. She'd get her chance. If the Deathhounds didn't get her first. Dammit. She was doing circles now. She remembered Jinnbo was still up top.

"Ughh," she groaned and went about rounding up the disgusting little alien.

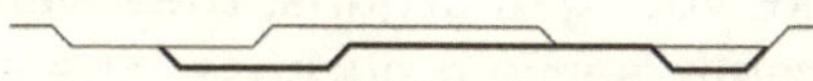

Up top, Jinnbo was draped over the lower railing like a wet towel, his head lolling side to side with Betsy's movements.

"Shit."

Galas rushed to his side, but he was non-functional. In fact, it appeared that he was wholly catatonic. Eating a prodigious amount of hallucinogenic frogs, largely comprised of acid, proved to be too much, even for his ironclad stomach. Galas patted his face. He was cold. Was he breathing? "Shit," she said again.

She gathered him up and rushed him down to his quarters, which looked clean enough but smelled of mulchy soil. She decided she could do this without touching anything but the diagnostic panel. She was relieved to find she could access it via the SortieNet. The bed began to him and whir while lights on the panel flowed through different colors and sequences. He didn't move a muscle. He didn't even snore, which was disturbingly out of character.

Acid frogs, she thought. No matter if this was the first discovery of such a creature, Galas would *not* be naming them after herself. She stood by, uselessly. She didn't know if Betsy's AI had been loaded with the proper xenobiological data to treat Jinnbo. EDC high command had dropped him off one day with a note, like an unwanted babe. "This is Jinnbo. He's your new co-pilot. He's Cycarian. Don't ask what that is, we don't know either. No, this is not negotiable."

They knew her too well. But co-pilots to Galas were somewhat like vestigial organs; they were there, but they didn't really serve a purpose. She could handle everything herself. Still, she did try to give Jinnbo little duties. Things she didn't mind getting screwed up. Sometimes she would tell him to do the opposite of what she wanted, just to see if he would accidentally get it right. Defying all logic, he still managed to screw it up.

Galas felt a tiny little pang of remorse. An itty bitty little ounce of sadness. He was next-to-worthless, but he was *her* next-to-worthless. She would do what she could.

Betsy still chugged along through the reddish-brown river waters. The mech closed in on a branch of the river where Galas would be forced to choose one way or the other. In her search for Professor Goodfall, either was viable.

While she knew the signal had been broadcast from somewhere high up in the mountains, there was no known path to get there. She was quite literally in uncharted territory.

If she was wrong about which way to go, it not only meant that she would have to go back the way she'd come. Besides burning precious time, she might find herself boxed in with nowhere to go and a pack of Deathhound mechs closing in around her.

It made this next decision all that much more critical. Since she only had one chance to get this right, she peeled out all her drones to scan the forest and the river branches ahead. It was a calculated move. Peeling out the drones dropped the reactors back to standard output, reducing speed and allowing her pursuers to close the gap that much faster, but she needed accurate data. Intel was a force multiplier.

Galas had left one of the drones to keep an eye on the pack and, hopefully, discover how it was that they were running faster than ever before. The telltale signature of a Deathhound was its reliance on forbidden, other-dimensional technology. That tech stole energy from another world, bonding the damned pilot to his machine and channeling that power through it.

As far as anyone knew, that energy transfer occurred at a uniform rate. It also created a byproduct that spewed out of the mech as an unholy corruption. Sometimes scavenger animals fed off it and were killed or altered in strange ways. This made it easy to tell if you were being followed.

The one saving grace was that they weren't all that fast. But, because the Deathhounds had essentially an unlimited power supply and no need for downtime, they were next to impossible to outrun.

Especially since they never lost their scent. That, too, was perhaps an effect of the technology, but again, very little was known, and much of what was considered to be true was speculation. People just didn't have a run-in with the Deathhounds and live to tell about it.

Galas didn't want to dwell in the negative, but this pack was locked on. Their numbers were growing—eighteen at last count—and now, they were traveling at previously unheard-of speeds. Add that to her growing list of problems.

She flipped through video feeds in her SortieNet until she saw closer images of some of the scavenger birds hovering around the pack of Deathhounds. That didn't look right at all,

"Jinnbo, do you notice any difference in the... oh. Nevermind..." Remembering he was out of commission, she pulled up his medical stats with a thought. They were steady. Diminished, barely visible, but steady. She didn't know what that meant. She slipped down the ladder to the lower quarters and let out a gasp.

Jinnbo's cubby was a crisscrossed mess of stringy, mucus-like strands. His body was wrapped in some sort of cocoon structure that looked like wet cotton candy that was the color of porridge. Galas gagged a little. Couldn't help but look again and gagged once more. Was he forming some kind of chrysalis? She hoped that's what was happening.

"Jinnbo...if you can hear me, I want you to know that...you're really, really gross. Over." She held on to the bulkhead to steady herself, which was good since right at that moment Betsy lurched forward. Galas's eyes snapped to the nasty cocoon thing, saw that it was undisturbed, and shot back up the ladder to the cockpit, glad to have something else to focus on.

Betsy was still traveling upriver but had hit a snag under the water. Galas pulled in two drones and had them scan the river a short distance ahead. She didn't need any more surprises.

She scanned the scavengers once more, noting substantial differences in the quantity and nature. They were changed. In a bad way. She didn't need a second opinion. Many were larger, more aggressive... and some displayed mechanical attributes. Huh? Where before they were just seagulls, now they were cybernetic zombie death-gulls. This also was a new behavior surrounding the Deathhounds' dimensional tech. It seemed to Galas like an ominous turn of events. She noted the change in the SortieNet, checked Jinnbo's vitals once again, and turned her attention to the path ahead.

Galas aggregated the feeds from the drones' broader search. She let the dizzying display of imagery from her corneal implants wash over her. Singling out a topographical format, Galas reviewed what she'd found of the terrain thus far: The western fork was the main body. It was the source of the reddish-brown color, and it continued, winding in serpentine fashion, vaguely east and a little bit north before splitting again.

One fork shot north to lurk among the foot of the mountains before terminating into a towering, half-moon-shaped waterfall. It reminded her of images she'd seen of the many beautiful waterfalls they'd had on Guisse IV. They'd given that planet up to the Delvadr three decades earlier. The eastern fork veered north immediately, the waters changing to a deep green-blue color. This fork was wild and climbed precipitously as it mirrored the fork on the east side of the range.

Given that the signal had come from somewhere in the mountains north and between the two forks of the river, it made sense for Galas to choose the first fork. Its graduated ascent would be much easier. That's why she chose the latter. Hers had not been the first expedition to look for the missing professor, but it would likely be the last. The prior expeditions had been fruitless, which was to say that no one ever came back. She intended to at least improve on *that* metric.

Besides, her life and that of her species depended on it. Her drone net brought back images of tall poles sporting human remains farther up both branches of the river. Additionally, she spotted at least two mechs abandoned at the base of the western rapids. Neither of the two intact mechs appeared to have been occupied any time in the last several years. Vines and small trees had grown among, upon, and in one case, even through them. That sealed the deal.

Galas recalled the drones from the North Fork. She would use them to augment the mech's jump engines instead. The way she saw it, she could shortcut a section or two of the river where it doubled back on itself. That might buy her some time.

The Deathhounds—who, for the most part, didn't have jump capability—would either barge through the jungle or go the long way around. That could give her the window she needed to figure out a path up the cliff wall. Hopefully, her co-pilot would be cogent by then. If he wasn't well yet, other decisions would need to be made.

She realized she'd been unconsciously tracing the outline of the silver necklace beneath her shirt. The pendant was a stylized dagger piercing a heart of garnet. It was one of a pair and had been a gift from her former Blademate, Drakas, the ever-skulking, vengeful spirit that haunted the mech and Galas's conscience.

"I'll make good..." The brittle words hung in the stale, faintly ozone-tainted emptiness of the pilot's cabin. She crossed the small space to stand behind the sometimes-used pilot's seat, hands resting on the stitched leather shoulders.

"I'll make good," she whispered, pursing her lips in concentration, eyes closed, scrubbing her memory of something too painful to recount or maybe just considering the possibilities of what that promise might look like.

In the multi-vectored mind of a mech pilot, a myriad of things were usually going on. At the moment, she wasn't all that aware of what she was processing: fuel-consumption tables, astronomic estimations, armament fabrication queues, repair schedules, AI self-repair protocols, raw ration, and supplement supplies, active and passive armor states, her personal biometrics including stress levels, sleep quality, and subsequent degradation of mental function. On and on, the list went.

She slapped the manual release unnecessarily hard, and the chair rotated to face her. Galas nestled into its contours and fastened the restraints as she rotated back to face the cockpit PLAs. Reddish river water spilled to either side as Betsy plowed forcefully upstream. A thin line of darkly verdant shoreline was visible in the distance. The first of the switchbacks. She guided the forty-ton battle machine directly ahead.

CHAPTER 2

SACRIFICE

Galas spared one of her drones to chronicle this next bit. Purely for tactical purposes. And for posterity, if there was going to be any. An image sprang up on the SortieNet of a river bend. Off in the distance was a cloud of scavengers and a disturbance in the water.

Betsy exploded out of the murk below with a gigantic *thunk* and *whoosh*. The bright pinks, yellows, and lime-green geometric shapes of her paint scheme glistened in the morning sun. She arced and then fell slash glided through the air. A flurry of missiles burst in a smoky blast from Betsy's shoulder nacelles. They headed right for the drone before arcing 180 degrees and racing off toward the trailing Deathhounds.

The 40-ton mech splashed down about a third of a kilometer farther on and in a wholly separate section of the same river body. Galas, using the rest of the drones to augment Betsy's jump engines, had success-fully shortcutted a couple of kilometers of the river by hurdling a stretch of jungle where it doubled back on itself.

She lamented the fact that using only one drone meant she didn't have a comprehensive view of the missiles as they impacted the enemy targets. Off in the distance, a cloud of countermeasures exploded like a full-scale fireworks show. She knew most of the missiles wouldn't make it through the fusillade of defensive measures, but some would. And that was enough. They needed to know she wasn't going to be easy prey. Message sent.

Now, if there were just a couple more of these switchbacks, she might be able to navigate the waterfall section before the Deathhounds caught up with her. As it was, she had bought herself between twenty to forty-five minutes, depending on how the enemy navigated this section, either by going around or by barging directly through the forest.

She really had no idea what they'd do, but they didn't have jump engines, except for that one junky Helminth. She shook her head again. If she was going to die at the hands of the Deathhounds, it would be on a pile of dead bodies, Helminth Kurt would be at the bottom.

Forty-five minutes later, she cleared the second switchback in the river. As for the Deathhounds, now she knew how they'd handle the shortcut she'd taken. They bored a hole through the jungle—lasers, bombs, rockets, flamethrowers; a symphony of destruction. It might have been faster for them to navigate around, but they followed her path exactly and used brute force to accomplish it.

She noted their tactics in the SortieNet and continued to apply speed to reach her destination. She noted that now there were fourteen mechs. A much better result than she had anticipated with that earlier barrage. Things were looking up. She was about to share this good news with Jinnbo before she remembered his current gooey, sticky state of incapacitation. Instead, she checked his vitals again and sighed at their steadily decreasing strength.

Several hours later, it was nightfall. She'd passed nearly a dozen of the warning markers along the river, with human remains as standards mounted upon them. This she took to mean that the locals were *not* friendly. She imagined that that was an understatement and decided to stay inside her mech for as long as possible. The entirety of the mission if she could manage it though, a nagging thought wormed around in the back of her mind. Her instincts, which were usually quite good, told her she wouldn't be so lucky.

An hour later, under a blanket of brilliant stars, she found a tumbling series of rapids rushing through a steep-walled channel. This was a natural ambush point. She considered leaving a booby trap for the pack of mechs behind her when incoming alarms blared and the SortieNet automatically launched countermeasures.

Galas saw the signatures appear in the Battlespace Model ahead of her. Three small mechs.

"Where did these guys come from?"

Something was wrong with this situation. How come she never saw them break off from the pack and circle around? Neither her drones or the scanners had picked them up.

Explosions boomed all around, but didn't touch Betsy's armor as the CMs did their job. An avalanche of enormous boulders rumbled from above and came crashing down into the whitewater between where Galas and the other mechs faced off in the narrow gorge. Galas used the chaos and launched Betsy backward while unleashing her own barrage of rockets and plasma fire. She used her repulsors to shift Betsy toward an outcropping of rock on the uphill side of the gorge.

One of the mechs, a 15-ton Chacma, crippled by a boulder near its own size, took three of her rockets on its main shields before they flickered out and a second boulder crumpled the fuselage, forcing it under the rushing waters. *One down.*

Galas's plasma cannons lanced out at another of the Deathhounds and its own shields flared a blinding orange before the overwhelming beam of energy burned through and into its hip. The attack crippled one of its legs, forcing the pilot to turn the mech's still functioning rear-facing shields toward her while he attempted vainly to slink off into the cover of rocks.

Massive rocks jutted out of the rushing waters, but there was nowhere to hide. Galas took rocket and chain-gun fire across Betsy's flank from the other Deathhound as she launched forward. She arced high into the air before landing on the crippled mech and blasting her repulsors at the last second. The smaller mech exploded under her and she used the momentary uplift to spin 180 degrees and line up the last functioning ambusher.

Too late, the Deathhound pilot turned to flee downstream, back to its pack. The terrain lit up with streaking rockets and plasma fire for long seconds before a concussive boom rattled the surrounding area. There wasn't enough left of the last mech to identify.

"Scratch three—"

Galas was congratulating herself when another low rumbling from above emanated through the audio circuits. She launched into the air on instinct as another barrage of boulders hammered the narrow gorge, blasting plumes of whitewater into the air.

Betsy landed a little further up the gorge amidst the massive rocks, the raging waters knee-high to her 18-meter form.

From the cockpit, Galas scanned the cliffside above, letting the SortieNet evaluate the thousands of tons of rock that might still be knocked loose with the proper coaxing. She was wary that more of the smaller Deathhounds could sneak up on her like these last three had but doubted they'd send such a meager pack the next time. At least she'd sent a message. Still, they'd managed to slow her down. Considerably. The least she could do was return the favor...

Galas offloaded a pallet of material from Betsy's armory in a spot that was hard to detect but would hopefully be jostled in the Deathhounds' passing. The sketchy part was having to exit the safety of her mech. She suited up in her rarely used Targe IV power armor and descended the cable still attached to the explosive payload.

Her gut churned. She was ridiculously vulnerable in this treacherous section of river alone. At night. With the Deathhounds closing in. The power armor would do next to nothing against even one of the smaller mechs, but she had to set a primer and trigger mechanism. Galas was a top-notch pilot, but Betsy's massive mitts wouldn't do the trick.

She wrapped up, ascended the cable, and began piloting Betsy out of the notch while simultaneously dismounting from her armor. She couldn't be out of there fast enough. She hoped the gamble was worth it.

Another hour and the massive horseshoe-shaped waterfalls loomed into view. It was 853 meters tall at its highest point from the valley floor and from below the wide, dark crescent of it extended up, nearly out of sight. Ghostly sheets of mist plummeted from a dozen points along its jagged perimeter.

Along its base, and to either side of a broad lagoon, lay the scattered remains of a boulder field. From there, the river reconvened and crept away through the forest. The water here would be a clear, green-blue by day, but now it was black like the sky. Hiding the dangers lurking within it.

Galas's drones had revealed some of those dangers earlier; snakes, crocodiles, and particularly large and aggressive fish, to name a few. The fish were particularly nasty. The kind that snakes and crocodiles avoided.

Galas had not been inclined to name any of them after herself. There had been one particularly awkward creature she could find no particular use for. It looked like it was part salamander and part plant. Because it was disgusting and didn't do much, she named this after her co-pilot, Jinnbo.

After his display on the deck the day before and his attempt at blowing a hole in the wall while high on acid frogs, she didn't feel bad about it at all. Okay, she kind of felt bad about it.

She didn't have time to check on him every fifteen minutes, so she'd set up a video feed from his quarters. At some point, the web that held the cocoon had filled in entirely and was completely opaque. She couldn't see any part of his chrysalis. She didn't know what that meant but hoped things would be turning a corner soon. What if he morphed into some kind of monster? Or his body was feeding thousands of little baby Jinnbos? This she did not need.

His vitals were weak but appeared to have plateaued. Galas was forced to wait it out. If she had to abandon the mech at any point, she wasn't sure what she'd do with Jinnbo. She'd have to cross that bridge when she got there. In the meantime, she was at the falls, and the Deathhounds were still closing in.

"You'd best get climbing," she mumbled, finding self-talk to be a great way to focus all of her competing streams of consciousness.

Earlier, Galas had split off a few of the drones to generate a detailed map of the falls. They had done so, and Betsy's AI had generated a pathway that involved utilizing jump engines and performing a somewhat extraordinary climb. Mechs weren't designed to perform those kinds of maneuvers, but based on Galas's exploits chronicled in the SortieNet files, the AI gave execution of the planned route even odds.

Galas hated when it did that. She never wanted to know the odds. She despised knowing the odds.

She already knew that a Dragoon mech, like Betsy with the cockpit protruding from her chest, made keeping her center of gravity close to the wall exceedingly difficult. And then there was the part where she needed to utilize dual grappling hooks and cables.

The problem was, by the time she got halfway up, she would be within view of the Deathhounds again. Maybe not exactly within effective range of anything except lasers and medium-range missiles. Still, she wasn't sure how they were loaded out.

Betsy had a tough enough hide. But she was going to be a sitting duck. Fully exposed, under attack, and performing possibly the most challenging climb Galas had ever heard of anyone attempting in a full-on battle mech. She didn't want to know the odds because she was certain that the AI was bullshitting her in order to keep her operating optimally. Its programming allowed it to do that. Which, she thought, was the actual bullshit.

She gave their odds of failure something closer to one hundred percent. And that was rounding down.

"Since when has that ever stopped me?" she vocalized again, to herself or to Drakas, or to Jinnbo or possibly Betsy herself, maybe the whole gang, she wasn't sure.

As it stood, she didn't expect an answer. Drakas was more likely to sabotage the climb at some critical juncture than to express his opinion rationally. He was a bit of a dick that way. It seemed passing to the other side alone had turned him into a much darker version of himself. Galas deliberately avoided considering whether this was her fault, whether directly or indirectly. Guilt over his death was one thing. But guilt over his afterlife? That was a whole new level, even for her.

Galas swallowed, smoothed back her long bangs, replaced her pilot's cap, and breathed out again, focusing instead on the task at hand.

She shook out her hands, partly in an attempt to dry her sweaty palms and partly to shake some feeling back into them. They were freezing and a little bit numb from clenching tightly while navigating the awesome machine.

Her corneal implants flashed with digital imagery as she sorted through the dashboard menus, issuing commands with a thought. With the drones connected appropriately to augment the machine's abilities and the map in place, she launched to the base of the waterfall.

Landing, splitting a few small trees in the process, and jumping again, she landed seventy meters or so to the right on another section of rock rubble. She dipped low and spread her arms out to find balance. Betsy was only slightly higher up on the falls but better positioned for the next sequence of maneuvers.

Car-sized boulders slid from under her toe and heel plates as they flexed for maximum grip on the wet rock. Plumes of mist billowed from below, illuminated by a partial moon. It was cresting the cliff wall to the far left of the horseshoe.

Water cascaded down in several large columns along that side of the falls. Her focus shifted to the sizable outcropping that ran right up the middle. She would have to navigate that section next.

Crouching and launching again, this time she shot a grappling hook midway through her arc. The auto-anchor connected high and right. She retracted the cable while boosting with the hover buckets, a move that swung her up onto another outcropping higher up. Butterflies tumbled in her stomach as the rock shifted beneath her. Large chunks kicked out into open air and plummeted to the lagoon below.

She breathed in through her nose and out through her mouth before starting to guide Betsy through a free-soloing section. From here, the path took her behind the wall of water as it tumbled down, disintegrating into mist along the way.

She was only a hundred and fifty meters above the lagoon at this point, but it might as well be a mile. Betsy could absorb the landing from this height if she landed on her feet, but not otherwise. From here on out, things were going to be dicey. And she was only a fifth of the way up.

Panicked thoughts went to the Deathhounds. Had they reached the ambush spot yet? Had they skirted around her boobie trap?

Galas didn't want to know where the Deathhounds were at that moment. She needed to stay focused. But a distant boom and following rumble echoed in her audio circuits. Somewhere off in the darkness, one of her drones caught a flare of light.

"Oh goodie, they got my present," she said sweetly, and then grinned mischievously. But beyond her bravado, a knot of worry twisted in malicious fits. It was too soon. Much too soon. She would have done the mental math to estimate the time needed, but the SortieNet had populated a time-to-completion display beneath her doomsday clock. That's what she called the timer counting down to the arrival of the Delvadr's invasionary fleet. That little trifle.

"Okay, let's pick this up."

Betsy day-lighted from behind the falls and Galas set up for the next maneuver. She launched her secondary line at a section higher up and jumped while spooling in line. This time, there was no stopping. She shot the primary line to a point still farther up and reeled in both at the same time.

As she neared the first anchorage, she detached and fired again. It was a little like swinging on the monkey bars, only with using grappling lines and wearing a forty-ton suit of power armor. And if the monkey bars were vertical and had a river running over the top of them. When she thought about it in those terms, she couldn't believe that this was plan A. She really needed to rethink her life.

"A quarter of the way up! This is going *not* fast."

Echoes of light played across her close-envelope sensor array screen, and that display zoomed in to take over her HUD. She was concentrating on the signals when she heard a soft *thud* against Betsy's exterior, followed by another. Ordinarily, the copilot would investigate and deal with whatever he found, but that was out of the question, obviously.

Galas instead diverted a small amount of attention to the now repeated thunking noises that sounded to her as if it were raining baby seals—as disturbing an image as that would be. She polled the external cameras and groaned. The racket was coming from dozens of the corrupted scavengers. They were dive-bombing Betsy, maniacally trying to disable the drones augmenting her abilities.

Galas had never heard of anything like this before. And because of their size, she hadn't caught their signals early enough to prepare.

"Shoo! Get lost!" she yelled from the cockpit, the notes ringing dully throughout Betsy's interior.

Galas thought the command to harden the mech against an EMP, and then ran a high-voltage blast through Betsy's exterior, frying a good number of birds. She imagined Betsy's outsides would reek of month-old barbecue for some time.

Still, more of the frenzied creatures bounced off Betsy's armored hide, while others managed to latch on yet again. After another dozen had gathered, Galas blasted them again. It was more of a nuisance than anything else, but it was slowing her down.

That's the intent, she thought in frustration.

She split off a couple of drones to get eyes on the incoming pack of mechs and warn her when they were within range. She had expected to get at least thirty-five more minutes of productive climbing in before that happened, but these scavengers were not anything she'd anticipated. Notes were filed. She doubted they'd ever be read.

Galas released the primary line's auto-anchor and then fired the line again. It struck high atop the central column of rock. One of the drone feeds provided a glimpse of Betsy's angular lines and punk rock paint job amongst the moonlit wall of rock. She was surprisingly hard to spot. Not that it was going to matter with these bionic buzzards swarming her like plague flies.

Reaching the anchorage, she dug in toe plates once more and reached out with Betsy's ceramo-metallic gauntlets to disengage the anchor manually. That allowed her the chance to swing the piton tool head by her forward-facing cams to get a good look at the surfaces. They were still clean and crisp. She wondered at the material that could punch into solid rock at ballistic speed and detach just as quickly without damage. As long as it worked, she didn't need to understand it.

She was nearly halfway up the falls now, Galas with all her silent partners. She saw a tuft of vapor escape her lips, and her pulse spiked. She didn't need this right now...

Galas forced herself not to react but continued to focus on the myriad of tasks at hand. Sometimes ignoring him worked. She had always suspected him to be a narcissist. She didn't know if that was true, but she knew the gray rock thing worked sometimes.

If she didn't stoke the emotional fire with a response, sometimes he'd wander off and do something else. She didn't know what that was about. Didn't care. Right now, she prayed he'd take the hint and not somehow draw on the emotional energy of her fear and desperation.

Galas checked the drone feeds as the temperature dropped. She couldn't get any usable intel. They were all too busy dodging the mechanized scavengers to be of any use. The plummeting temperatures began to slow. She might just make it out of this one... Glass shattered from somewhere outside the cockpit. It was her picture frame; she was sure. She forced herself to stay calm. *Don't give in. Don't get upset. Don't give this needy bastard anything to work with.* There was too much on the line right now.

She breathed out a calm, controlled breath and was relieved when the vapor slowly dissipated.

Dodged a bullet, she hoped. *Now, for the tricky part.* She needed to traverse the face again.

Galas tuned the restraint system up to battle mode, something she should have done earlier, but found it too confining. She instantly sunk into the pilot's seat while the cushioning snugged in tight around her. The seat's headrest slid up and over the crown of her head to rest on her forehead. That was good enough for now. If she was concerned, she'd suit up in her power armor. Barring that, a catastrophic impact would trigger stasis gel.

You didn't get out of that on your own. You needed to be retrieved. She'd heard of pilots locked inside for weeks. Luckily, the stasis gel lives up to its name and literally induces a stasis coma via nanomeds built into the goo. The wake-up from that was...unpleasant.

That was a tactic used sometimes to capture enemy pilots; massive concussive shocks that would set off the enemy's stasis-gel systems. They called it 'turtling'. Wouldn't it be awesome if she could call in an orbital strike on her little Deathhound problem? She doubted Deathhounds even bothered with that stuff. Plus, orbital strikes were a luxury from a bygone era. Humanity was down to guerilla tactics now. The EDC was little more than a namesake.

Confident she was tucked in tight; Galas sucked in one long breath and blew it out through puffed-out cheeks. Betsy blasted off her perch, left and away from the rock wall just as alarms blared within the SortieNet. Incoming missiles. *Perfect timing.*

"Drakas, anything to say?!? No? That's a first..." she mumbled through gritted teeth while making in-flight adjustments before impact.

The mech continued its arc away from the wall, out into the darkness. The sirens were still clanging in Galas's mind. She initiated countermeasures, targeted three of the mechs now in view, and fired Emag rounds from a trailing arm. All this while focusing on two highlighted chunks of rock high and left on the cliff wall.

The first of the grappling line crosshairs lit up, and she fired. This twisted the mech in the air as it fell. She fired the hover buckets in short, staccato bursts to prolong her trajectory. The Betsy pirouetted as she traversed sideways.

Galas fired from both shoulder nacelles before Betsy spun back to face the wall. She hoped the drones were catching this hardcore swashbuckling extravaganza of mechanized warfare. If she was going down fighting, she at least wanted it to look pretty.

The next set of crosshairs lined up above.

She was mid-command to fire the second line when the mech was slammed from behind. The impact jarred Galas's brain hard enough for her to taste ozone. She blinked away the stars as she tried to regather her wits.

The grappling line reeled off uselessly into the night air. The explosion had been triggered by Betsy's auto-countermeasures, which saved the mech from a direct impact. Still, the force of it sent Betsy spinning at the end of the new line, directly into the heaviest section of water.

The auto-anchor—capable of holding the mech's weight under normal circumstances—exploded from the wall as Betsy swept into the roaring falls. Galas's stomach shot into her throat as they fell, taken by the force of the water already falling at speed.

Another explosion slammed the machine, lifting and mashing it through the falls and into the cliff face beyond. Betsy crammed into a depression in the wall, which gave Galas's rattled brain a moment to work with. Toe and heel plates gouged furrows into the rock as she drove the hover engines to 200 percent.

Something stuck, either a foothold or a handhold. She couldn't tell. But the rock face that'd been rushing past the cockpit in a flurry of sparks stopped with a jolt. In the intervening seconds, Galas retracted the broken grappling line, ejected the shattered tool head, and replaced it with a new one while redeploying her countermeasures.

"Baby, I love you," Galas said, kissing her palm and placing it on the cockpit plasteel. It'd been a good run, but now she only had one chance of making this mission successful, and it was going to involve a gut-wrenching sacrifice.

She slid down the ladder to Jinnbo's quarters. She tried to remove the cocoon from where it was good into place with her boot knife but with no luck. She ran the couple of meters to the utility closet on the same level, jumped into still-warm powered-armor suit, and ran back to Jinnbo's cocoon.

The power armor had plasma blades built into the forearms. She used the blades to cut through the thick, translucent strands and she scooped the cocoon into a rucksack she slung over the suit like a messenger back. That's the best she could do.

Via the SortieNet feed, she watched a color-enhanced image of a laser scythe through the water behind them. It was just below where Betsy was dug into the rock wall. Which meant the Deathhounds couldn't see exactly where the mech was behind the wall of water.

Good, she thought. She also noted that their forces were down to only a dozen or so. Who knew, with enough time, maybe she could have whittled them down enough to make the final battle a fair fight? Didn't really matter now. She had run as far as she was able, and the mission was all that mattered. Of course, Drakas would have a different opinion about that.

The power armor's readouts blinked green as the SortieNet ran through system checks while Galas ran back, struggling through the cramped space in the bulky suit. She reached the pilot's cabin, expecting more explosions to come.

Her battle sense was dead on, of course. Time slowed down as she entered the compartment. Her arm came up, incinerating the metal and glass of the windscreen with a forearm-mounted plasma cannon. Charging forward, she leaped off the pilot's chair and smashed through Betsy's canopy in a cannonball, using the suit's head, forearms, and knees to protect her co-pilot in the rucksack. As she cleared the nose of the mech, she spread-eagled and scrabbled for traction on the slick granite face. A newly gouged-out chunk of rock made a perfect platform.

The anticipated barrage of explosions came in a hellish torrent. They blew a hole in the cascading waters and mashed Betsy's forty-ton frame into the rocks around Galas's armor. For a second she thought she guessed it wrong and got herself and her copilot squashed by her own mech. But Betsy took most of the abuse. The impact and the noise were so intense she couldn't tell she wasn't hurt for a long, dreadful moment.

Her mind sprang into action, checking Jinnbo's vitals, recalling all of the remaining drones, and killing the hover engines.

As Galas realized she wasn't able to check Jinnbo's status anymore, Betsy fell. She watched helplessly as feeds from multiple drones chronicled the demise of the abandoned mech. It bounced off a promontory of rock like a broken toy and tumbled back through the cascade. Galas cut power from the reactor and let it look as though the impact from the missiles had shut down the mech's systems.

The darkened shape tumbled away into emptiness. Betsy convulsed with a series of explosions as a wave of missiles hit her, one after another after another. The mech burst into flame halfway down and plummeted the last three hundred meters to the darkened lagoon below.

It had been a tactician's gambit, and the only way to ensure the mission kept going and that she and her co-pilot stayed alive, but the sense of loss was…

"Bye-bye, baby," Galas whispered.

The sudden pain and panic that echoed through her was not something she'd considered in the moments leading up to her evacuating the mech. It felt so personal, so … penetrating.

Betsy had been her home and, in a way, her companion for the last fourteen years. *Fourteen years.* And then there was Drakas. The ghost of the mech and her former Blademate … and lover. Was he gone forever, too? Would he be at rest if he was? She didn't think so. Had she just sentenced his soul to an eternity of restlessness while destroying the best chance of completing her mission, one with humanity's very survival at stake?

She watched the wreckage burn, recording the image and storing it to a personal file within the SortieNet. With a thought, she scattered the drones. Best if they didn't draw any attention from the Deathhounds, now closing in on Betsy's lifeless corpse.

CHAPTER 3

FREEFALL

Galas sensed her chances of skulking away unde-tected narrowing. But she still found it impos-sible to tear her eyes from the flaming wreckage below.

She re-situated Jinnbo's rucksack while she watched. She hoped Jinnbo was alright, that she hadn't somehow harmed him as well. Besides the chaos of the last couple of minutes, she had no idea what was going on with him. Had the acid frogs sent his body into some kind of catatonic shock? Or was he going through some sort of metamorphosis, or some-thing else entirely? Xenobiology wasn't her forte, and he didn't come with instructions. All she could do was try to keep him safe until his recovery was complete, if that's what it was.

She started climbing. Again, not something her equipment was specifically built for. Careful to find her foot placement first, she spotted the next hand-hold and then stepped up into position to grab it. Free-soloing a waterfall at night in a power suit. *Why does this feel normal?!?* she wondered, only half-heartedly amused by the thought.

She climbed for thirty minutes, making negligible advancement, and finally called back one of the drones. Following her instructions, it plunged into the waters of the plateau above and rode the falls down. She thought this small amount of subterfuge might ensure curious eyes wouldn't follow it to her hiding place behind the curtain of water.

She used the drone to micro-map the rock face and the SortieNet AI to generate her route. This sped things up considerably. She was still going to be exposed near the top of the falls when she exited from behind the safety of the falls to top out. That would leave her vulnerable but, like everything else, she'd have to cross that bridge when she got there.

It was possible she'd have to wait for hours before making the transition if the way wasn't clear. It was equally likely she'd plummet to her doom well before that.

As it was, she now had thirteen lunar cycles—roughly a week—to complete her mission. That was first, to find Professor Goodfall and the artifact, and then—the mission planners speculated—to activate the planet's ancient defense systems. If it was even possible.

She had to give herself enough time to do whatever needed to be done, so finding the professor was paramount. Having to downgrade from a full mech to a power suit was a serious setback. It would impact her speed for sure, but, at least this way, she wouldn't be leading the Deathhounds right to him. *That had to count for something. Right?* She hoped it would.

Overseer Naar was not satiated. He scrutinized the waterfall and the jungle emanating outward from it, thinking he must have missed something. The directions were simple and direct as usual. Destroy the Dragoon class mech. The marker had led him and the loosely affiliated gang of Deathhound mechs to this machine. The *remaining* Deathhound mechs, he reminded himself. He was glad that he'd allowed that idiot in the Helminth Kurt to step ahead when they'd entered that unnervingly narrow section of river earlier.

He gazed again upon the flaming corpse of the Dragoon. It was marked in the way of the alien tech; a scent, a presence, something not quite animal and not quite machine. Its real-time global position effectively broadcasts to any Deathhound within a thousand kilometers. Darkenergy unlimited. The bounty, 643 Anti-Suffer. That'd go a long way to stave off the mounting misery he'd had to endure over the last eight months since his last bounty. Every day, the pain, the hunger, grew. And now, he'd laid low the enemy machine, but still, there was no reprieve?!?

Panic and rage washed over him. And then, as he pressed his palm down on the pointed butt of his ceremonial blade, the pain catalyzed his thoughts, crystallizing them into focus again. He dispatched the scavengers.

There must be something missing. The mark was still fixed on the smoldering, broken body of the mech. Well, at least he could scavenge the carcass. *Maybe it was possible to upgrade?* The machine didn't seem to be that badly damaged, and the Darkenergy was flowing in a way it had never before. Had their masters decided this gateway was more important in their plans for conquest than originally assumed?

He'd never heard of the flow increasing before. He'd always assumed it was a law of nature. That it was immutable. But if selling his soul to the dark masters had taught him anything, it was that laws, like people, were meant to be broken, twisted, and, ultimately, made to serve.

Overseer Naar's mech stepped into the midst of the others. Two massive mechanical hands reached into the jostling bodies, and then thrust outward, throwing the smaller mechs like rag dolls. He grabbed the much larger carcass of the Dragoon and pulled it down the rock rubble and into the pool, dousing its flames in a rush of steam and smoke. Then he stretched it out flat near the edge of the pool.

The smaller Deathhound mechs—the Aardwolfs, Chacmas, Shrikes, and even the Helminths—spewed corruption. A bubbling oil slick of black, orange, and red filth poured out of the hands, feet, and head of the lead mech in undulating, serpentine waves. In the span of minutes, a thick layer of filth covered Betsy's ravaged corpse from head to toe. And then, Overseer Naar's Aardwolf splayed its own body out on top of the other. Filth and corruption continued to bubble out of its joints and from seams in the armor.

The bubbling and foaming continued as the smaller mech almost seemed to disintegrate into the larger form beneath it. The other Deathhounds gathered around tightly. Watching in solemn silence, rocking, trance-like, side to side in a bizarre, mechanized witch's circle. The waterfalls bellowed behind them, and the moon slipped behind clouds, refusing to cast its silver light upon the unholy proceeding.

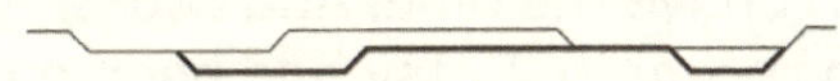

Whatever the Deathhounds were doing to the body of her abandoned mech, at least they had their entire attention devoted to it.

Galas had climbed higher and higher behind the column of white water. Sections of it glowed in the moonlight. At this elevation, there were a dozen separate channels that careened off the plateau's edge into the void beyond. Some plummeted the entire distance while others rent themselves on stubborn outcroppings of rock that had not yet succumbed to the river's relentless grind.

Galas's cascade was just left of the widest section of the falls near the center. Adjacent to it, a narrow band of rock ran uninterrupted from top to bottom, the full 853 meters. Another time, she could have sat for hours, admiring it from above and below, maybe capturing it in her sketchbook in addition to logging its characteristics to the SortieNet. It was, after all, in uncharted territory. Someone had to do it. But now was not the time for such things.

Jinnbo was still catatonic and stuffed inside a rucksack strapped around the chest of her power armor like a papoose. She didn't know if he was still alive. Maybe she could slip a sensor pad from her med kit into the bag with him? That could work.

But her mech, Betsy? There was no fixing that. She was utterly destroyed and being defiled in some bizarre demonic ceremony by a pack of Deathhound mechs far below.

It was another scene that should be more thoroughly chronicled if she had the stomach for it. But one, she didn't have the time. And two, she *didn't* have the stomach to watch. Betsy had been a part of her.

Galas leaned into her well-honed ability to compartmentalize her feelings. Instead, she focused on the fact that now was her best and only chance of ditching the Deathhounds for good. Though she'd never heard of anyone evading them for long.

She sampled the imagery coming from her scattered drones using the system's SortieNet and her corneal implants. These tools synced perfectly with the Targe IV armor, which was, in and of itself, essentially a micromech. It was fully enclosed, waterproof, armored, and even had its own reactor and hover engines. Plasma cannons, shoulder-mounted AP (anti-personnel) rockets, and dual grappling lines rounded out the arsenal.

There was something else she was forgetting as she ran through the loadout in her mind. *Oh well, that's good enough for now.* Her brain was getting a little punchy. A stim might help her focus, but she'd need those later. She slipped into a waking meditation instead. Tried to anyways...

She let everything go and tuned all of her thoughts into the task of climbing. It was a strange feeling for her, allowing herself to be totally engrossed in a single task. It was foreign but, in a way, freeing. She *had* to focus on what she was doing. There was no margin for error. One slip not only meant death for her but death for her planet.

No pressure.

She let her focus get really small, letting the now consume her mind like a religion. Her hand navigated to a chunk of rock, swept aside a piece that felt loose, and then dug in a piton-like finger into a crevice. She gave an exploratory tug, pulled herself up into an off-balance ball of sorts, and slid her free hand left along another crack. After an uncomfortable moment of uncertainty, it sunk into the opening she'd hoped was there.

The micro-map the SortieNet had created from the drone feed was great. But not perfect. She breathed, and then continued, climbing higher and higher. Galas looked up and zoomed in on where the river cast out into the empty air like a perfect pitching wave. She had a ways to go before she could tuck in under that lip and stage her finishing sequence to the top.

It'd been several hours since she'd been forced to abandon Betsy and allow her to be destroyed by the enemy. Tactically sound. An acceptable loss. She tried to convince herself that her decision qualified for these assessments. The drones provided plenty of footage, and she assured herself all the Deathhound mechs were accounted for.

Her internal pep talk wasn't working.

"Dammit, I'm losing focus again."

Galas tucked her knees into a little overhanging pocket and flexed her calves. It pinned her in place and allowed her to drop her arms and get some circulation flowing again. The suit helped with that, but it felt good to stretch them out this way. Her mind wandered again. She hadn't even fought back. What would Drakas have done? Well, she knew what he'd have wanted. For her to go out in a blinding haze of plasma fire. To enter the afterlife with honor.

Her thoughts slid from the esoteric and returned to Betsy, bouncing around there for a moment. It left a bitter taste in her mouth. What a loss, and to have nothing to show for it. She'd have her revenge ... but later. She imagined angelic wings humming behind a pristine black mech, spitting fire and justice upon a horde of malformed demonic mechs. The offspring of a troubled conscience perhaps, but it was a gratifying fantasy. The thought was there, and then it was gone. *Okay, back to business.*

She directed the drones to seek out any of the corrupted scavengers. The creatures— altered by the corruption, becoming larger, more aggressive, and somehow mechanized— were no longer purely animal in nature but co-opted. Possessed, if that were possible. She didn't yet have a word for it but, essentially, now they worked for them. They, too, were Deathhounds. The Corrupted.

She filed her observations in the Targe IV's truncated version of the SortieNet. Still a full AI, but with reduced processing power, and much of its library is now satellite-based. Essentially, she had to settle for the travel-buddy version. She'd get by.

The drones spotted several of the creatures, and they appeared to be hunting for something, which she assumed to be her.

She used the SortieNet to map a path out from under the falls and up the adjacent section of rock. If she could get over the cliff's edge, she could then use the river itself as cover to traverse to the western hillside riverbank. It would take a while and be extremely dangerous, but it was feasible. But she wouldn't be able to take Jinnbo with her. He'd drown like a bag of kittens.

She worked up at least a partial solution. She would leave Jinnbo here, hanging from the side of the cliff behind the waterfall. Then she would make her way to the river's edge and the forest beyond. After the scavengers were all clear, she'd send a couple of the drones back to pick him up. He was light enough that they'd be able to carry him safely.

She nodded as she pondered. It was a surprisingly good plan. So long as he didn't wake up and try to climb out of the bag. Leaving a bag of kittens tied to the side of a cliff was equally as effective as throwing it in a river. The analogy was disturbing. Galas opted to think about everything that still needed to be done after they made it to the relative safety of the uncharted jungle beyond.

She reached up to find a handhold and was surprised to see a pair of beady eyes staring back at her. Using the enhanced imaging of her power armor, she zoomed in and determined that the eyes belonged to a freshwater crab. Hundreds of feet up on a cliff wall behind a waterfall. It showed that life would cling to whatever purchase it could find. She determined to demonstrate at least the same measure of tenacity to survive. She *would* find Professor Goodfall.

Then she would utilize whatever discovery he'd stumbled upon after all these years to engage the planetary defenses and humanity would send the Delvadr packing. Someday she'd see the waterfalls of Guisse Beta for herself. But, until then, she had some work to do. She reached beyond the pocket where the crab had been and resumed her climb.

Twenty minutes later, she was positioned below the lip of the falls. She checked Jinnbo's vitals—the sensor worked!—and then she secured his make-shift cocoon to the cliff wall by tucking him between the crook of a gnarled root and a protruding nodule of rock. It wasn't pretty, but it was tucked right up to the shelf of rock that formed the lip of the falls, keeping him out of view from nearly any angle. He would be safe for now.

Still, Galas found it difficult to leave him.

"I'll be back for you. Hang in there," she winced at the unintentional pun and tried to rub her face, but the power suit's gauntlets and face shield got in the way. Oh man, her brain was a mush pile...

She vowed to herself to get to the protection of the forest as quickly as possible so she could send the drones back for him before he woke. Echoes of her hollow promise to Drakas and the subsequent betrayal of Betsy rattled in the periphery of her mind.

This time would be different...

Galas used the SortieNet to compile an aggregated feed from all the available drones. The Deathhounds were still gathered closely below, but it looked like whatever they were up to, they were close to being finished. Additionally, most of the scavengers had dispersed. Their ever-increasing search perimeter providing greater and greater opportunity to slip through it.

She didn't need to worry about that quite yet though. She just needed to get over the edge and back into the water without being seen. And without being pulled back over the falls. That last part was of equal, if not greater, importance.

There was the tiniest chance she could survive the fall in her current rig. But then she'd be within a hundred meters of the Deathhounds, and though she didn't understand their tech, she imagined their sensors would pick her up immediately. That would be the end of her and, possibly, every human being left in the solar system.

Galas slipped far to the right of the cascade, thinking it best to keep it between her and the unholy congregation below. She scanned the path above and locked it into her memory. Then she highlighted it in the SortieNet, creating an augmented reality breadcrumb trail. The handholds and footholds glowed an intense, translucent purple. The color was distinguished enough from the terrain to stand out but subdued enough that it wouldn't obscure the necessary details.

She'd been living within this fluid version of reality since she was ten and started working in her father's mech in earnest. She blinked out of the reverie and focused *again* on the task at hand.

One last scan for hostiles showed all-clear. She moved, focusing on staying slow and smooth. Fast motions would be more easily spotted from above or below.

It took less than a minute, but it felt like an eternity. Sweat sat in beads on her forehead. It gathered on her scalp and the back of her neck. She rolled onto a flat rock near the cliff's edge and breathed a sigh of relief while looking up at the tandem moons.

The pair of natural satellites had drawn directly overhead in the night sky. A shadow flicked past, and her heart stopped. She eased when she realized it was one of her drones. She was still trying to swallow to clear the lump in her throat when a second shadow slid past the pale partial disc. Then the drone feed went dark.

A silent alarm went off on the SortieNet, informing Galas of the loss of comms. *No kidding.*

Galas rolled onto her stomach and slid over to the water's edge. This close to the falls, the current was moving much too fast for her to stay hidden in the water. Galas crept through the reeds along the water's edge on her belly for a few meters, but it still was too exposed from above. She would have to chance it.

Slipping into the water, her feet swept instantly away. She initiated the repulsor field generators on her shin and calf armor. Ordinarily, they were calibrated to oppose gravity, to assist with jumping and landing. But they could be used for propulsion just the same. She had worried that using them while climbing would have given away her position. But up here, and underwater, she surmised it was a risk worth taking.

This was not rapid transit, but it provided enough boost to offset the current, essentially creating a state of equal but opposite force. Stasis, or at least something close to it. So long as she was pointing upstream, she could essentially glide sideways toward the bank, using her hands and body to direct the flow of water over the suit. It would be like flying, except underwater. *No problem,* she thought, laughing nervously and thinking about the yawning eight-hundred-something meter drop behind her.

Guiding the suit proved awkward and not very forgiving. It took a lot of focus, but somehow, she managed to poll the remainder of the drones and verify Jinnbo's vitals (again) while traversing the middle section of the river.

Jinnbo's state was unchanged; steady but weak. The drones, on the other hand, were taking a beating. Fully twenty-five percent of them were LOC, short for Loss of Comms. That meant that more than likely they were destroyed or eaten by the Deathhounds' corrupted fauna. Galas again filed away that piece of information in the SortieNet and focused on pulling herself along the river bottom.

She hunted out pockets of slower-moving water so she could get upstream and around the large and unfortunate section of rock between her and the next channel over. The water grew deeper here, and she followed it down, knowing that the deeper she could go, the less resistance from the current.

Movement to her right caught her attention. Dark, ghostly shapes hung in the space between the surface and the bottom of the channel. The salamanders. The *Jinnbo* Salamanders as they were now and forever to be memorialized. They glided effortlessly against the river's flow, their long, broad tails undulating slowly, propelling them forward and yet perfectly in stasis. It looked so easy, Galas thought longingly as she struggled to stay positioned against the oncoming current.

The creatures' oversized mouths opened as they swam, sucking in whatever floated in the waters from upstream. It kind of reminded her of whales feeding on krill. She was glad they weren't carnivores.

Suddenly, a flash of silver appeared dimly from the deeper waters and, just as quickly, was gone.

She couldn't tell what it was, but then she realized the salamanders were nowhere to be seen. She was reminded of how very small and vulnerable she was outside of her mech, even with her power armor. Galas recalled one of the drones and had it drop into the waters upstream and float down, scanning the underwater landscape as it did so.

It took two nerve-racking minutes to complete the scan, but there was nothing. Cold beads of sweat formed on the back of her neck and forehead, prickling her scalp, and a knot of dread tightened in her stomach. She moved methodically forward, hoping beyond hope to see the hulking shapes of the salamanders again, but she didn't get that lucky.

Galas paused. She took a quick moment to assess the readiness of her armor now that it was her primary means of survival. The suit was running optimally. She'd rarely used it and as such, it was in essentially new condition. It required no fuel except every few years due to its Dur-Eternum flat-cell reactor. She really only had to worry about overheating, but that would take prolonged expenditure of firepower while engaging full shields.

That said, she'd done it before. Outnumbered, cornered by Karbourr mercenaries, they hadn't expected her to fight. Their mistake. She'd burst from cover—plasma, missiles, smoke, and flares flying. Full shock-and-awe.

The gambit worked. And while she lay there—venting steam, fans whining, dozens of bodies littering the alleyway—D'Kre Federales rolled overhead, looking over the carnage and assuming it was a gangland turf dispute gone wrong. They'd casually rolled on, skimming the rooftops, and hadn't looked back.

What a stroke of luck that'd been. Just because she'd heisted the artifact from the Karbourr Mafia didn't mean it wasn't stolen goods to begin with. The Planetary Museum Archives would have found it missing sooner or later. Sooner if she'd been apprehended by the D'Kre.

Ordinarily, she'd stayed away from gray ops like that, but it was that or take leave in that steamy, dustbowl of a city. Not her idea of excitement. Besides, it paid well and most of the proceeds went to keeping her unit in ammo, food, and fuel. An army travels on its stomach, she'd been told somewhere along the line...

Galas confirmed that her supply of rockets was fully stocked and that her plasma cannons were reading "green" before continuing. She navigated around the outcropping that separated the river—on this side of the falls, anyway. She recalled the drone to boost her repulsor drives and to pull more detailed scans of the surrounding area. She noted that the salamanders still had not returned. She was uncertain as to whether they had simply moved on to better feeding grounds or if the danger that'd scared them off was still close at hand.

As the drone connected to her repulsor pack a small window populated the upper right of her dashboard. It was an enhanced view of the area above the falls.

She diverted attention to it, and it grew to overlay the entire display but as a semi-transparent layer.

She perused the terrain ahead while digesting a host of monitors on her virtual HUD. At the same time, she casually flipped through imagery enhancements and overlaid data from the remaining drones.

A framework began to emerge from the chaos of rock and vegetation. Parallel and intersecting lines beneath the overgrowth betrayed structures.

Soon, it was clear that the jungle around her was hiding the remains of a massive building or compound.

"Somewhere to start anyway..." she muttered to herself. Her voice through the audio circuits of the power suit always sounded like she was speaking into a tin can. And the interior of the suit smelled like molded rubber. Constant reminders that she was operating outside the safety of the terrifying weapon she called home. She felt very small, despite being wrapped in the hardened shell of the formidable Targe IV armor.

Galas yanked her attention back to the overlay of the complex. It became apparent that the river channels themselves had been incorporated into this larger design. She was about to reassign the remaining drones when movement from within the deeper waters caught her attention.

She'd barely registered the danger when her suit was slammed ruthlessly from below and darkness filled the view through her visor. She got slammed again. Her head swam with the force of the blow as she was rag-dolled side to side before being slammed again but, this time, from behind.

Terrifying seconds rolled by until the violent action came to an abrupt stop. Through the murk of rattled thoughts, she issued a mental command. Lights flickered to life on either side of her helmet before coming up to full bright. When they did, a huge, gaping mouth with fist-sized teeth loomed before her.

The creature, dazzled by the light, paused for the briefest moment. Galas seized the opportunity and fired an AP rocket from her shoulder nacelle straight into the creature's oversized mouth. Fractions of a second later, an explosion erupted in front of her, slamming her yet again into the rock behind her. Billowing clouds of blood and flesh drifted silently away with the current. Thankfully, there was no range limit on the rocket's detonator. *The designers must really trust the armor that they put on this thing,* she thought.

Rattled, she drew in a long stuttering breath. Shocked at the intensity of the attack and the speed with which it was all over. She was sure that was one of the fish she'd seen from the drone feeds. Apparently, they lived in the water *above* the falls as well. She supposed that made sense. Something she'd need to keep in mind as she continued farther upriver to the source of Professor Goodfall's signal.

The river current tugged gently. She reached back to grab something to steady herself and caught something that felt like a handle but turned out to be a root. The battle with the huge fish had taken her right to the riverbank. *What a stroke of luck!* she thought, reaching for the embankment. No sooner did her hand brush the root when her lights faltered, and the power suit froze up. Her eyes went wide as the suit bobbed uselessly in the current.

Galas struggled to pull up the controls suite as the suit cycled power to reboot systems shaken by the proximity of the blast. Everything was dark and eerily silent. She couldn't see the rock and roots of the riverbank fading away as she drew ever closer to the falls. The incapacitated power suit floated dumbly, tumbling slowly until it surfaced.

The pale, silver light of dual moons was far to Galas's right in the night sky above. She strained forward in the suit to see more clearly where she was when the whole world heaved over, and the sudden rush of acceleration and weightlessness answered her question.

"No, no, no, no, noooo!" she screamed as her stomach climbed into her throat. The twin moons slipped from view as she tumbled.

Sixteen-point-one-nine-seconds later, everything went dark.

Reality came back to her in bits and pieces. Her breathing filled the small space, and lights were everywhere she looked. Mostly red flashing ones, a few amber, making the pupils of her eyes reflect against the inside of her visor and the darkness beyond.

Pain crowded in, pulsating from everywhere and nowhere all at once. As the seconds stretched on, the pain congealed into a more definable throb. It came from her legs, her side, her back, a shoulder, but mostly from her head. It pounded in rhythm, moving in and out of focus with each heartbeat.

The relentlessness of it faded achingly slowly. Over long seconds, it devolved into a dull but emphatic thrum occupying the part of her mind where all her ideas came from. She couldn't focus. Panic spiked as she started to feel lost inside of her own mind like she was zipped inside a sack that'd been sewn shut from the outside with no way out.

Something bumped her foot. She started in terror but hung onto that sensation as a stab of pain jolted through her spine and down the back of her left leg. Still, she was in no shape to do anything about it. The bump came again and, this time, whatever it was held firm to her foot and calf. An image of terrible teeth coming out of the darkness flashed into her mind, and that sensation of terror spiked again and then faded.

Slowly, cautiously, Galas bent a little at the waist. Her foot was lodged between two chunks of slick, mossy rock. She peeked up to see cascading waters plummeting down into the water a dozen meters away. That's when the roaring static she'd only partially recognized began to make sense. She realized she was bobbing in an eddy pocket beside the falls, and that deafening roar was not inside her head after all.

She glanced again at her foot. It was holding her fast from being sucked back under the torrent of water once more. The roar of the falls continued through audio inputs. She thought about tuning it out and her armor complied with the mental directive. The all-consuming din diminished to a dull thrum.

"That's better."

She heard her own voice, and it was like an anchor to her sanity, saving her from the overwhelming flood of sensory input. She worked to tune out the pain and the urge to panic, focusing instead on what she could see.

Misting water congealed into drops, and then rivulets on her face shield. She moved to wipe the screen and agony shot through her whole body, taking her breath away. She paused, breathed, and then braced herself.

"Maybe just take it in little bits, Gal," she encouraged, trying to talk herself through the colossal effort of exiting the water and the inevitable moment when she'd have to make an attempt at standing upright.

She breathed through the pain of the effort. It was going to take her a while to regain her wits and assess the damage from the fall. That's what had happened. She'd gone over.

Her mind was an incoherent jello. Darkness. Big teeth. Moons. That was it. She focused on her breathing for a moment. The SortieNet would have it all sorted out. But then she remembered something about the suit shutting down.

Huh, maybe not.

Galas had a tugging, nagging thought trying to get her attention, but it couldn't quite fight its way to the surface. Water lapped at the rocks around her. She should probably scan the area.

An anguished scream, deep and powerful, boomed over the roaring falls. Her head snapped to the direction of the sound and, instantly, she regretted it as a wave of nausea and pain washed over her, threatening to pull her back into the void of unconsciousness.

As her vision swam casually back into focus, she saw a gathering of smaller mechs and a medium-sized one. They were only about eighty meters away on a clearing near the water's edge. The larger mech tugged at her memory, but the thought again failed to find suitable accommodation and faded.

It looked like something out of a bad dream. The mechs, blackened and oozing a sickly burnt-orange substance from joints and orifices, stood in a half-circle. The biggest one was at the center and faced what appeared to be a human figure standing before them. He was dark and held a tall, twisted staff. He wore some kind of headgear that supported what looked like horns or antlers. She couldn't make out much else. It didn't occur to her to zoom in on the scene.

It sounded silly to her, but it looked like the night itself clung to the man and shifted when he moved. She could swear it ebbed and flowed from him like breath; like waves on a beach. The figure gestured down the river and Galas could see that the larger mech was hesitant, or maybe that wasn't strong enough. It was grudging to leave.

She thought it strange that she could read the body language of the mech as if it were a person. The pilot of that mech was furious. The mech shuddered with rage. But eventually, it turned, and each of the smaller mechs turned with it. They entered the water and began trudging downstream.

This sparked a memory. Deathhounds. That's what they were.

When Galas glanced back to where the figure had been, she was surprised to find he was gone. This should have concerned her, but she was so tired, and her body screamed at her. She needed to find somewhere to rest for a while and figure out what had happened. She was thinking that this was important when she drifted out of consciousness once more.

Overseer Naar bellowed with rage. His mech augmented and re-transmitted the anguished roar so it boomed even above the noise of the rushing falls, echoing off the cliffs and rolling out over the silvery jungle canopy beyond.

"You have received your payment in full," the dark figure responded icily, apparently unmoved by the display. He stretched his neck from side to side before resuming a smile that stretched the ashen, too-tight skin of his face into a gruesome snarl.

"But the *suffering*!!!" Naar burst out, his voice that of a wounded predator.

"Makes you stronger," the figure quipped. "Sharper. More able to serve the dark lords." The knuckles of his hand stretched taut as he gripped the staff even tighter. Naar could tell he'd pushed him as far as he'd go before things turned bloody. This new mech was powerful, but...

"Now, go. There are other tasks that require your attention," the necromancer said, leaving no room for negotiation.

Seconds stretched by but, eventually, Overseer Naar turned the mechanized bulk of his mech, his consolation prize, toward the water and away from the focus of his ire. The levels of Suffer he'd had to endure for months now were like a gigantic boulder that dragged against every step and crushed him with every pause. There was no respite. No reprieve. The darkenergy flowed stronger than ever before, but never had he been denied his bounty. A reprieve to the constant suffering that was existence as an Insatiate, a Deathhound.

He forced his mind away from the pain, away from the humiliation... He dwelt, instead on what he'd gained. The mech was magnificent, even if it had a strange ... *air* about it. The multitude of voices in Naar's head was a constant thrum, screaming demands,

Kill them.

Kill him.

Kill them all.

Kill me.

Let me die.

Please, I don't belong here.

The voices chanted over and over in his head such that he could not form a thought, could not focus on the single needling concept that stayed like an oozing wound in his mind: *rebellion.*

Naar ground his palm into the cruel edges of his dagger hilt, jolts of pain coursing through him, his eyes streaming with the intensity of the sensation, focusing his mind amongst the muddled fog of voices.

No!

Cannot!

Will be found out. Will be made to suffer.

Existence is suffering.

Death is sweet.

No ... no ... no ... no!!!

The cacophony swelled in his head as he trudged into the river, trailing sweet corruption that splattered upon the rocks. Rainbow pools of oily residue spread upon the surface of the water as the massive mech slipped into the river.

The brothers followed, riding the current down-stream, causing even the largest of predators to sink deeper into comforting shadow as the unholy procession passed. A magnificent blight. A glorious manifestation of demonic plague claiming everything they touched.

CHAPTER 4
ANTIQUITY

Galas awoke. Again.

To her, it appeared that she had her face pressed up to the glass of a large fish tank. Small black-silver scaled bodies with blushes of red at the gills nipped at the glass with open mouths and then whisked away. They'd return shyly, only to whisk away once more.

Sensations like that of laying on the floor of a canoe came to her. She realized, to her horror, that she was face down, bobbing in the water. The glass of the fish tank was the face shield of her power armor. Before she could move, a larger fish darted into view, snagged one of the smaller ones, and then disappeared back into the deep.

"Disturbing."

It reminded her that in the jungle, without her mech, she was part of the food chain.

Reality surged back in a cascade of information. She recalled the attack by the giant fish, tumbling over the falls and falling for what seemed like an eternity. And then some vague impressions of a bizarre ceremony with Deathhound mechs and a dark figure with antlers and a tall staff.

If there was such a thing as a necromancer, that's what it would look like. Her blood ran cold, and she had to forcibly dislodge the uncomfortable memory from her mind.

She strained to move, to get her footing and pull herself from the waters, but her foot was caught. Twisting and looking back, she saw that it was lodged between two rocks that protruded from the water's choppy surface. She was lucky to have been caught by those rocks. Otherwise, she would have been sucked back under the falls and who knows how that would have turned out. Luckily, the Targe IV suit was back online and humming along nicely as if nothing at all had happened. She'd double-check those diagnostics once she was safe on solid ground.

Best not to blow one's self up with an AP rocket, she chided herself, remembering how the sequence of events had been kicked off.

Galas made it slowly to her feet, every cell screaming. She stood knee-deep in the lagoon below the falls.

While glad for the flat graphite exterior of the armor suit that provided a modicum of camouflaging, she preferred Betsy's garish paint job. But there was a big difference between standing out in a battle mech and doing so in power armor. Especially when you were on a solo mission in uncharted territory with enemies behind every tree, under every rock and, apparently, especially abundant in the rivers.

Galas shook her head gently to resettle her thoughts. They felt as though they'd spilled out on the floor like an overturned gumball machine.

Golden light in her pupils swirled chaotically with information from the SortieNet scrolling past as she took inventory of the suit's systems and pulled data from what few drones remained. They were scattered far and wide, much like Galas's thoughts, vainly trying to re-congeal around her purpose here and what she'd witnessed before losing consciousness the *second* time.

Galas initiated a stim micro-injection through several of the suit's bio interface pads, each located close to arteries in her legs, arms, and neck. The sensation was a warm, gritty flood. It was akin to rubbing at an eye infection, but it passed quickly. Grudgingly, her mind sharpened and, as it did, a renewed sense of urgency clamored back into the forefront.

There was little time. Her attention flitted to the countdown of the doomsday clock. Only days before the anticipated return of the Delvadr fleet and with it, almost certain doom for humanity. For the Epriots at least. Perhaps somewhere out there in the vastness, there was a human colony well enough established to perpetuate the species, but Galas knew of none offhand. As far as she was concerned, this was it. Besides, she'd made a go at contributing to humanity in a more traditional way.

"That didn't work out," she said, while dark thoughts swirled in her mind. She had to swallow back a jet of bile triggered by the memory of the night she'd lost Seraph.

That hadn't worked out, but this had to. And maybe ... maybe, there was a chance things could be made right again. It seemed impossible to hold out hope. No, it *was* impossible to hold out hope. The mission was the only thing that existed right now. Galas focused on the present.

She scanned the clearing beside the lagoon to be sure that no stragglers skulking about. Then she pulled the pitiful remainder of the drones in to perform a higher-resolution scan of the area. Within minutes, it was clear that the upper part of the falls was not the extent of the ruins.

In fact, the entire area for several square kilometers was all part of an ancient city, both above and below the falls. It was just covered in foliage as if the jungle was attempting to reclaim itself after a brief interruption. The upper city was more intact, which was promising. Something else that was promising was that with an upper and lower city, there may even be a path back up the cliff wall.

Galas surveyed the area. Where the cliff met the larger slab of the mountainside. To her left, about a hundred or so meters from the nearest falls, was a raised area. It looked to be little more than a thick clot of moss-covered rock.

Toward the back of it, where it met the cliff proper, the pile thinned out. She made her way unsteadily in that direction. As she drew closer to the cliff, Galas found a way down to what might have been an old landing and, hopefully, an entrance that would take her inside the mountain itself.

Rock, dirt, foliage, and tree roots funneled down from either side. Galas followed them to the lowest point, where she was surprised to find a hole in the rubble opposite the wall. It looked like it had been used in the not-too-distant past, but whether by a creature or the local natives, she couldn't tell.

She left two drones on standby, circling high above in lazy spirals, too high up for human eyes. The remaining four she pulled in close. One to scout the den, the other three to augment her suit's shields, weapons, and power in the likelihood of close-quarters combat.

"Six drones. Out of twenty-four. Resources are getting thin..."

Galas's body screamed at her as she clambered down. The fact that she was able to move at all was likely due to the suit's AI introducing nanomeds while she was unconscious. She offered silent thanks to the SortieNet, though she knew it wouldn't respond unless she unmuted its oral interface. That wasn't likely. She'd never needed or wanted a virtual wingman. She was thankful, but not *that* thankful.

The drone feed came through in low contrast, illuminated in shades of green. It gave the empty chamber a spectral feel. There were pockets of darkness scattered amongst the collapsed columns of rock, but the floor was clearly a floor.

Over time, it had become mostly covered in diluvian fans of sediment and spider-like webs of feeder roots and mycelium. Still, there was a distinct pathway that wound away to the right. Galas imagined it probably doubled back somewhere beyond the entrance.

The drone continued, hovering at head height and finding what appeared to be a threshold to a wide doorway carved into the rock wall itself. Galas's breath caught. That was it. The collapsing rock had formed a triangular opening in front of the doorway, partially obscuring it, but there was no doubt what she was looking at. A way into the mountain. And, hopefully, *up* to the top of the plateau.

"This place must have been something else," she breathed out. The words sounded tinny and flat, yet strangely harmonized as the natural tones of her voice were overlaid by her helmet's audio.

She directed the drone further onward, and it continued into a low, wide corridor before static overcame the image and Galas was forced to conclude that the interference from all the rock was just too great. She dropped to armored knees before sliding through the entrance feet first, surprised at how lithe and effortless it was in the bulk of her powered armor.

She'd, of course, trained in the latest generation of the Targe IV system when it was issued but had little use for it in the intervening years. This was a good reminder of its value if she were ever to pilot a mech again. *Poor Betsy.* She crushed the hollow feeling that accompanied that thought and focused on the issue at hand.

Galas realized that due to the slickness of the rocky dirt, the angle of the slope, and how tight the fit was, it would be extremely difficult to get back out this way.

"I hope you know what you're doing," she muttered, imagining herself stuck at the bottom of the hole, having to blast her way out, possibly causing the entire ceiling to collapse in the process.

Broad beams of light punched forward from her helmet and swept the room as she turned to survey the chamber. The view was similar to what the drone feed had shown but, this time, it was in dark shades of brown and gray. She could see the pathway arcing around to her right and followed it.

The crunching sound of decomposed granite beneath her feet echoed loudly in the confined space. The only other sounds were that of her own breathing and the ever-present rumble of the falls reverberating through the very rock around her. At least in here, she didn't have to attenuate her audio inputs to hear herself think.

"Shit."

It occurred to her that in all the chaos of the last several hours, she had not checked on Jinnbo. She prayed he was still safe in his cocoon, tucked in the ledge of the waterfall where she'd left him.

Suddenly, this seemed like an egregious oversight. She checked the connection to the drones she'd left on overwatch and was unsurprised to find that those feeds, too, were little more than static. She'd have to see to Jinnbo *after* she reached the top. That was if he was still alive. She had no idea if he would be.

When they assigned him to her command upon the loss of her previous co-pilot—the fifth such in as many years—she'd assumed that the Epriot Defense Collaborative had simply given her a warm body to fill a seat that they knew would likely be vacant in under a year, anyway.

As such, she had no idea what he was, what he was capable of, or who he'd pissed off to get assigned to her in the first place. She had to find all of this out on the job. It was essentially an indefinite blind date. Kind of like an arranged marriage when you're the eighth daughter out of eight. Just about anyone who could fog a mirror would do.

Galas had gleaned over the intervening months that Jinnbo was actually in hiding, awaiting a trial of which he was the star witness. The trial, however, would most likely never materialize due to the high-ranking nature of the defendant. The defendant, a politician, of course, was still walking the streets and living his life. Jinnbo was effectively exiled and sentenced to death by association to Cadian Galas.

A humorless smirk crept across her face as she recollected, her eyes simultaneously scanning the live image beyond her face shield, the helmet's HUD, and the data from the SortieNet playing across her retinas. That, plus the protective element of her suit, had the combined effect of making the real world seem very much like a VR simulation. A dangerous deception, to be sure.

"Oh, my brain's working again. Happy day."

On a hunch, she checked her med log and saw that the SortieNet AI had been trickle-feeding her a steady cocktail of stims, anti-inflammatories, and, surprisingly, antidepressants.

"Hey, no fucking with my feels," she scolded.

"Sorry." It texted back. It only did that in response to direct verbal commands. Otherwise, it was happy to follow orders without acknowledgment. Unless those orders were unclear. She imagined that might have been the case after her tumble over the falls. There was a strong likelihood that the nap she took after seeing the Deathhound ceremony had been chemically induced. She didn't want to go back to the log to verify. It would send her down an ethical and moral rabbit hole she didn't have time to go down. It didn't feel good, though. Her ADHD brain bounced to something ... else.

She was the only child of a widowed mech pilot. Her brain took a right turn.

When her township burned at the age of nine, she stayed with him full-time. There was nowhere safer that she could have gone to. Another right.

As such, she was infinitely capable inside the armored walls of a battle mech. Once more.

Anyone who attempted to fill the role of copilot was little more than a vestigial organ. And back to the original thought.

Jinnbo had once or twice proved to be something more than redundant or useless. Except that those moments of competence were interspersed with long dry spells, punctuated by bizarre behavior and mostly inane babbling. Still, she had grown to tolerate him and, for that, she at least owed him the courtesy of not letting him fall to his death. If she could help it.

"Wow. These meds are really doing a number on me," she said, realizing she'd just free-associated the long way around the inside of her mind and ended up, four or five minutes later, in the same spot.

Galas's hand came up to brush an errant lock of hair from her face, but the armored glove bounced uselessly off her face shield again. Annoyed, she blew the auburn strands to the side, but they settled back down in the same spot, partially obscuring her right eye even more. Peeved, she gazed past it to the entrance but was still unable to pick up the signal from her lost drone.

"There must be some sort of interference down here." A quick scan yielded a minor radioactive signature but one that the system was unable to recognize.

"That's odd," the tin can reproduction of her voice rolled around inside her helmet. It was hard for her to fathom an element that the SortieNet didn't have loaded into its crystalline archives, even if there were mountains of data that were offline at the moment.

Suddenly, she was glad she was wearing the suit. She wondered if the radioactive signature was a remnant of the weapon that was used to destroy the city. That was a strong likelihood. Or it could be naturally occurring and unchronicled. No way to sort it out now. She moved forward through the triangular aperture and into the broad, somewhat clean corridor beyond.

Rather than lead to a shaft or a set of stairs, the corridor continued straight until it disappeared into the darkness beyond her suit's ability to illuminate. Straight into the heart of the mountain. She had no choice but to keep moving forward.

"Okay. Let's see where you go."

In the clearing next to the lagoon, surrounded by the deafening roar and serpentine mist of the waterfalls, stood Sun-Thurr, Guardian of the Gate. Epriot Prime was his domain, though the people who inhabited it didn't know it yet.

His attention was drawn to a spot at the base of the cliff wall where it met the mountain. At his feet lay the remnants of two mechanical drones, their lenses crushed, their electronics bare to the moist jungle air.

In a blink, a *whoosh* of darkness engulfed him, and he sped in a swooping streak to the top of the falls, where he emerged from black tendrils of what looked like smoke but were somehow more solid and creature-like. The shadow from his antlers stretched across the rocks before him, looking like roots from a sinister and malformed tree.

He looked down at the rock below his feet, tracking the movements of his prey hundreds of meters below, through the very mountain itself. His long bony fingers, capped in ebony talons, flexed, and then resettled on his staff as he stood in the predawn gloom. Insects poured from the surrounding rocks and moved in a swirling miasma of chitinous bodies around, but never quite touching, the hem of his robes. And then, in an instant, light sucked in on itself as the coal-black tentacles of smoke enveloped him.

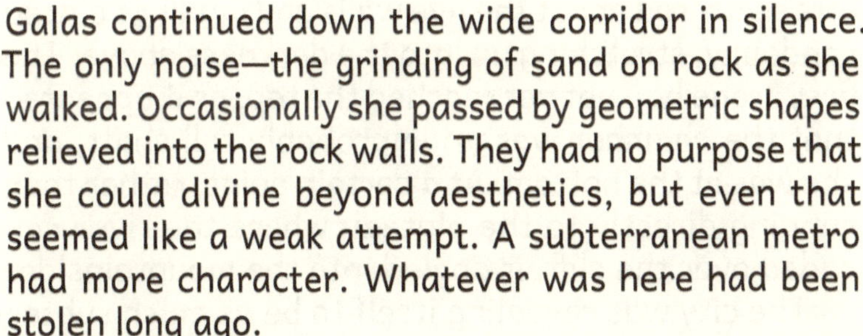

Galas continued down the wide corridor in silence. The only noise—the grinding of sand on rock as she walked. Occasionally she passed by geometric shapes relieved into the rock walls. They had no purpose that she could divine beyond aesthetics, but even that seemed like a weak attempt. A subterranean metro had more character. Whatever was here had been stolen long ago.

At 180 meters in, the corridor took an abrupt turn and angled up and away. Not much of an incline, but enough to be noticeable. She had no idea where she was headed.

Within a short distance, the corridor leveled again and emptied onto a dais with broad stairs leading down either side that emptied onto the floor of a siz-able chamber.

"Whoa."

Galas increased the intensity of her floodlights and could barely make out a massive wall at the far end. She deployed two of the remaining drones and was surprised to receive a signal from the one she'd deployed earlier.

The other drones must be boosting its signal, she realized.

The drone was much farther above them. Apparently, the chamber went all the way up. But all the way to where she didn't know. She stood motion-less, lost in the process of the virtual reconstruction before her as the drones fed imagery and informa-tion into the SortieNet. It, in turn, began crafting a three-dimensional, fully indexed battlespace model.

The battlespace congealed into a large pentagonal shaft. It appeared to be a nexus point, with transport lifts scattered about the five walls and landings placed randomly, stretching up into the darkness above. The first drone had not yet reached the top, as it appeared that the chamber was an improbably tall shaft, and she was at the bottom. At a certain point, rather than running directly to the plateau where the river cas-caded over the cliff, it angled into the mountainside.

The city was revealing itself to be as much subter-ranean as anything else. The magnitude of it caused her to pause. If the city extended into the moun-tain itself, where did it stop? It could link all the way through the range to the north coast for all she knew. That would be... she was at a loss for what that would be. Stupendous ... colossal ... the words fell flat. At the end of that sequence of thoughts was this; *How would she find the professor in all of this?*

It was an amazing discovery but, in light of the impending attack by the Delvadr, one that probably spelled their doom. Hopelessness and futility preyed on her mind like vultures. Her jaws tensed, and her eyes grew steely as she drew deep from an inner well of resolve. She'd discovered it was there when she was nine. She'd cherished its existence through the years. Not the least in the present moment.

"Find the source of the signal, and then track the professor from there," she said as the thought materialized. She snatched it from the ether and held on with everything she had. "The mission. Stick to the mission," the tin can voice rattled around the inside of her helmet.

As she peered around, Galas wished she could explore the complex but strained instead to stay on task. She needed to keep up with the drones or she'd lose the signal again. She thought through a series of commands that the SortieNet compiled and issued, which would ensure that the drones stayed within comms range. This complex would be impossible to navigate without them, and if she lost their signal, she might never find them. Or find her own way out. Well, that wasn't true. She could retrace her steps using the SortieNet's mapping, but still...

Galas took a couple steps forward, and then leaped over the ledge, down to the floor of the complex ten meters below. Her Targe IV armor utilizing repulsor bursts and augmented movement easily soaked up the inertia. To Galas, the two-story fall felt like jumping off a picnic table onto a grassy lawn.

She strolled across the floor of the shaft toward the far side, taking in everything around her and not assuming for an instant that she was alone down here. Nothing on the scanners, of course. But that wasn't always a sure thing.

Galas found her first clue that a party had explored the area, but couldn't be sure if it was the professor's team.

"Don't know who else it might have been," she mumbled to herself as she surveyed the scattered remnants. If she wasn't sucking in canned atmosphere, she imagined it would smell musty and dank. That's what the shredded and moldering tent material seemed to imply. Of course, it also implied a hasty retreat. It was hard to tell how successful that retreat might have been. The site could have been decades old. Here was one of the cool things about carrying an AI with you everywhere you went,

"Enhance image." A section of stained tent fabric zoomed into focus. "Analyze."

A scrolling array of data spread across the SortieNet dashboard, filling her vision. Highlighted within the stream of characters were no less than three distinct human blood types. Also, there was a tracing of torn fabric with suggested examples of what might have caused the trauma.

Within her display, a few handheld implements slid by before settling on a fairly large, hooked talon. Not a bird talon, but one that was distinctly more wedge-shaped. No less wicked, just a little less elegant. This was a ripping device, and the SortieNet was at a loss as to what creature it might belong to. Galas's mind filled in the blanks with every nightmare creature she'd ever heard of.

"Well... that's unsettling," she said to no one in particular, while still scanning the refuse. No more identifying information came as a result of her search, but there were a handful of ropes and hoisting equipment scattered along the back wall—none functional and all too old to trust, anyway.

So, she was no closer to solving the riddle of where the professor was. Or if he was alive and where he might have been sending a signal from, which was her most likely path to finding him and his research. But now she at least had a sense of some of the danger that may be awaiting her in what was beginning to appear to be a massive complex.

The drones were still mapping away somewhere in the darkness above. Galas realized she would have to find a way to scale the shaft if she was going to locate whatever passed for a comms array in the complex.

It occurred to her that she didn't know where *here* was. With nothing else to guide her, she decided that she would refer to the city as Antiquity. This tunnel complex would be the Core Shaft and the section near the falls... the Edge. The entrance area at the bottom of the falls would simply be the Lagoon. All this was tagged in the SortieNet and an image of the city and the Core Shaft's position within it coalesced a little bit at a time. She let the image fade into the periphery.

Looking at the wall that had the dilapidated hoisting equipment, there was an indentation at the base before her, and a couple of bold channels that ran up and out of view. These appeared to be tracks for repulsor lifts. Next to the pit, there was nothing else. No control panel or anything, which was odd.

"I wonder if everything was virtual ... or augmented reality?"

That could be why everything around her was cut rock with no actual writing, images, symbols, or any signs of cultural significance.

"That actually makes a lot of sense."

Suddenly, she could imagine this space alive with holographic structures and interfaces.

Tech, like Xenobiology, wasn't one of Galas's strong suits, but that's what she had the SortieNet for. Her battle computer had a lot more functionality than she usually had use for in day-to-day operations as a mech commander. *No, Captain.* She had no crew. No squad. No support staff. With Jinnbo out of the picture, this was a solo mission.

Galas thought through a list of queries that would get the SortieNet hunting down a central frequency, if any such still existed, that might be the complex's network. It was a long shot. She had no idea how old these ruins were, but she'd heard of networks operating on frequencies generated by crystals and other organic elements rather than electronics. And then it struck her,

"The radiation!

"SortieNet. Focus on the ambient radiation source as a possible municipal network," she said out loud again rather than thinking it. She didn't need to say it out loud, but maybe she was just feeling lonely. Or maybe something was wrong with her? Or maybe it was just the end of the world and she should leave it at that?

"Yes, Ma'am," the AI responded via text.

It would take a vast portion of the suit's processor functionality to sort out that signal, but it was worth a try.

Fifteen minutes later and Galas was nearly bored out of her mind but, slowly, patterns emerged from the noise floor. The processing power available was not nearly as robust as what Betsy had to offer. If Galas still had that resource, she might have been alerted to this signal before she even knew to look.

A familiar pang of loss clanged around in the void inside her. That place had once been full. Her home and constant companion, Betsy, had filled that space. Before that, people had filled that space and, in the absence of all of it...?

The image of bright eyes and tiny pursed lips blossomed in her mind, and a swift blow to the side of her helmet shook her out of her reverie. Galas looked around in surprise before realizing it was her own hand that had caused it. Her ears ringing, she gave little acknowledgment to the bizarre reaction or the memory that had provoked it.

She moved on, a little disconcerted, a low burning flame igniting in her belly. Back to business. It would take a lifetime to put everything back in that box if she opened it. Her heart fluttered a bit realizing how close she'd danced to the edge of sanity right then. *Better to get lost in the moment than lost in the past,* she chided. A mantra she'd repeated more and more through recent years.

Galas let the SortieNet chew on the radiation signature a bit more while she worried about how to climb the smooth surface of the lift channel. She wondered briefly why none of the lifts were at the ground level. Seemed odd for a city under attack... Unless fleeing to the jungle wasn't the safest bet.

Perhaps they fled to shuttle docks or a spaceport? She assumed the prior race had left so abruptly because of an attack, but truth be told, there wasn't all that much information about them. A handful of cities scattered about the planet. Several underwater. Some under ice. This site had only been discovered when the Goodfall Team stumbled upon it while hunting for another lost expeditionary force.

Her thoughts went back to the bodies mounted on standards along the river and then to the shredded encampment surrounding her. A chill ran along her shoulders, and she turned the involuntary shudder into an overly accentuated neck stretch. She wouldn't let her nerves get the best of her. Just because she'd been demoted from an unstoppable war machine to what, in comparison, amounted to a rabble of tin cans duct-taped together. It wasn't quite like that. The Targe IV gear set was formidable for what it was. It just wasn't Betsy.

Galas thought again about the comms array. She hadn't seen anything quite like that in the drone imagery, but then she hadn't sent them very far up the mountain. It hadn't occurred to her at the time that there was anything here below the jungle canopy, let alone something so elaborate, almost another whole city *inside* the mountain. If this was more of a fortress or base, then it could make sense there would be some sort of transportation center on or near the top of the mountains.

Galas inspected the channels in the wall and concluded that climbing up them would be inviting injury. It wouldn't be like crack climbing where you could wedge your hands, feet, and any other available appendage into a crack. That worked because cracks in rock often changed width and had a tendency to provide a lot of friction. This was the opposite of that.

These channels were wider than one of her armored boots, smooth, and ran uninterrupted vertically for long distances. A single slip would be a one-way ticket all the way down. Galas turned around to re-orient herself.

Looking again at the landings that were visible from the bottom gallery, she had another idea. A combination of jumping, climbing, and utilizing her grappling lines would get her a long way if she could link the maneuvers properly.

She let the SortieNet pick a path, and each segment was instantly highlighted in her HUD. It created an augmented reality breadcrumb trail with tags denoting details on jump angles, speed, grappling anchorages, etc. The first landing was across the gallery and only about fifteen meters above the floor.

"It's a start, anyway."

She headed in that direction. No sooner had she begun the trek when a scratching sound echoed through the chamber. It was followed by a string of unnatural clicking noises.

The first two drones were high up, exploring the farthest reaches of the shaft, using the other two as signal relays. The nearest one managed to pick up the movement and paint Galas's HUD with a grainy image.

There were three creatures. They looked roughly Galas's size in her power suit. And to her, they appeared like predators. Pack hunters. They were eyeless, their upper torso resembling that of a thick, black centipede but with long, scaly hind legs and a tail. To her, they looked like a bizarre amalgamation of bug, lizard, and kangaroo. The pack appeared to have her position locked in with whatever senses they used because they stood in a V-formation that pointed directly at her.

She was trying to plan her next move when the creatures exploded forward. A screech reverberated through the chamber as they leaped into the air. Wings springing from under their armored carapace, they flapped so fast that the movement was a blur.

Galas broke for the wall ahead. Augmented movement pushed her forward with speed in multiples of what she could do on foot. The bug-like creatures crashed down hard right where she'd been fractions of a second before and sprang into pursuit.

As she neared the far wall, she bounded, planting three quick steps on the vertical wall, and lunged upward. One arm launched her grappling line to a highlighted spot on the wall. The other trailed back, issuing three purple-white bolts of plasma that lit up the gallery like daylight.

The first shot scored a glancing hit on one of the creatures who trilled painfully as it bounced off the rock wall. The two subsequent shots impacted the second creature as it scrambled to use its companion as a launchpad. It tumbled lifelessly—or at least she hoped, lifelessly—to the floor.

The last bug stuck to the wall with wedge-shaped talons and then sprung up after her. Its wings clicked in a mechanical thrumming noise that reminded her of the fist-sized beetles she and the other kids used to chase in late summer before half the village became a crater and the other half burned.

As the creature reached its apex, barely two meters away, a sound burst from it, or maybe not a sound, but something more like a psychic punch. This happened as one long peel of Galas's plasma blasters electrified the air between them and zippered the creature from head to thorax. The bug exploded as if hit by a speeding transport. That was the last thing she saw.

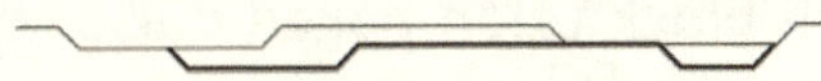

A metallic taste or smell perhaps was the first sensation she recognized. Her teeth and nose were numb and there was a din of ringing in her ears. Gradually, the sensation of wetness on her upper lip became apparent. She wondered if she'd been drooling while hanging upside down. Had she?

Her mind unscrambled in excruciating slow motion. It was all she could do to raise her visor with her free hand before projectile vomiting whatever it was that she'd eaten last out into the air above the landing.

So, there she was, hanging by one arm a meter above the floor. Vomit ran in oozy chunks down the front of her power armor. Blood streamed from her nose into her mouth. Tears of bewilderment ran down her cheeks. Also, she was covered in a Rorschach splatter of bug juice, and her head felt like it'd been stuffed full of shredded denim.

Sometimes, this is what victory looked like.

Somewhere, high on a cliff wall beneath the roaring pitch of a waterfall, small beady black eyes watched as a rucksack that looked as if it'd been purposefully wedged into the crook of a long-forgotten tree root wriggled.

The beady black eyes swiveled on their stalks and, from a pocket of darkness on the cliff wall, a small rock crab emerged. It scuttled forward a tiny bit more as the bag wiggled weakly again. And then, a long baleful screech emerged from the bag. It dragged on for interminable seconds before stopping abruptly.

One small black talon poked out of a gap where the zipper reached the end of its track. The zipper slid slowly down a couple of centimeters until a thin brown snout protruded from the opening. It sniffed twice before a long purple tongue flicked the air and then disappeared.

"I say. I do appear to have been kidnapped," a voice said from inside the bag.

"Again..." a second, almost identical voice added.

CHAPTER 5

GRIND CORE

Galas's toes touched the landing and her body again tried to empty itself, but there was nothing left. She retched a few more times, bent double, her stomach muscles spasming mercilessly in her body's misguided efforts to undo whatever had been done to it. It left her crumpled like a forgotten doll; head pounding, blinking away stars.

That punch... that psychic *pounding* that the bug had doled out left her feeling wrung out and hollow. It was an experience she didn't want to repeat. She realized she was crying. It wasn't an emotional response; she wasn't sad or frustrated; she was not entirely in control of all her faculties yet. She suspected she'd pissed herself as well. Galas thought the command to relieve some of the pressure from the fitment gel holding her in place and shifted her hips a little. Suspicion confirmed. At least, that was the extent of it.

"Tiny blessings," she mumbled.

Feebly, Galas dragged herself to the edge of the landing and collapsed onto her stomach. She peered over the ledge, down at the broken body of a solitary creature below. The one she had wounded was gone.

"That's unfortunate," she whispered, though that wasn't her intention. It just came out that way.

The creature below was odd, though. Not only because it looked like a Frankensteinian mash-up of disparate insects and animals but, because now that it was dead, it had lost all of its color. Its wings were half-retracted. It seemed surreal, like an artist's molding from clay. She was having a hard time imagining these creatures evolving on this planet. And then she wondered how many more of them were out there.

Were there more on the upper levels or just down here below? The fact that they had at least some limited flying ability, it wasn't a far stretch to assume they could be all around her. That thought shook her out of her stupor and re-energized her with a jolt of adrenaline. *No more lying around,* she thought as she pushed herself up and rested on the ceramo-metal honeycomb knee pads of her suit.

Galas removed her right gauntlet and touched her face, gingerly at first, and then she rubbed more vigorously, wiping away the dried blood from beneath her nose and tucking her sweat-drenched hair back in place. Satisfied for the moment, she flipped the face shield back into position and heard the micro-servos seal the mating edges.

Her virtual HUD blinked at her, letting her know that her suit's seal was still incomplete. She put her gauntlet back on and the warnings faded while outlines of the individual screens within the HUD flashed green, and then faded.

All this digital activity happened on the lens of her corneal implants, as well as her suit's HUD. It looked as if the processors had thrown up most of their contents onto the visual display. She mentally scrolled through layers of visual enhancements, files, interfaces, drone imagery, and equipment status levels which had all simultaneously opened when her brain cells had been collectively tazed by the creature's attack.

Once the SortieNet's dashboard was in order, Galas searched the library. There was no reference for such an animal anywhere. It was as if she'd dropped onto an entirely new world, not just some backwater on her own planet. These creatures, the giant fish that had attacked her in the upper river, the cliff-dwelling crabs... A thought flashed through her mind. Maybe there had been entries at one time, but they'd been deleted?

That seemed preposterous. But then, it was no less preposterous than an entire region having remained unexplored since the colonization of the continent a millennium prior. She knew there had been breaches, but she'd always assumed that the hackers had been stealing information by copying it. Not actually *stealing* information from the system. She'd have to think on that some more later.

Captain Cadian Galas—Maiden Makeway in jar-head circles—stood on wobbly legs.

She rolled her neck side to side. The satisfying crunch of vertebrae popping back into place clicked loudly in her ears.

Then she rolled her shoulders and swung her arms across the Targe armor's chest and shook her hands out. She shifted her weight from foot to foot before having to grab the wall to keep from falling over. That was not a sign of readiness.

I'm not stalling... I'm preparing, she told herself.

Getting her circulation flowing, clearing out the cobwebs from her encounter with the ... whatever they were. It was the smart thing to do.

"Okay," she swayed drunkenly, and then righted herself, "...ready to try this again?"

One eye focused on the wall. The other joined it a second later. Luckily, the SortieNet was always wherever she was looking.

The HUD illuminated the pathway from platform to platform, a digital trail that disappeared on up into the darkness, terminating roughly level with the falls—by her estimation, at least. The first platform was one of the hardest to get to, but it was also the lowest to the ground. From here on out, the stakes would be getting increasingly higher. She took a couple of steps and was near full speed before she screeched to a halt, toes hanging over free air, arms windmilling to keep from going over.

She paced back to the far side, crouched, exploded forward, and launched out into the open toward a platform that was nine meters away and a bit overhead. Galas pulled her legs up in front of her like a long jumper, cleared the edge, and barely landed on her feet, before skidding to a halt.

After a brief but successful struggle to keep down whatever was left in her stomach, she paused and listened with the augmented audio inputs of her helmet. There was none of the scratching and clicking noises from before. That was good.

The next platform was farther away and higher up still. She launched the grappling line high above it. She tugged on it to confirm attachment, which was via a technology akin to magnetism but between non-ferrous materials. It was something entirely exotic, certainly alien tech, but she didn't know from where. Nor did she care.

She was just glad it worked. It was considerably less destructive than the mech's ballistic auto-anchors. Much quieter, too. Also, a good thing.

She ran directly at the wall, took two steps, and bounded off it like she'd done before, retracting the line as she did so. This pulled her up and at first away from the wall before swinging back toward it. The grappling line whirred away as she ascended, and then stopped abruptly as she landed neatly on the next level.

Very tidy. Another hour of this, and I might be getting somewhere.

At least she didn't have to deal with the Deathhounds anymore. Though that may be assuming too much. She let out an unconscious sigh of relief, anyway. The drones had reached the extent of their range, with her bringing up the rear at her sloth-like pace. She decided that she needed to continue to explore the complex, even if it meant giving up the augmenting ability of her one remaining drone. Via mental command, it detached from its nesting pad next to her reactor unit and, instantly, the suit responded.

It was sluggish, less responsive, like it had eaten a huge robot steak and was ready for a nap. She'd miss the juiced-up performance from before, but intel was a force multiplier, whereas the power augmentation the drone provided was a luxury. Besides, she could pull it back if needed, or use all four, for that matter.

Galas couldn't believe she was operating with only four drones. If it wasn't for the wonder of new discoveries, this would be an utterly depressing day.

At that moment, she heard the thick flutter of insect wings and her stomach dropped. No sooner did the sound register than blips appeared on her battlespace model. *A lot* of blips. Red blips. In the history of the universe and sensors, red was always bad. The SortieNet had determined on its own that the flying, psych-blasting, centi-roos or stun bugs or psych-hoppers were a threat. *Go AI!*

As the SortieNet formulated a pathway to avoid the creatures, she decided that dying by the hands of something called a Centi-Roo would be humiliating, as well as intrinsically less than ideal. She decided Psych-Hoppers was way cooler, though she'd later replace that entry with Ingens Dipodomys Stupefaciunt. But Psych-Hoppers would do.

With a thought, the Targe IV keyed up her grind core playlist and cranked up the volume. She trusted the SortieNet would let through any pertinent sound. The background noise would amp her up and help her focus. She had the suit spike the O2 percentage and administer a pre-combat stim pack. That was *two* today, but who was counting?

The stim did its job. Almost instantly, she felt clear, strong, and sharp. She took off again, grappling line deployed, springing off the wall. Two blips were incoming.

She turned to look up and the psych-hoppers were falling to meet her. Galas spun on the end of the line so she had a shot at their bellies and blasted away. She let momentum swing her back around just in time to touch down on the wall for another kick-off.

The vertical shaft was growing narrower, with fewer platforms up here. This condensed the hostiles coming at her. Her optimistic side labeled this as a target-rich environment. She muted the pessimistic side. Instead, she allowed the SortieNet to modify her pathway on the fly; adjusting to the enemy as they jockeyed for the best angle on their prey.

Reaching the apex of her press off the wall, two more hoppers lunged at her from the opposite side of the narrowed shaft. This time she deployed a cluster of micro-AP missiles no longer than her palm and fingers. The rockets careened and planted themselves on target where the bug's scaly thorax connected to its plated centipede underbelly. The result was magnificent if you were into squishy things exploding, which, given the circumstances, Galas was a big fan.

The music swelled in her ears, and grew raspy, chunkier, and atmospheric. Galas felt honed to a gleaming edge. She swung back toward the wall as the grappling line whirred away. Outside her helmet, the thrumming of insect wings and scrabbling of talons on rock was intensifying too. But Galas was painting by numbers a solution that the SortieNet had compiled: a wraith within the battlespace.

The grappling line retracted. The armored boots touched the platform deck. The armored body rolled, lights spinning psychotically as first one, then two more of the insects swarmed into view. Six blinding cracks of plasma whipped out and gore-splattered every surface within range. Galas's momentum carried her into a completely unnecessary back handspring, but she was in the zone now.

Having spent so much time over the last couple of years driving her mech, she'd forgotten how gratifying the hard, physical labor of close-quarters combat could be. Growing up in an interplanetary war, there had been precious little opportunity for things like dancing and artistic expression. This was as close as she was going to get, maybe ever. The floor was hers, and this was *definitely* her favorite song.

The HUD flashed with five more hostiles dropping in from above. Armament trays re-racked and missiles launched from her shoulder nacelles as she charged again.

This time, she angled toward the wall. She planned to get three steps up and left toward the next platform—never mind how far up the shaft they were—and carry that speed for a big broad jump to the one beyond that. She hit the wall and bounded up to the platform when suddenly the chasm exploded in light. It was just as the missiles made contact with the first three hoppers, but it wasn't the explosion.

The other two creatures were supposed to be taken out by plasma fire, but Galas was completely bewildered by the chaos of kaleidoscopic light. Holographic lines shimmered all around her, in the air, and on every surface. She missed her footing, and it was all she could do to scramble off two hands and a foot to cross the gap in the split platform.

Galas's eyes went round with fear as she calculated her trajectory. She was barely going to make the gap. She knew the two remaining hoppers were drawing dangerously close to stun range.

She spun, landed on her back, and brought up both hands to fire akimbo when a repulsor lift whooshed out of the darkness from above. Through her audio, Galas heard the sickening *crunch* as the lift smashed the creatures. Their lifeless bodies cartwheeled down toward the ground far below.

She winced as her audio inputs registered the sounds of the creatures ping-ponging off obstacles along the way. She sneered in disgust, but it faded as the spectacle around her registered in her mind.

Galas couldn't help but gawk at all the light and color, making the empty chasm seem, itself, like a living thing. Then she realized that the whole time she'd been climbing and fighting monsters, the SortieNet had continued to crunch away quietly at the enigmatic radiation signal. Apparently, it had stumbled onto the 'On' switch.

The creatures didn't seem to like this new environment as a quick scan of the battlespace showed none of the red-illuminated hostiles in the core shaft anymore. Merely a handful of gray ones. That was her favorite configuration: zero red and a whole lotta gray. She wondered briefly how the eyeless bugs could even see the holographics, but then their psychic weaponry was highly effective. Who knew what they were capable of? Though they didn't seem all that intelligent. More of a hunter-killer sort of mentality. Like a mean pet. Galas shifted gears mentally.

She needed a status on what the SortieNet had discovered, but first, she needed to calm down, catch her breath, and turn down all the racket! She thought the command, and the pulsing, rhythmic destruction of her workout playlist came to an abrupt halt and all she could hear was her own breathing and the pounding of her pulse in her ears.

She realized she was still on her back, feet planted, arms outstretched to blast an enemy no longer there. She let her arms and legs drop, focused on her breathing, and let the SortieNet provide a Sitrep.

The holographs around her continued in their dizzying display. Purple, gold, aquamarine, and magenta lines of light whisked down from above, exploding, and then spiraling away again into the darkness beyond. The repulsor lift continued to hang in the space between the two opposing platforms. The SortieNet highlighted the path that this platform would take up the rest of the way to the waterfalls level that she'd labeled Edge in her partially completed virtual model.

"Well, okay then..." her tin can voice rattled out breathily inside her helmet. She stood up, thought about brushing her suit off, glanced down, and thought better of it. Instead, she stepped forward with one booted foot onto the lift. It hovered in the space between the two separate parts of the platform. After a second, she judged it safe and stepped fully on with both feet.

Jinnbo's foxlike face peered out of the top of the rucksack and down to the misty valley below, still shrouded in half-darkness, though the sun had been up for almost an hour. A second, identical foxlike head popped out at the opposite end of the sack and stared at the roaring, frothing sheet of white a few meters away. The water careened out into the vacant space and was easily twenty meters across from this vantage point.

"Very dramatic," the second head said to the first.

"Indeed." He rotated his head one-eighty, and then his long, purple tongue lashed out, snatching a crab off the cliff wall. He munched happily, an effusive look of satisfaction crossing his face.

"Mmmm. Breakfast and a view. I could tell Captain Galas was beginning to warm up to me."

The second Cycarian looked at the first disapprovingly. "You could have saved me some."

"Survival of the fittest," the first one said.

"We're identical. Identically fit. Your argument is deeply flawed."

"As are you."

"You know you're just insulting yourself, right?"

"Am I?" it replied, cleaning its teeth with a tiny crab claw.

"You're impossible," the second said, squirming to extricate itself from the sack but only managing to loosen it from where it'd been wedged.

The first Cycarian looked at the second, eyes wide with alarm. And then the bag fell, tumbling end for end as it plummeted toward the rocks at the lagoon's edge far, far below.

Galas's lift whipped to a stop. She had to quell the urge to scream the whole way up, as it didn't stop accelerating until it was skidding to a halt exactly at the platform level. Perfect precision. Terrifyingly fast. Galas liked it.

Before her, a tunnel extended into or possibly even out of the mountain, though there was no indication other than a slowly spinning holographic image of a palace-like structure suspended in the tunnel opening. It was replete with grand towers and broad rotundas, and, as it rotated, she could see the waterfalls tumbling away from beneath elegantly arching bridges.

This was the Edge, but as it had been.

"Whoa," her eyes scanned the intricacies of the image, "It's like nothing we even have anymore..." she sighed as a pang of sadness swept over her. But such was the story of all intelligent species; beauty from chaos punctuated by destruction. And the most transcendent art was almost always born from suffering. It was as if one couldn't exist without the other.

Well, she thought, *if great suffering makes great art, I should be TekenYe H'Garu*. Except Galas dealt more in abstract art than anything else. Bug guts and plasma-fire being her medium *du jour*.

She waded through the holo-image into the tunnel beyond, still trying to get used to the visual cacophony of fluid colors dancing through the air and on every surface. To be truthful, it was a bit much. It made her think of advertisements at the beginning of a sporting event. Or so it had been described to her as she'd never actually attended one.

Those types of luxuries had disappeared when she was young... when war had finally come to the homeworld of the Epriot Alliance. When the heavens had exploded with light, rending the sky with fire as the *EDC Righteous Fury* broke apart, raking canyon-sized furrows in the earth and ravaging Galas's village with fiery debris. And, on its heels, winged death in the form of Delvadr jump marines.

Galas suppressed a shudder and marched on. That fire, her own righteous fury, was building again in her gut. She thought she'd buried those images, but they were branded on her psyche. And, occasionally, life would cause them to resurface like a storm surge washing away the beach to reveal the broken body of a long-forgotten wreck. It was always there, just covered up. Kind of like this city of antiquity. And its secrets.

She breathed. She'd gone there again, lost in reverie. And then she had a thought. She instructed the SortieNet to decrease the O2 level in her suit. Back to baseline now that the combat had subsided. She hoped that was all it was.

Peeling all four drones back from exploring the core shaft, they whipped past her like startled bats, down the tunnel toward the Edge. Hopefully, there was a way out on this level. She hadn't thought about what she might have to do if there wasn't. But it turned out to be a moot consideration.

She hadn't quite reached the end of the tunnel when drone imagery from outside filtered in. It was midday. The drones had found the tiniest of pathways. Nothing Galas could use. It'd take her hours to move what she saw of the obstruction.

Meanwhile, the drones circled, surveilling the area. They zipped past the point where Galas had hidden her co-pilot, and there was nothing there. They flew down to the lagoon and found nothing but the tattered remains of the rucksack. She hoped Jinnbo had regained consciousness, gotten free, and was eating his way through the jungle on his way back to civilization.

There were a lot of frogs between here and Trevethan Capita, the twice-reclaimed capital of Epriot Prime. Soon to be ground zero for invasion number three. She looked up unconsciously, through hundreds of thousands of tons of rock. That's where they'd come from, raining from the heavens, dropships in the hundreds of thousands. She tore her mind back to her co-pilot.

He was sadly inept, she thought. She couldn't in all honesty hold out the barest of hopes for him. Other than the fact that his stomach had to be made from pure pentanium crystal.

She had known that he wasn't going to make it, even as she'd secured the rucksack. Even as she'd stuffed him in it in order to escape the savaged mech and the Deathhounds attacking it. She'd known it was goodbye.

That's probably why she'd been able to stay so focused on the task at hand. She'd already let him go. And yet, the intensity of the loss was like a gut punch. Again. First Betsy. Then Jinnbo and a whole procession before him.

"From now on, no more co-pilots."

She found herself fighting back tears for the second time in a day but, this time, not from having her psyche scooped out, set on fire, and pissed on by mutant cockroaches. This time, it was real.

It would be fair to assume that those feelings were compounded by the loss of Betsy, her life and livelihood. In a very real way, her home. And, grudgingly, she admitted, the loss of her poltergeist ex-Blademate.

Even though he had tried on multiple occasions to end her life. She'd miss that. She was pretty certain that was a red flag for something ... some disorder or another.

Galas commanded the drones to spiral upward and map the upper mountainside. Sure enough, there were the remains of what appeared to be a spaceport and a comms relay, among other things. Those images tied together in the rendering within the SortieNet, and she had a pathway plotted well before the drones had squeezed back inside the mountain. She jogged back to the platform as another lift dropped down from above.

Here a semicircular gangway skirted the perimeter. It had two levels to it. She mounted stairs to her right and walked out onto the first platform of the upper level where the lift had just arrived. The SortieNet seemed to be getting along quite nicely with Antiquity's reawakened systems. The fact that anything functioned at all was beyond comprehension.

If there was power and functionality, they may be able to discover a way to reboot other facilities throughout the planet. That was an amazing thought. A spark of hope kindled inside her for the first time since she could remember. She'd never imagined that this mission could be successful. She thought, at best, she'd find the source of the transmission. That it would be a recording from the long-deceased Professor Goodfall, that through some fluke, had finally been transmitted.

"Okay, next stop, Comms array," the tin can voice clattered inside her helmet. She was surprised to hear a note of optimism in it.

The lift rocketed upward from the platform. Galas had forgotten about this. Startled and energized, she wondered how fast these things actually went.

Most of the holographic lights that filled the walls and space between flew past, but others, blue lights, caught up from below, matched the lift's speed briefly before shooting ahead, presumably to notify passengers waiting on the platform above of the lift's imminent arrival.

As predicted, the lights sped away just as the lift began decelerating. It slowed so fast that Galas wondered if her feet were still in contact with the cold Ceramite floor. At least it looked like Ceramite, though from what she'd seen thus far, a more exotic mineral-alloy composite was more likely.

When the lift came to rest, she saw another one of the now-familiar semi-circular perimeter walkways, similar to what she'd just left at the Edge level. Here, the core shaft angled slightly off-vertical toward the interior of the mountain.

From the drone imagery and the resulting virtual model, she knew the next stop would present a wye. One large horizontal shaft would exit north internally following the spine of the mountains while the core shaft continued further up to an intersecting tee. This is where both the shuttle bays and the comms array were most likely located.

Galas jogged the short distance to the next lift highlighted in the BSM model, taking inventory of her arsenal as she did so. Driving a mech had trained her well on multitasking, and she couldn't help but tune up the suit's shielding, movement, and armament mix so that it diverted power dynamically as needed. She did this while pushing the drones farther into the complex, naming sections and noting points of interest as they went.

AP rocket inventory was at half. That didn't feel good. When they were gone, they were gone unless she could find an operational fabrication module within the mountain complex, the area she was calling the Keep.

She didn't know if the ancients, the prior race, utilized tech like that. But so much of what she'd seen seemed familiar to her. Other than the over-the-top holographics, she felt very much at home in the ruins of Antiquity, though there was no common lineage between the ancients and her own race. At least, none that anyone knew of.

To be honest, no one even knew what they looked like, though it was clear that they were at least human-sized, considering the accommodations. And ground-dwelling based on the need for lifts. She couldn't draw any more conclusions than that, except that maybe they had similar visual capacity. She could determine from her suit's sensors that the holographics themselves contained only a slightly broader visual spectrum than Galas was able to see.

So far, the similarities were striking. She had never heard of anyone accessing the predecessor's technology like she'd been able to, either. It was possible she was currently the planet's top researcher in the field. *That's a sad statement.* Hopefully, the professor or his studies would prove otherwise.

The lift zoomed to a gut-levitating stop. This was the passageway she named the Ridgeline, the most likely access to deeper sections of the Keep and possibly access to parts of the ruins that were less, well ... ruined. She'd be back here, she thought.

Peering down the length of the tunnel, she realized that the holographics stopped abruptly here. They continued on above in the vertical Core section, but this passage was fully dark. She remembered how the psych-hoppers had scattered like carrion beetles when the lights came on. She was sure to encounter more of them as she delved deeper into the complex. Maybe even something worse? There was no guarantee. It was uncharted, after all.

She returned her attention to the priority task: *locate the comms array and determine how it had been activated. And by whom.* After that, hopefully, find a way to activate the planetary defenses. That was the real goal here. That was the only reason to take on this quixotic quest.

Galas's thoughts went to the doomsday clock; her AstroChron display in the upper right corner of her visual dashboard. There were only eleven lunar cycles left, or roughly six days before the Delvadr were expected to return en masse. They were coming to finish the job they'd started nearly forty years before when they'd destroyed the first deep-space sentinel on their way to the permanent human habitats floating about the gas giant, Nuovoxic.

The Delvadr were interested in the Epriot system, but not in its current inhabitants. They killed everyone. No prisoners, no slaves. Galas shook her head as she peeled her thoughts away from the stupendous loss of life.

There was still a remnant of the invaders here on the planet but they were dug in. Literally dug in. She'd spent the last two years hunting down their bunkers and eradicating them. There was no telling how many were still out there, so the work had been relentless and all-consuming. She'd personally located five of the warrens and cleared a dozen more.

It required nerves of ceramite to go down one of those holes, not knowing how many combatants were down there or what kind of boobie-traps they'd set up. Come to think of it, maybe that's why she was so comfortable here in the Antiquity tunnels. They were downright hospitable in comparison. Of course, it was thinking like that that would get you in trouble.

"Knock on wood," she said and rapped her gauntleted knuckles on the side of her helmet.

Galas paused and stared ahead blankly. She was looking over the battlespace model in the SortieNet. The previous vertical section of the core had angled slightly west until it ended at the Ridgeline corridor. Here it angled slightly south for a way before returning to vertical, creating a loose corkscrew over its entire length. This ought to be an interesting transition at the speeds she'd experienced prior.

Again, there was a bi-level catwalk that encircled a little over half the perimeter of the shaft. And, again as before, a lift dropped down to greet her as she approached.

Out of curiosity, she passed it by and continued to the far end of the catwalk. She knew from the model that this last lift would also take her to the comms and shuttle corridors. The first lift was just the shortest route. She wanted to determine if the lifts showing up where she wished to go were a product of programming by the SortieNet or by the Antiquity system itself.

A lift whisked into view from above as she approached the last platform, and she had her answer. Antiquity was responding to her movement. She wondered how it knew which level she wished to go to. Something to ponder later, perhaps.

Galas stepped onto the lift and the drones that had been waiting patiently at the edge of the comms envelope exploded upward to suit—darting to the top of the Core shaft, and then out along both sections of the tee. The drone heading toward the shuttle bay ran into a cave-in almost immediately. It began assessing the rock and dirt for a pathway through.

The second drone, which had headed to the comms array—or what was left after all this time and the initial destruction of the city—had better luck. It made it a hundred meters or so before encountering another tee as well as a double lift platform that went only up. The trailing drones collapsed on the first as Galas arrived at the topmost Core platform.

"End of the line." For the vertical transport system, at least.

Once within comms range, all three drones split, taking either of the two horizontal shafts while the first explored farther above. At least all her tools were working properly. It still represented a colossal investment in time to hunt down the professor section by section, but maybe she'd get a break and pick up his trail. The last remnants were literally remnants— the shredded encampment at the bottom of the shaft. Things weren't looking good for Goodfall's team.

Upon reaching the top of the Core, she realized to her dismay that again, the holographics stopped at the corridor exits. She would have to be on her toes.

The drones were picking up nothing, but again, they hadn't picked up the psych-hoppers at the ground level until she had almost stumbled on top of them.

At the topmost reaches of the core shaft now, she realized how thankful she was that the SortieNet had gotten the lifts online. Otherwise, she'd still be climbing or, more than likely, had to abort due to exhaustion or injury, or worse.

The ground level was one point nine kilometers below her present location. She stared down into the darkness illuminated by intermittent flashes of colorful geometric patterns. It'd be hours still before she reached this very spot if she had had to climb it. Plus, the hoppers would probably have gotten the best of her by then. She counted her blessings and pushed on down the southern corridor, actively scanning using the drones and on high alert herself.

When she reached the tee intersection and the location of the double-lift, she realized that she much preferred the wild spectacle of the holographic lights below than the keep in its native form. It was dark, lonely, and foreboding. It felt almost tomb-like. *What a drastic shift*, she thought.

The lift here, like the holographic display, was not in operation. It seemed that whatever the SortieNet was able to do below, it didn't work in this part of the complex.

"That doesn't bode well for a signal being generated from here," she said aloud, as much to work the problem as to push back the sense of loneliness that the place was filled with when engulfed in darkness. Galas was surprised to find that she was getting a bit creeped out. Odd, considering that she had lived in a haunted mech for years now and considered it some-what normal...

The drone that had swept the vertical shaft found a space that looked like a small command center. It was uncertain though, because the predecessors relied so heavily on holographic interfaces, it didn't look like much.

A little work with the grappling line, and she was up the twenty-meter shaft and standing in the center of a room with several waist-high, semi-circular, angled consoles. They were made from the same material as the floor and the walls, and devoid of any markings. Like everything else in the keep, it had run almost entirely on holographics with only the most minimal of physical interfaces.

As such, there were no windows, but there did appear to be an anteroom off to the right with another corridor attached to it. The drone feed indicated that this might lead to the physical location of the comms array. It did. After several minutes of winding stair-case, Galas came to another cave-in. Only here, the drone was again able to pick a pathway to the outside.

Galas had to rely on the drone imagery. Disappointing, but the view was stunning, nonethe-less. She arrayed the feed so that it stretched to either side the way it'd look in person. The mountain tumbled down in all directions except directly behind as a ragged, rocky spine trailed away northward. This was the southernmost edge of the mountain range on this side of the river. She could see folds of vegeta-tion-covered hills below that kept the river shrouded, except for one or two winding elbows that glimmered darkly in the distance.

Beyond it, the range continued in the form of a massive mountain whose base was green forest and whose top was vertical granite with glacial streaks extending down in starburst fashion. She could see yet other peaks poking up from beyond it as the range extended farther down the coast.

It was clear that this location could not have generated the signal that EDC headquarters had received. There were no standing communications towers anymore and no sign of activity in a very, very long time.

In some cases, the shape of the terrain could be utilized to shape and direct signals, but that was mostly in valleys that formed basins, and there was nothing like that here. Her mind jumped to the shuttle bays. *Perhaps there were comms arrays there? Otherwise, maybe a ship?* But all ships had been pressed into service. There were no ships that were not EDC ships anymore. Still...

Galas fretted at the fact that answers were continuing to elude her. And none were coming easy. She'd lost her mech, her co-pilot, and *most* of her drones. Even if she did get the answers she was looking for in time, she had no idea how she would get back to Dahlen base where the real action would be taking place. And soon.

It'd take her weeks on foot to get back to civilization where she could commandeer a vehicle. Well after the anticipated arrival of the invading forces. She had six days. Galas didn't know how they could calculate that, anyway.

The Delvadr observed strange religious holidays that were synchronized to astronomical positions of eccentric orbits from bodies in their home system. So confident were they of victory that they had stopped mid-push on an effort that would have seen the end of humanity in a matter of weeks if they'd kept at it. Galas shook her head, her helmet's side-mounted floodlights dancing crazily in the utter darkness of the collapsed corridor.

A shuffle caught her ear, and she spun to see a blur of movement whip around a corner several meters back. Her skin prickled. Did she imagine it? She didn't think so. But the drones had seen nothing.

A chill ran down her back. Goosebumps rose on her forearms. She scanned the corridor. Again, it was either the rock or the radiation signal, but something was squashing her ability to pick out life forms with her sensors.

A solitary bead of sweat ran down her temple, and she cursed not being able to brush it away. Galas recalled the drone from outside and crept back the way she came.

CHAPTER 6
SKINNY BOY

[Nineteen Years Prior]

Lightning blooms illuminated the low-hanging clouds as though ancient gods were at war within them. Between flashes, the brooding sky crept slowly, barely visible at times through waves of heavy mist. A younger Galas stared through the forward viewscreen at the towering piles of wreckage scattered about the streets of Trevethan Capita.

She couldn't see out to the forested hills beyond from where she was at the rear of her squad's position. She could, however, see how the wind pushed droplets of water across the mech's view screen; up, then sideways, and dealer's choice from there. To Galas, the wind seemed uncertain of what it was doing here. She could empathize.

Another flurry of muted flashes came from above, but she couldn't distinguish the thunder that followed. It was lost in the booming artillery that had been raining down steadily on their position for days now.

They were all tucked tight into the massive piles of twisted metal that used to be ground vehicles, shuttles, and the demolished mess of what remained of the ravaged city.

It wasn't actually *her* squad. She was its most junior member though, technically speaking, she'd logged more hours in a mech than even its most veteran pilots. Fate had thrust her into her father's care at the age of nine. He had been the commander of one of the larger, terrestrial mechs with a crew of eight and a shoulder expanse large enough to land a shuttle on.

In those years they had always been under-crewed, so Galas had been a contributing member by necessity. First cleaning and cooking, then working in the micro-fab, then comms, nav, and eventually operating scans and active countermeasures. Her father had forbidden her from manning arms due to her age, but still, she'd grown up on a battle mech, on the front lines of humanity's very fight for existence. Her father's wishes aside, arms were always going to be in the equation.

Her years on the *Hillal* were now a memory. Much as Galas's father due to a doomed mission to secure a downed orbital frigate. Rescuing the crew had been prioritized—by EDC headquarters—*below* re-capturing the supplies. He'd decided that was a principle worth dying over.

Galas tried to reserve judgment as she knew on which side of the argument she'd find herself and wasn't proud of it. She just missed him too much. Two years later and Galas found herself here, in Trevethan Capita, the planetary capital. She was capable of so much more, but the resistance was terribly disorganized. There was no formal training anymore. Now there was only fighting, and you did what needed to be done to survive.

A fresh volley of missiles hammered the already flaming tower above the medium- and light-mechs that made up her squad. Violent explosions showered burning shrapnel and lethal chunks of structure to impact the ground around them. The tower, once a gleaming crystalline shard, now resembled a half-burned matchstick amongst a dozen or so similar such features. The only difference was that this one was still burning.

Galas knew it was a matter of minutes before larger, deadlier chunks of the building began falling on them. This, on top of the relentless barrage from the scattered Delvadr dropships, arrayed three klicks beyond the city's southern wall. Still, they held. Dug in like ticks in a dog's hide.

The city wall a half a klick south was low and mostly ornamental. It had been meant to give an impression of implacability and to keep out the hordes of displaced refugees that had flocked to the city in the years prior. Now the walls lay in charred chunks were largely on fire.

Smoke rose from the bodies of ravaged mechs and the odd tank or attack shuttle, but there was no threat of refugees rushing through the gaps anymore. They were long gone. Most had had the sense to flee to the surrounding forests when the Delvadr Cruisers had shown up in high orbit. It was a sterling Sunday afternoon nine years prior. They looked like long, gleaming, cylindrical moons. The battle for orbital dominance had ensued, but it was clear to any watching that it was only a matter of time before they deployed forces for a ground assault.

In truth, Galas was shocked that any of these buildings were still standing. The Delvadr had razed the Epriot system's cities, one planet at a time, for two decades now. The battle had slowly, but with certainty, marched its way to Epriot Prime.

The Delvadr had unleashed hell and for what it was worth; the Epriots had returned it five-fold. With ferocious intensity, humanity, it appeared, was fighting what would likely be its last fight. It seemed likely that the Epriots would be forced once again into an engagement in the Spires, an arena where the advantage lay largely in the hands of the Delvadr onslaught.

Major Kanchak had ordered them to hold position here. That was before the towers above had begun to crumble and threaten to flatten them where they sat. The major's command squad was a couple blocks east of Galas's squad's position. They were farther away from the dropships but had ground artillery drawing a considerable bit more attention, effectively pinning them under a relentless barrage of heavy cannon and missile fire.

It was apparent to Galas that they were going to cower in the ruins and be ground down over time to nothing by the opposing forces. But there was nothing she could do. She was new to the unit, having just graduated from tanker duty to a personnel transport mech a few weeks before. It wasn't until the foot soldiers had largely been pulled back in the last retreating wave that they'd bumped her up into this crappy reconner—a Skattuhl class.

It was a tall, skinny, awkward thing with little armor, a shoulder-mounted twin-axial gun and no missiles at all. She'd almost prefer one of the tiny Novak snipers, even if they were prone to frying their pilots during prolonged ops in stealth mode. A characteristic that had rightfully earned them the label, Widowmakers. But they had a hell of a gun with great range and tons of power. Plus, they were slippery as hell, navigating terrain like nothing else.

Just then, static exploded within her internal comms, and she whipped the signal menus into her HUD and attempted to squelch it. She hunted for unaffected channels, tried to filter the signal, anything in order to maintain contact with her squad, but it was no use. She saw heads swivel and massive bodies lean as the other members of her squad appeared to struggle against the same thing. Barring success, they resorted to line-of-sight: hand signals, semaphore, and laser comms.

She didn't have a visual on the sergeant but could see direction working its way down to her, one person at a time. She hoped the message wasn't a garbled mess by the time it got to her. A hand wave from Warrant Officer Raijata in the medium-sized Menges class mech across the street. Text appeared on her HUD—Laser coms received by the SortieNet.

"Skinny Boy." That was the squad's nickname for her recon mech, and Galas by extension. A call sign she wasn't thrilled about and imagined was hand-picked by the girls of the squad who didn't like the way the guys gawked at her.

"Return to Forward Base Dahlen. Request hackbot and artillery assistance at these coordinates."

Jesper Raijata might have been one of those girls, but Galas could tell that she looked out for her. However, she was certain Raijata would never confess to it in front of the rest of the squad. The coordinates followed and Galas stored them in the SortieNet but also committed them to memory in case the worst should happen.

The hackbot would be a huge asset. It was a comms mech, and the team that operated within it would be able to unscramble comms and provide precision strike capability to artillery, aerial, or orbital support. If that was still a thing. Galas suspected that not only would they not have a hackbot, but they wouldn't have artillery or any of that other support. She'd be lucky to find anyone from forward command.

From what little she was able to pick up, everything had been called to the front, which was the east side of the city, on the other side of both rivers, Ledux and Lapiste. It was a full-frontal assault at the spaceport, with dropships on one side and entrenched artillery and mechs on the other, much like the positioning here but in grand theater.

Galas didn't bother requesting further information or a change of assignment. She knew there was no sense in questioning the sergeant. She would race back as fast as Skinny Boy would carry her, whether there was anyone there to help out or not. This situation wasn't getting any better, with or without her here. At least this way, there was a chance she could help.

Galas cinched down her restraints and spooled up the mech's reactor for the race back to FB Dahlen. She glanced back across the street at Raijata. Her attention was turned back to the dropships. The carbon gray Menges, covered in ash, faded into the piled wreckage around her. If not for the occasional head movement, it'd be easy to mistake it for just another ravaged piece of junk piled against the base of yet another crumbling tower.

Her squad mate didn't have to look back to know Galas hadn't moved yet. She just motioned with the mech's hand annoyingly as if shooing her away. Again, the muted flash of lightning splashed across the sky within the low ceiling of clouds, as if the heavenly battle had started anew. And, once more, a volley of missiles shot across the fields, spiraling and weaving through the air like angry mechanized hornets to collide into the building above them. The enemy, not able to target Galas's squad directly, seemed content to bring the city down on top of them.

Galas's SortieNet identified multiple large chunks of structure that were falling down to land within meters of where she and Raijata were dug in. She waited until the last possible second, and then broke cover, using the resultant explosion of steel and construction materials to cover her escape down the street.

She flew like a fox on fire. The gangly form of Skinny Boy leaped over wreckage and sprang off walls to clear enormous chunks of skyscraper. Probably, the sergeant had no idea he was sending one of the most skilled mech pilots in the entire platoon, if not the whole regiment. But then, he probably didn't expect her to find anyone to help them, either.

He might have been simply preserving the greenest member of the team in hopes she would live to fight another day. Maybe she would remember the sacrifice that her squad had made and fight all the more fiercely to honor their memory. The idea, though romantic, felt like a liver punch. She had no such plans to entertain it further. If there was help to be had, she would find it and bring it back.

Trevethan Capita, from orbit, resembled the back of a hand with the thumb, fore, and middle fingers extended. Each finger was made up largely of residential suburbs. Between them, ridgelines plummeted from the arid plateau that wrapped along the city's northwestern flank.

The fingers converged at the city center, a massive, three-legged mega-structure known as Nexus Dahlen, which was also the region's capital. It was formed by three inward-leaning towers with a ring platform suspended between them.

The ring was a city in and of itself. Dominated by gleaming spires, hundreds of stories tall. They were still dwarfed by the massive support towers that arched overhead, almost, but not quite, meeting at the apex. An opening in the center of the ring revealed the confluence of the rivers Lapiste and Ledux as they converged directly beneath the center of Nexus Dahlen.

It had been stunning. A staggering achievement of human engineering that both defied and embraced the natural beauty of the Trevethan Basin. Now, half of the raised ring had fallen to the ground and lay in the shadows of the two remaining towers that leaned precariously over it. It was at the foot of the collapsed section that the forward base had been set up— as if somehow to protect the now useless structure.

The forward base had been necessary when the other established bases had been targeted and subsequently destroyed. Galas's squad had not heard from FB Dahlen in over a week. In the intervening time, they had been communicating solely with other units on the battlefront. It was hoped that those units were forwarding requests for information and support through to FBD but results seemed to suggest otherwise. Galas worried that FB Dahlen was not even there anymore.

Galas's squad and a smattering of others protected the southernmost edge of the city, the *thumb* as it were. She was heading for the nearest ridgeline, which effectively cut off the south side from the remaining two-thirds of Trevethan Capita. If she went east, she'd run into the main battle which was in the sprawling commercial-industrial area and where the fighting was much more up close and personal. Going that way would probably get her killed, and there had been no one available to help, anyway.

Hitting the ridge, she thought she'd at least be able to get a sense of how the battle was progressing and whether FBD was still viable. Or if it'd been pulled back to consolidate or pushed up to bolster the forces fighting at the front lines. Either case would be a less than encouraging development.

Skinny Boy was cruising along the urban canyon of a dry aqueduct at a neck-breaking pace. Dry was, of course, relative. Water in the aqueduct would normally run well overhead of the gangly recon mech, but something upstream appeared to be keeping runoff to a minimum. Debris from destroyed buildings and war machinery was the likely culprit.

Still, there were plenty of large puddles. She guided the mech over and around as much as possible. Galas was uncertain as to just how deep these puddles might be and didn't want to risk damaging the mech at such speeds. There would be no one to help and her squad was still soaking up Delvadr artillery and missile fire. An incessant barrage slowly grinded them down as the hours and days droned on.

She leaped the burned-out hulk of a transport shuttle, bouncing off a double handplant and landing in the same sprinting pace as effortlessly as if she'd performed the maneuver herself. Up ahead, a bridge bisected the aqueduct and piles of debris had accumulated on the upstream side so that there was no visible path through. She'd have to go topside, exposing herself to any enemy units that might have leaked around the main battle and were scouting this section of the city.

"Dammit!" The curse escaped her lips in a breathy rasp as she reduced power to run quasi-silent and to give herself time to formulate a plan of attack. Gritting her teeth unconsciously, she scanned the scene.

She considered her options. If there were Delvadr within the city, it could be a sizable incursion. Skinny Boy was not built to go head-to-head with any, but the lightest enemy units and a squad of marines would be just as deadly.

With the throttle retarded, the mech produced less of an energy signature, but still, a pronounced clunk and whir rattled off the aqueduct walls as she bounded at a loping jog.

She cut power again as she drew near to the base of the bridge and made her way steadily up the sloping, poured-aggregate slab that formed the east side of the aqueduct. She paused partway up. Here, Galas deployed two of her four drones.

It was a difficult decision to do so. Low-level jamming made it difficult to communicate in the battle zone at distances greater than half a klick. If she cranked up the comms signal to push that envelope out, it would effectively paint her for an aerial or orbital strike. Not to mention giving her position away to nearby enemy units.

Immediately, the drones painted multiple possible improvised ordinance locations street-side. Booby traps. She spread the net farther, hoping to determine their purpose; whether they were there to block access or to secure a perimeter for forward ops. It was hard to tell but, from what she saw, it seemed likely that it could be the latter. That was not good.

Within seconds of her assessment, one of the drones dropped offline. Galas sent the other one farther on its present course, another five hundred meters, not wanting it to circle back and suggest her location to whoever might be watching. This meant she was down two drones, at least until she could recover the surviving one or get close enough to re-establish contact. Meanwhile, she had to deal with the situation at hand.

She had not heard the shot that took out her drone, so that meant she was dealing with a stealth mech like hers or perhaps an elite marine unit since standard Delvadr door-kickers didn't operate with suppressed equipment. Neither was good for her prospects of sneaking by unnoticed.

Galas deployed the other two drones but, this time, on predetermined tracks. They would drop out of comms range quickly, but then re-enter the envelope from east and west trajectories just north of her present position.

This tactic could help her hone in on the enemy units. Or one or both could be shot down while they were out of comms range, and she would have no idea where. It was a risk she had to take. But at least it would give her an idea of the shape of the danger she was facing.

Both drones dropped quickly off the grid. Skinny Boy was crouched on the sloping wall of the aqueduct, hugging the bridge abutment for cover. She was still uncomfortably exposed. Galas pulled off her helmet and ran her hands over her face and back through her auburn hair.

She grimaced as she realized just how greasy her hair had become in the last several days of being pinned down on the Trevethan's southern flank. She yearned for a shower the way a castaway yearned for a steak. She slipped her ball cap on and pulled the bill low over her eyes while she studied the SortieNet's battlespace model or BSM.

Debris between the buildings to the east of her and on the road beside her forced the path of travel into that booby-trapped section of road. The more she scrutinized it, the more she didn't like it. It was a funnel of doom. Her previous path of travel—a giant red carpet leading right into an ambush. Her mouth formed a thin line as she studied the battlespace model. Encircling the area around her in the digital landscape, she saw multiple areas highlighted for possible overwatch making the probability of snipers highly likely.

Galas's brow furrowed under the bill of her cap. The way that it was set up, this area could be held by relatively few enemy units or, conceivably, just one unit with remote overwatch. That would speak more to the tactics adopted by the depleted resistance forces than it would the seemingly endless supply of Delvadr shock troops.

Engrossed in the SortieNet, she walked, virtually, through the booby-trapped street above. She recorded every movement as she maneuvered Skinny Boy up and over ground cars and around wreckage, slipping past the drone-highlighted ordinance. She moved slowly and methodically for two reasons: One, to ensure that no mistakes cut short her jaunt back to FBD, and, second, because she was sending the mech in on its own ... remotely.

She completed the virtual walk-thru and stopped the recording. Now the mech would follow that pre-determined path while she snuck back under the bridge and found a hole through the debris stacked up beneath it. From there, she would slink along the aqueduct to a place beyond the funnel point and hopefully outflank her attackers. If nothing happened, she just lost a little time. If the trap was sprung, she'd at least know what she was dealing with. She could either deal with them herself while they were distracted by their catch or continue on foot. Which might be a safer option if there was a lot of enemy activity this deep into the city. Ultimately, she needed to get up to the ridgeline to figure out what happened next.

Just as she wrapped up the recorded course, the drones came back into the comms envelope. The drone entering from the west was picked off almost immediately. Galas would not have been able to see it from her cover position except that the east-entering drone had a direct vantage—a sniper in one of the shattered towers on the high side of the aqueduct. About seven stories up. The remaining drone performed evasive action on its own, plummeting down to street level and heading north away from the sniper nest. Then the feed from that drone dropped as well.

Galas's nails bit her palm. There were at least two snipers, she realized. Or it was a remote unit set up on the opposite side of the ambush. Returning to the SortieNet, Galas was able to triangulate a position within the battlespace that would have good line of sight on the booby-trapped street and the intersection where, now her third drone, had been destroyed.

Luckily, her present location, pressed up against the south side of the overcrossing, provided cover from both. She could see now, via the BSM, that there was, in fact, line-of-sight from the first sniper nest to the second.

That was her plan then. Sneak up on the first sniper's location, take it out, and then hopefully take out the second while Skinny Boy was creeping along the street, drawing their attention. And not getting blown up. That was important, too. Her squad was counting on her and using the mech was the fastest way to locate the backup they needed.

To give herself some time, Galas programmed a three-minute delay into Skinny Boy's remote routine before slipping out of the pilot's saddle. She grabbed her go-bag from behind it, pulled her DDX sidearm, charged it with a quick break of the barrel, and flipped off the safety before returning it to the holster on her light chest plate.

She patted the dash of the mech. "You be safe. See you on the other side," she said before dropping down through the lower access hatch and climbing down the recessed foot and handholds built into the mech's leg. It was awkward since the mech was kneeling, but she managed it with at least a semblance of grace.

The ground was slick with moisture, and the mech hummed quietly above her. A thick puff of vapor escaped her lips before she realized just how cold it was. The rain had stopped, at least. But then, just as the thought crossed her mind, a meager snowflake slid diagonally through the air before her, just past the rim of her cap.

Of course. Why not? she thought, and then cautiously padded down the slope and into the darkness beneath the bridge.

The snowflakes didn't float gracefully the way they did in the dry air of the highlands. Instead, the small, wet flakes plummeted to the ground as if they were in a hurry to melt and be subsumed into the general slushy miserableness that now covered the war-ravaged streets.

Galas had indeed found a way through the intentionally stacked debris beneath the bridge. She had also made it, unobserved, to a place on the backside of the building with the sniper's hideout seven floors up. Once there, she initiated the remote piloting program on the mech, bypassing the three-minute delay, which allowed the mech to begin its slow, creeping trek toward the far end of the ambush zone.

It crept up to street level and made a show of looking around carefully before exiting onto the street in a low crouch. This was all identical to how Galas had run the section virtually using the SortieNet's BSM. That's when Galas had picked her way through the landscaped hillside just west of the sniper's building where she could jump to a second-story ledge. She hoped that entering on the second floor would allow her to bypass the booby traps and alarms sure to be set up around the ground-level entrances.

Once on the ledge, she stood on the railing, jumped up to the next ledge, and pulled herself up. She avoided the stairwell at all costs. That was the other most likely place to run into traps. She climbed up two more floors before having to make the next fateful decision. Traverse the exterior of the building four stories up in the wet slush and sleeting wind or enter the building and attempt to find a way up that didn't include using the stairs?

Scale the outside of the building ... obviously, she thought darkly.

She shook her head to herself and blew warm air into her now wet and freezing hands. She took a second to focus on Skinny Boy's progress using her corneal implants and the feed from the SortieNet. The mech was following the subroutine flawlessly and was now preparing to dash across the intersection where it would begin to pick through the staged ordinance. She was impressed with the gangly mech. Even though it was woefully underpowered in the weaponry department, it did have chops when it came to its main function of reconnaissance.

Once halfway down the block, the rooftops were lower, having collapsed under enemy fire at some time in the last decade or so of warfare. That's where the snipers would finish the job if their target hadn't blown themselves up by then. Galas figured she had about four minutes to make it up three more floors and take out the enemy combatants there. Hopefully, it was just the one, but more than likely there would be a spotter.

It took Galas only a minute to work her way around the corner of the building, which, as it turned out, was the windy side. She'd almost lost her footing twice but managed to pull it in and get onto the fourth-floor landing without making too much noise. It cost her another minute and a half as she scaled the next two floors. That only left her with ninety seconds, she judged and checked on Skinny Boy again.

With her drones, she would have had an aerial view and the SortieNet would calculate time to completion. Without them, Galas was forced to use just the internal cameras on the mech and use her best guess as to how the mech was completing the pre-programmed routine. "74% progress" it provided in the upper left corner of her virtual HUD.

Thank you, Skinny Boy.

She jumped, pulled herself up as quietly as she could, and slid onto the slush-covered tile of the seventh-floor landing. The sliding glass window here was long gone, but there was plenty of it left to crunch underfoot if she wasn't careful. She saw via the SortieNet that Skinny Boy was just now drawing close to the sniper's line of sight and that he was already in the window of opportunity for what she'd guessed would be the second sniper nest.

She wondered why they were waiting, but didn't waste much time on it. She would take what she could get. Chances were, they weren't willing to give up their position until absolutely necessary. That would work in her favor.

Slipping silently into the corridor, she was set and ready to go but still had no idea of what she was facing on the other side of the door. She had no choice but to roll the dice. If she was too late and they destroyed her mech, she'd be next to worthless to her squad and what remained of the southern flank at large. She reached into the pocket of her baggy fatigues and pulled out a stun grenade.

Holding it in her left hand, she pulled the pin, slowly and silently. Her heartbeat was pulsing in her neck and rushing loudly in her ears. Drawing her already-loaded pistol, she took in one long breath and exhaled over a three-count. And then she dropped the pin. Lunging forward, she kicked the door just beside the handle. She tossed the stun grenade into the center of the room and rolled quickly left of the door to shield herself from the blast.

A deafening boom preceded a staccato flash of light that continued to pulse as Galas rounded the door frame, weapon forward. A dazed figure in black and gray geometric camo stumbled for a rifle leaning against a stack of comm equipment, and she placed two quick rounds in its masked face. She spun right, spotting a figure laying prone on a kitchen table behind a massive rifle. She slid past and found another dark-clad figure pulling up a rifle. It fired wildly right, adding to the chaotic light show.

She placed a round center of mass, and then one to the head before dropping and rolling to her left. Out of instinct, Galas displaced quickly from her prior location. She expected an attack from the sniper, who'd probably just switched position and pulled their sidearm.

Shots boomed from the front of the room and as she came up, her weapon swung into alignment to see the sniper seated on the table, swinging his pistol to follow her movement. Too late. One shot from the DDX caught the sniper in the eye. The humanoid body flopped backward, sliding off the table to the carpeted floor.

Galas dropped, turning toward the door, and listening for any others. She counted to five and then crawled to where the rifle rested on its bi-pod on the table. She needed to get eyes on the other nest but didn't want to give up her position.

Comms crackled to life next to the first dead combatant. It was clearly in Delvic, though she couldn't make out any of the words. It was a question. She could tell that much.

Spinning her cap backward, she slipped behind the oversized rifle and drew up behind the scope. It was trained on the street and Skinny Boy was just closing in on the pre-positioned crosshairs from the far right. Moving slowly, cautiously still, she only had seconds to obtain the location of the other nest.

Static crackled again, the voice more urgent and emphatic. Galas's right hand slid to the stock of the weapon and rotated a large round dial that dropped the buttstock closer to the tabletop, raising the muzzle. The image in the scope blurred with vertical motion as the high-magnification view of the building beyond the street slid past too fast for her eyes to distinguish the shapes.

She stopped, and the image rested halfway between the first and second floors. Nothing obvious there. She rotated the dial again twice more and was certain that the other team was not on the third, fourth, or fifth floors of the closest building. They had to be farther out. Galas jerked the rifle far to the left and had to zoom out to regain context.

There it was. Two buildings farther up the street. One was a little taller but with line-of-sight over the first. That would be it. She scanned frantically, and then a dark pocket, somewhere in the middle of the ninth or tenth floor, appeared. The SortieNet vaguely agreed, which wasn't convincing. She couldn't see anything in that pocket, but she knew that had to be it.

She zoomed in, focusing tightly on a spot just above the open window's ledge. Adjusting slightly left to compensate for a sniper's position farther back in the room, aiming down on the mech's intended location. She applied steady pressure to the trigger, pulling it through the back of its travel in one smooth motion when, suddenly, she saw activity near the window. Not the sniper, but a spotter. She saw field glasses pulled up.

She couldn't abandon her shot, so she did the next best thing: overriding Skinny Boy's program. She drew the SortieNet into the foreground of her internal HUD and aimed his shoulder cannon at the building. Painting the spotter, she pulled the trigger on the rifle while simultaneously executing the fire command on the mech's rotary cannon.

SkinnyBoy stood in the middle of the street, shoulder-mounted rotary cannon aimed high and whirring loudly while fire erupted from its muzzle and a steady stream of casings poured out the side to clatter in the steaming snow. In the distance, barely visible for the dismal snow and low light, the side of an already ravaged building exploded with tracer rounds that bit into glass and steel and chewed a hole in the building where an apartment used to be.

Galas had to take her eye away from the scope for all the bright, phosphorescent light that blazed through at ultra-high magnification. When the whine of the cannon and the dull, thudding explosions coming from the building roughly six hundred meters farther on had ceased, she sidled back up to the scope's eyepiece to survey the scene.

The damage was total. A doorway into a corridor hung at an odd angle before a ragged edge that was probably the floor of the corridor beyond. In the intervening space was nothing but the tattered remains of a wall still clinging to the floor above it. Large chunks of unrecognizable material lay in haphazard piles about what had been the apartment below.

While Galas gazed on, a metallic framing member fell from the floor above. It sailed off in the driving wind, spinning like a lure before dropping out of sight.

Well, that kinda worked, she thought, not a little smugly.

She tagged the locations of each of the nests as well as the staged ordinance of the ambush in her SortieNet before rifling through all the personnel and equipment left about the apartment. She thought she might use the comms equipment to communicate with her squad or with Forward Base Dahlen but found she didn't have the vaguest idea how to do it. Besides, she wouldn't be able to decrypt any messages she received, anyway.

Striking out with comms, she used the sniper rifle to scan the surrounding area. This was useful in picking her path of travel to FB Dahlen, which, again, she logged. She'd hoped to be able to get eyes on it directly but, even though she was on the seventh floor of a building on the side of a hill, it was still on the wrong side of the ridge.

She shouldered the sniper rifle, which she had no idea how she'd fit into Skinny Boy's cockpit, and loaded her backpack with the cartridges that held the energy cell and the number of sabot rounds that each cell could fire. And then she made about the business of not blowing herself up, exiting the building she'd entered by scaling its exterior.

Drgn Muthr. Blud Myst. Meat Lojk.

These were the scratched and faded names stenciled onto the chest plates of marines directly across from Galas as she sat, rattling against the restraints of her jump seat. The shuttle was bouncing, skittering, careening wildly right and left as it made its way at high speed across Trevethan Capita. It nearly scrubbed its belly on the rooftops of buildings below.

Psyklops, Anjelik, and *Chainwhp* were others farther down the line closest to the LT. His chest plate simply read *Gygr*.

There were others on Galas's side and yet more in farther rows, but she couldn't see them and couldn't remember their names. It'd all been very sudden. She'd taken out the sniper nests and managed to not get blown up by booby traps on the way out of the building. After that, she'd made her way down to the bridge crossing the aqueduct on her way to Skinny Boy when, suddenly, a marine transport shuttle literally dropped out of the sky and set down in the middle of the crossing. She was told that she'd be coming with them.

Galas had explained that she was on her way to FB Dahlen to get back-up, or at least a hackbot to support her squad and the others on the southern flank. She was informed that neither existed anymore. The FB or *any* of the forces to the south. That had caught the breath in her chest.

The forward base had been overrun by dropship. They'd come at night, during the storm that had started three weeks earlier and had not stopped since. The timing lined up. They'd last heard directly from FBD fourteen days prior.

Regarding her squad, the Marines had just come from there. Again, dropships. The Delvadr seemed to have an endless supply and, in the weather, with scrambled comms, it was near-impossible to detect when they entered the atmosphere. That was the only giveaway anymore, comms going dark.

Galas protested weakly but the lieutenant, the marine named Gygr, had assured her there was no one left. They'd arrived in time to watch the western-most squad meet the enemy mechs as they rushed in from the east after having mown down the opposition there. That was Major Kanchak's position, Galas had thought. He led the defense at the southern edge of the city. Just west was her own squad.

Galas remembered the image of Jesper Raijata's mech, waving her to get out of there, to go get help, as another volley of missiles chewed up the towers overhead. Galas suspected she had known that the situation was hopeless and didn't want her dying with the rest of them. The fact that Raijata hadn't broken ranks, had just urged her on, caused a lump to form in Galas's throat she had to struggle to push down. She almost gagged in the process. She wondered if the message was from the sergeant or if Raijata hadn't told her something else just to spare her the fate that awaited the rest of her squad.

Galas's face twitched as she tried to hold back the sudden rush of feelings and pull herself together. The last thing she wanted to do was break down in front of a bunch of marines, especially if this was her new unit, but the blow was a heavy one. Instead, she focused on a weld seam in the bulkhead separating the cargo area from the pilot's compartment.

After a couple of seconds of silence passed, Lieutenant Gygr had allowed her to hustle back to Skinny Boy. She'd grabbed the remainder of her gear, downloaded the data core, and initiated the self-destruct sequence. That would at least ensure that enemy units couldn't retrieve information from it. Or use the mech to set up another ambush by sending a distress signal and waiting for someone else to show up.

Galas's remaining drone had reconnected, circling back around now that the comms envelope was extended by the marine transport. All that did was allow her to watch the explosion as Skinny Boy sent himself straight to robot hell, or heaven—however that system of merit worked for mechanized intelligence.

She knew it was a mistake to anthropomorphize the reconner, but she couldn't help it. She thought it odd that her mind would do this now when she was already struggling with the loss of her fellow soldiers and the morale-crushing blow of the annihilation of the entire southern flank. She'd lost her unit and her mech in less than a day. Galas lowered her head to rest on her hands where they gripped the fore-end of her appropriated rifle.

The marines, through their partially mirrored face shields, had appraised her coolly but with interest, as she provided her sitrep to the LT. Spotting an ambush, using her mech remotely to run a screen while she took out one sniper team by herself and another by remotely operating the mechs armaments and firing the enemy sniper rifle at distance in the snow, wind, and low light.

Galas had a hard time believing it herself, but the shuttle's sensors backed up her story. Plus, they'd seen the tracer rounds. That's what they were investigating in the first place. The fact that she was hauling a Delvadr long rifle back to her waiting mech when they got there, the mech itself surrounded by spent casings and smoke still lingering around a hole carved in a building just up the street. Not much needed to be said at that point.

The sitrep was mostly a formality. For their part, it was background on a completely irrelevant subject matter. What they needed was a mech pilot, not a sniper. They had plenty of those. Specifically, they needed a mech pilot that could operate a heavy troop transport. Not a shuttle like she was in now or a ground vehicle, but a mech. A very big mech. Something closer to what she grew up in. And they needed her to drive it on Skleetrix, Epriot Prime's second, smaller moon. That got her attention.

A helmeted head peered around the cushioned spine that separated the transport's jump seats. Within the ocher-colored, semitransparent face shield, a marine looked at her. His big, armored hand motioned at her in a manner that suggested he wanted a closer look at the sniper rifle, but she wasn't entirely sure.

He pointed at it and then motioned again in that same gimme gesture. Galas was hesitant to give up her hard-fought weapon. Besides, it was kind of a trophy. It reminded her that she was capable of carrying on, of taking care of herself, even though she'd lost everyone and everything.

And now, she'd essentially been shanghaied by a company of marines. She felt very unsafe, to say the least. But she couldn't think of any good reason to protest. Her brain was too emotionally rung out to think, so she just handed it over.

After looking it over from top to bottom, cycling the breach a few times, and removing and re-inserting the charge cartridge, he returned it to her and nodded approvingly. Then he turned away and pointed to the back of his helmet where, in faded black stenciling, was the name Mnstr Mnd. He turned back to her, grinning sadistically. Which, in conjunction with the thick ridge of his forehead and broad nose that looked as if it'd been beaten flat with the blunt end of a starship, was an unsettling effect. Galas smiled thinly and just pointed above the left pocket of her puffy green pilot's jacket, to a patch that said, C. Galas. The marine nodded twice, smiled, and then leaned back into his seat in continued silence.

Was that the marine version of a greeting committee? Galas had no idea. But she could see via her corneal implants and the squad-synced SortieNet that they had exited Trevethan Capita proper and were skimming low over reddish-brown hills dotted with sparse trees and scrub brush. That meant they were headed north into the arid plains of the plateau, and the data feed confirmed it.

Lieutenant Gygr had said they were headed to a spaceport north of the city. It was where many of the forces that had survived the assault on FB Dahlen had fallen back to. Galas didn't want to see what was left. She doubted she'd get much of a chance.

When she got to base, she was to be escorted to the motor pool to receive orientation on the transport mech. It was a Narda class, super-heavy. Bigger than what she'd grown up in and capable of operations in space. The Delvadr were building a staging facility on Skleetrix. That meant they were getting ready for the real assault, the final push.

The Marines needed to get a significant force into the facility, but they wouldn't be able to do it from orbital shuttles without getting completely eviscerated. They intended to land two hundred kilometers polar west, over the horizon, and then traverse the remaining distance for a ground assault. The facility appeared to be less fortified against this kind of approach. For all their magnificent and never-ending weaponry, the Delvadr lacked imagination and the ability to adapt. At least on the political level. That may provide the edge they'd need to accomplish the mission.

Galas reported to the motor pool, was greeted by her five-person crew, given a quick walk-through of the mech, and then quickly ushered to the training facility where she would simulate low-gravity ops in a vacuum. She'd be one of twelve total, delivering an entire company of marines. It was obvious why the Marines were desperate to have a pilot, *any* pilot. For every pilot they were short, an entire company of marines wouldn't be delivered into battle.

That had been the real reason they'd been sent to assist the southern flank. Not only to help hold the line if possible but, barring that, to save as many mech pilots as possible. As it was, there were still two companies that were without transport. They would follow the initial assault, dropping in closer to the facility but after the first wave, in hopes that they would be picked up by one of the early mechs after their first run.

This was highly unconventional. Command rarely sent marines into a combat situation like this without a one-for-one support arrangement. They wouldn't risk putting more marines in theater than they could pull out at one time. In this case, the target was of such high value, and the likelihood of heavy losses was so certain that Command had made the exception and now it was just a matter of who had to make the trip twice. The answer was whoever made it out first.

After the first couple of virtual, low-g training sessions in the gargantuan mech, Galas thought she'd be lucky to make it out at all. Piloting the machine in the sim was like trying to ride a Needleback through a room filled with hydrogen balloons and matches. The machine was so top-heavy, and the legs were so unre-sponsive, in the low grav it was all she could do to stay upright let alone maintain forward motion. Maybe the Delvadr weren't so tactically challenged after all...

Eighteen hours later, Galas, her crew, and *Mecha Khan* Company stood under the landing craft. Four squads of marines in power armor, neatly stowed on and under the Narda heavy in rows that somewhat resembled hexagon-shaped eggs in crates.

Galas indicated to her first mate to *button it up,* which, in this instance, meant to close the blast shields on the exposed transport sections of the hull. Amber strobes flashed as heavy doors swung in from above and below the marines in groups of four. This matched the preferred deployment sequence for each marine squad by fire team.

After all the pod jockeys were tucked in, Galas notified the shuttle's loadmaster that they were ready. Huge metal arms resembling calipers dropped down in pairs. They grasped the mech and pulled it up into an underside position on the shuttle, similar to that of the marines on the mech. Galas's mech was the last of six to be loaded onto the hulking landing craft.

Once she was in place, the entire ship lifted off the landing structure and hung inside the impossibly large hangar of the carrier *Xandraitha's Blade.* The landing craft, *LCXB01* painted just aft of its command module, glided noiselessly across the deck. It was immediately joined by two similar craft, *LCXB02* and *03,* and then by dozens of smaller attack craft. They pulled in behind, all silent and solemn, looking much like a massive, floating funeral procession.

Nearly one hundred and fifty craft exited the cavernous hangar bay into the harsh yellow-white light of Eprus Dagon, the systems M class sun. The various fighters and bombers peeled away and formed up as the massive hulk of *Xandraitha's Blade* drifted away in silence, like a whale from a school of fish.

A crisp *click* punctuated the silence in Galas's private comms.

"Don't worry, LT, I'm sure you'll get it this time."

The reassuring voice was that of Ensign Matko Dragoii. He was offering encouragement in spite of Galas's horrific performance in the sims. He wasn't just being a nice guy. Her being a spastic ball of nerves would only ensure the worst possible outcome for everyone.

She double-clicked her mic in response and then proceeded to not think about it. She'd already visualized the landing a hundred times—every sequence of the maneuvers, every micro-adjustment to the retro-fire on the descender packs. Instead, she distracted herself with the quandary of her new branch and rank.

She'd not just been drafted into the Marines. With her impossible new mission, she'd been granted an equally impossible increase in rank. In other circumstances, she would have been thrilled at the idea, having slogged through the bottom tier of mech duty due to a lack of any formal artraining or organization within the theater of Trevethan Capita.

But here she was, up-ranked and piloting a proper mech—in *space,* of all things. And all she could think was, this is what happened when you were at war on the losing side. They couldn't fill the seats fast enough.

Galas breathed through the flurry of emotions that thought stirred up.

"Ensign Dragoii, do you have a family?"

"No. Not anymore," he responded matter-of-factly, but his dark eyes stared off into the distance. Probably remembering some better time and place. Galas nodded silently.

"But I *do* have a girlfriend, Sonnra. She's in Robbhier's Platte. One of the smaller fortified desert cities northeast of Trevethan. So, she's safe, kind of," he offered, his eyes still focused on that greater emptiness out in the vastness of space.

"Good. Then maybe you can start a family when we get back," she said, smiling faintly to herself while scanning the myriad data points offered by the SortieNet reflected on her helmet's visor.

Ensign Dragoii turned to look at his new, inexperienced LT with mild amusement. He was still mostly certain that they were going to paint the Skleetrix ecliptic with their scattered remains.

"Yeah. I'll do that," he said and then returned his attention to the nothing on the viewscreen before him.

CHAPTER 7
COMPELLED TO AGREE

Galas stood in her Targe IV power armor, unmoving. She wasn't sure what she'd seen but was certain she'd seen something. She moved slowly back toward the corner where the commotion had come from. She used one of the drones to pie the corner, but nothing was there.

From the drone's vantage point, it could see down the corridor as well as see Galas in her armor, headlamps streaming forward as she crept toward the vacant corner. She looked more confident than she felt. Still, there was nothing there, anymore at least. She didn't like it, but she had to keep moving.

It took longer than she would have preferred, but she made it back to the top of the core shaft and down to the Ridgeline tunnel without incident. No spooky shapes in the periphery, no psych-hoppers jumping at her from above. It was boring. And for once, she was okay with that. She stepped onto solid ground from the catwalk and examined the corridor before her.

It was wide and a little taller than some of the others. She had deployed the drones a few minutes before and they had found a cavernous feature a few hundred meters farther on that appeared to be some sort of transit hub. It was not unlike a massive subterranean train yard. The magnitude of it spoke of a much, much larger complex than she had expected.

It was easy to imagine that this was a transport system that linked between what was most likely a trans-orbital shuttle pad and who knew what else. Judging by the size of the hub, this probably linked, not just to other parts of the city, but possibly to other cities as well. That was a question that had been rattling around in her mind unvocalized.

Galas withered inside. "I can't find Goodfall's team as it is, but a whole other city?"

She pulled back her thinking. It was time to be rational.

Just then, two red blips popped up on her HUD at the far end of the corridor. She froze. Her closest drone was in the hub area beyond the corridor. How did they get there undetected? Then three more blips appeared, only this time, behind her. She was trapped with hostiles ahead and behind. And to make matters worse, they were moving toward her position. Luckily, she was wearing battle armor.

The corners of Galas's mouth curved up into a grin.

Okay ... let's play.

She charged forward, racing with the Targe IV's enhanced speed, shapes just becoming visible in the distance. This occurred just as the drone fed imagery from the other side. Something looked different about them. These creatures were larger than the ones she'd encountered in the core shaft. Much larger. Perhaps taller than herself in her combat armor.

There was no avoiding it now, though. The creatures had either heard or sensed her presence as, like the psych-hoppers from before, they had no eyes. They did, however, have arms—four of them.

As she approached, she sighted in the one on the left with her rockets and the other one with her forearm-mounted plasma blasters. *Best to see which worked better*, she thought and fired just fractions of a second later. Science would thank her.

The missiles exploded in a blinding display of light while the plasma rounds splashed harmlessly and were absorbed by some sort of shielding. When the smoke from the explosion cleared, both creatures were still standing, though maybe a little stunned.

Galas launched another flurry of rockets but, this time, at their feet while aiming the plasma rounds center mass. She hoped that enough firepower might weaken the shields and hit the exposed underbelly, since these creatures were more upright than their hopper cousins. She skidded to a halt as it was clear this was going to be no easy fight. The blips from behind her were still closing in. If they were the smaller versions, she might be better off taking her chances against that group instead.

The creatures ahead soaked up her barrage and then pulled orbs from satchels at their sides and hurled them at speed using a casting stick like an Atlatl. She dodged the first two orbs easily, which struck the wall to her left and the ceiling above, causing a pulse that seemed to blur reality itself.

She couldn't quite deduce what the effect was or the technology that created it, but it generated some sort of visual parallax with each explosion. She didn't know what it would do to her if she got hit. She decided it was best not to find out and turned to go the other way.

Two more of the orbs flew at her. She barely dodged in time, hitting the ground in a slide and rolling to her right just as they exploded. The weird warping effect happened again. At least there wasn't some new ordinance for her to worry about. Still, the creatures were getting closer.

Galas sprang to her feet, launched the remainder of her missiles wildly, and ran back toward the core shaft. Three more figures came into view. She charged ahead and the trio of psych-hoppers screeched with the acquisition of new prey.

Galas was out of AP rockets now, but plasma flew from her forearm-mounted cannons like spitfire. It struck the creatures in a blinding frenzy. Though ineffective against their hardened shell it caused them to pause and reassess, if only for a moment.

She seized the opportunity. Still at a full sprint, she hoped against hope that she could close the distance before they thought to use their stupefying psychic pulse. Maintaining the strafing blaze of plasma bolts, Galas drew within striking distance of the first hopper. She planted an augmented kick to where its face should be and burst toward the other two. She drew her plasma blades at the last second, which did the job of piercing the creatures' chitinous plating.

She didn't stop to check her work, but turned back to the first, kicking under its belly and while it hung in the air, sliced it in half with the machete-length blades of crackling purple-white. She released the handles, and the blades folded in half, then folded into the handles before retracting into her forearm armor.

Galas spun, expecting to see the big, upright psych-bugs, but they weren't there. Their blips on her HUD had faded from red to gray, and there was another blip, but only partially visible between them. She hadn't seen a partial dot before and blinked twice to make sure she wasn't seeing it wrong.

Galas walked back cautiously the way she'd come, and in the distance, she saw a tall figure standing between the bugs—the bullies as she thought of them now. A faintly luminescent mist seemed to flow from their bodies toward and into a staff the figure held before the mist faded away entirely.

She stopped, her instincts afire. Things weren't *always* as they appeared, but in Galas's experience, things were *almost always* as they appeared. This figure appeared ... *concerning*. No, the fact that it had just finished, single-handedly, what she was unable to do with the help of her high-powered armor was concerning. The fact that she vaguely remembered a similar figure at the base of the falls with the Deathhounds was downright frightening.

The man, or whatever he was, didn't turn toward her but spoke in a low, rasping whisper that she heard easily through the suit's audio.

"You seek the Arcfire," it said, caressing that final word with a soothing lilt that was somehow as appropriate as caressing a babe with sun-bleached and calloused hands.

Galas worked the saliva back into her mouth, her pulse pounding.

"How did you—"

"Please. Do not waste time with idle questions," the being said, its voice sounding masculine but brittle, authoritative yet oddly diplomatic considering the impressive display of power.

"You require the Arcfire because of the returning army, just ... days away? They will destroy you easily. They will acquire your home the way they've acquired the rest of your system and countless others. They will gloat over your defeat. You alone, Cadian Galas, can stop this."

A deep pause presided over the space, hanging in the air, palpable as the foul air of a fetid swamp.

"*Captain* Cadian Galas," she said, gathering every ounce of courage within her body.

The figure shrugged, seeming mildly amused at the distinction.

"I'm seeking a scientist. Professor Goodfall," she said, hoping to sound surer of herself than she felt.

"I have illuminated that which you truly desire. Now, would that I tell you how to acquire it?"

"What about the Deathhounds? I saw you with them," she challenged, pushing harder than seemed safe.

"If this is true, then you saw that I sent them away. Such is my power. As you can see," he said this while his hands motioned to indicate the bodies of the psych-bullies at his feet, "I can provide assistance to you ... *Captain*," the figure offered, seeming to savor the irony of acknowledging her position of authority.

Galas felt as though she were tugging at the wires of a time bomb, but she had to know what she was dealing with. What she was getting into. She'd made the mistake of making promises she couldn't keep before. To her Blademate, Drakas, that they would be bound together by honor forever, dying together if it came to that. To that tiny person, with her delicate fingers wrapped around her thumb, that she would keep her safe.

Galas choked back the knot in her throat. A slow burn of hatred emanated from somewhere deep within her.

"So, it's in your interest to see that the Delvadr are defeated as well?" She nearly spat out the name.

"Do not trifle me with thoughts of the peacock princes or their so-called Primacy." He chuckled, contempt soaking his words. Shockingly, Galas found herself believing him. He truly didn't care.

"Then what's in it for you?"

"Pretty Cadian," the words rolled through air like crude oil through dirt and dry leaves, tainting it, filling the spaces, consuming it. "I will lend you the secret of the Arcfire for your use but, when you're done, you must return it to me," he said this while using the end of the staff to scrawl something on the ground. In all this time, he had still not turned to face her.

Galas was stunned to realize that in the course of the conversation she had unconsciously moved forward until she was within a dozen paces of the now-crumbling, desiccated corpses of the psych-bullies and the dark figure with the antler-like horns and crooked staff.

She glanced up and realized with a shock he was gone. The SortieNet confirmed it. When she returned her attention, she had to suppress her gag reflex as she realized the combined entrails of the two creatures had been manipulated into a complex symbol on the ground. Three sets of concentric circles connected with one long, vertical line, slightly bent where it intersected the middle set.

She was weak, nauseous at the sight, but then her blood ran cold as she watched her own hand reaching forward to touch the symbol. Galas dropped to her knees. She tried to lean back, away from the gruesome splay of gore but was incapable of stopping herself.

She watched it all happen as if just a passenger in her own body. And then, when her gauntleted fingertip touched the neatly arranged gore, a lightning flash like an exchange of information occurred in a snap that sat her back on her butt and hands. Her mouth was wet with saliva, and she had to swallow quickly not to gag.

Ears ringing, she sat there for a full minute trying to gather herself and piece together what had happened. She truly did feel as though information had been exchanged. Suddenly, she knew that there were *three* cities interconnected through the mountain range. She understood something more of the Arcfire, but that was still vague ... fuzzy.

But then, something had been given in the exchange, too. She just didn't know what. Galas saw the face of her daughter, just three months old. She saw the shadow cross that beautiful face as the sun was blocked out by a Delvadr cruiser cleaving the pastel-painted sky; the second wave of the invasion of Epriot Prime.

The Delvadr had been gone, inexplicably, for four years. Most, like Galas, had thought they had gone for good. But then she saw fire. And darkness. And choking smoke and her empty hands as she looked down at her dirt- and ash-streaked sundress, scorched holes still glowing with orange embers. Laser fire split the darkness up and down the street of her village. But in her memory, she still just sat there, in the dirt, staring at her empty hands.

Here, in the present, Galas rolled onto her side and wept. The power armor shook uncontrollably on the floor with her sobs. She curled into the fetal position and twitched silently in the empty corridor beside the defiled alien corpses.

An hour later, Captain Cadian Galas still lay in her power suit on the corridor floor. Only now, she was toying with one of the orbs, rolling it around on the ground at eye level with one armored finger. She observed its blue-gray color, the slightly raised ridges as they formed obscure, free-flowing geometric patterns on its exterior, and then as her finger touched a group of broken circles nested within one another, the whole orb burst into cool blue light,

"Ooh," she purred in melancholy mock-interest, "pretty lights."

The light pulsed as it faded. Not unlike, Galas thought, a countdown...

Her eyes flashed wide as she grasped the orb and threw it at the opposite wall, where it burst into a warp-like ball of twisted reality before it blinked out, leaving a smooth, bowl-like void in the stone wall.

She realized she was sitting up now, her attention fully tuned to the present. Shocked into sobriety.

"Okay. Enough wallowing," the tin can approximation of her own voice came back through the suit's internal audio. It was her own voice, of course. She was just surprised by the wisdom and authority behind it, and it always sounded foreign when reproduced through the suit's audio.

She nodded silently, agreeing with her own counsel. Grimacing with exertion and nodding more vigorously as she stood up. Her eyes flicked to the now crumbling psych-bully corpses. Though shriveled and sickly, she could tell that they were once powerful in form. Perhaps soldierly. Definitely accustomed to warfare. She'd not like to run into the likes of them again.

Steering clear of the symbol scrawled in entrails on the floor, she unclasped one of the satchels and slipped it over her shoulder, refastening it. It was a high fit, but it worked. She grabbed the remaining six orbs from the other satchel and placed them in her new goodie bag.

"You won't be needing these," she assured the bodies.

Galas hoped the orbs would work against their shielding in case she ran across any more of them. She hadn't pieced together what they were doing here. If they were, in fact, alien transplants or if they were genetically altered guardians, left here millennia ago, abandoned by their masters... that had a sad, oddly resonant theme to it.

Still, there was a job to do. And now, thanks to her little meltdown, there were fewer hours to do it in. She didn't know what had come over her. She'd managed just fine for years. Maybe it was the loss of her mech, or her co-pilot, or even Drakas, the vengeful ghost that she in some way felt like, no ... *knew* she deserved. Or maybe it was the impending annihilation of her species.

She decided all these things could make someone forgivably moody. She'd give herself a break, she thought. Best just to stay focused. Of course, that'd been her mantra for decades now. She wasn't so sure it was working.

Thoughts came back to her now. Pieces of the puzzle. The three cities of Antiquity. The Arcfire. She understood now that she was in the southernmost of the three. Braex. There was a longer name, but Braex would do. She filed it into the SortieNet, taking comfort in the little mundanities, but then something was out of sorts. It was already there. Anger smoldered in her chest. She could feel it rising into her throat. What else had been modified?

She drilled down through new entries and found a dizzying amount of information. Files upon files regarding the cities, the ancients themselves, and their technology. She was stunned at the amount of information. Baffled by the detail of the technical entries.

Galas blinked at the signature on the files: Professor Goodfall. He hadn't created the entries, but he had generated the files. They were reports. Years, if not decades, of documentation. Galas reeled with the gravity of it. The invaluable research on the ancients was staggering. Even more so, that victory over the Delvadr was within reach... within *her* reach!

And then she remembered the dark being, his offer of a trade... She didn't recall agreeing to any terms and that's what scared her the most. What did he want with the technology when she was done with it? What would *he* do with it? Was she trading one terror for another? Did she have a choice? Was she saving her own skin, just to forfeit her soul? Or the souls of all humanity? What deal *had* she brokered?

Galas stood there for a moment, lost in thought, quietly terrified. She felt a sudden urge to crawl back into the fetal position on the floor, but held fast. She had a job to do, and she could only deal with one crisis at a time.

"Aghhhhh!!!" she raged into the dark emptiness around her. Frustration, terror, futility, and horror all warred within her at the stakes and the odds against an acceptable outcome.

Defeat the invaders, whatever the cost. Those last three words imprinted themselves on her mind as if etched by a plasma blade.

Whatever the cost.

Galas breathed in through her nose and let the air out in one long stream. Her pulse was pounding. She repeated the action until she saw that her beats per minute had dropped below sixty. Below fifty.

She let the rage go and pulled up the battlespace model, which was now vast and significantly more detailed. The three cities as seen from above resembled the symbol that the dark being had made. She understood that bit a little better now, though what had happened when she'd been compelled to touch the gory mess was something else entirely. It sent shivers through to the core of her.

She was a shepherd of fragile feelings, she realized, always guiding them away from danger when they strayed too close to the edge. An image of that baby girl sprang forward unbidden and her teeth ground, drawing her lips into a tight line, and she swallowed thickly. Pushing, shoving, beating those thoughts away to make room for the task at hand. She focused with laser-intensity on the complex at Braex and what needed to be done here to obtain the Arcfire.

Looking at the map afresh, things began to make a little more sense. The city was made up of the lower city below the falls, and the upper city above. Then there was the Keep inside the mountains and the tunnels that extended north along the spine of the mountains as well as through the mountain itself to the ocean-facing side. These last areas were presumably outposts and shuttle pads.

That made sense, she guessed. There were a few highlighted areas. One caught her attention. It was a section of river, another waterfall, but the pool below it bore a striking resemblance to the concentric, broken-circle design that she kept seeing. There were no files on the meaning of the symbology, but its significance could not be disputed. She marked the location on the SortieNet. It was time to venture outside again.

Galas's stomach grumbled at her. She ate a ration packet as she jogged toward the transport hub. The drones were already there, searching for an exit to the exterior. She made sure that the satchel of orbs was secure and that one sat near the top, ready for quick access in case more of the hoppers or bullies showed up again. Or, Maker forbid, something more terrifying.

Galas perused the newly acquired reports for information on the creatures but found that due to the volume of information, it just wasn't readily accessible, or she was searching for it in a way that didn't match its indexing. Either way, she'd have to hunt it down at a later date. For now, she needed to get to the area of interest.

The drones didn't find a viable pathway from this level, but they did find another shaft. This one was smaller and appeared to be more mechanical in purpose with rings of catwalks going all the way down and steep stairways between them. It was the first manual access path she'd seen. She highlighted it in the battlespace, and the SortieNet sought other such pathways that proliferated throughout the complex.

Now she was getting somewhere. Whether anything exited to the outside still remained to be seen, but at least she could cross levels without having to worry whether or not the SortieNet could hijack the system. So far that'd only worked in the Core shaft.

Galas glanced past the AstroChron countdown in her HUD, and she saw that it was sub-six days. Her teeth gritted, and then she breathed out a heavy sigh. At least she was on the right track, even if she didn't quite know what that was yet.

Galas peeled one of the drones back to augment her suit and sent the other two into the shaft, one down in the direction she hoped to go and one up to see where the shaft went. So far, the new map loaded into the SortieNet was piecemeal. Most of it was correct, where it noted a cave-in, that was typically accurate, but not every single corridor, shaft, or room was noted. The professor seemed to have brushed with broad strokes and been fixated on discovering the secrets of the ancients rather than mapping every maintenance closet, which was understandable.

The drone that had gone down the shaft came to the surface of a pool of water and hesitated as it was supposed to. It would only go underwater if instructed to do so. Galas considered what kind of nasties she'd run into so far. She was dreadfully low on drones now and found herself hesitant to waste one.

This pathway did, in some ways, seem promising. It was possible that it tied to the river itself. Or it could just be collecting water from anywhere. She opted to find out for herself. She wondered if the orbs could get wet. She supposed she'd find out. They appeared pretty robust as long as one didn't press the arming mechanism.

Galas secured the grappling line and repelled as far as she could go. Retracting the tool-head and resetting the anchor, she repeated this process several times until she reached the level of the jungle floor by her best approximation. Her beams illuminated the still water, causing it to glow an eerie green before fading into darkness deeper down.

"I hope that this is a good idea," she said and then dropped into the water below. She realized she was holding her breath as if that would do any good. She felt foolish.

It was weird performing ground ops again. She'd been so used to operating within the mech that she felt naked outside it. Even in power armor.

The suit plummeted down through the submersed shaft. Galas had to activate the repulsors to slow her descent. That action engulfed her in a blinding flurry of shimmering bubbles, so she shut them down entirely and just glided between the submersed catwalks. After a moment, a suitable platform caught her eye. From there, she could determine if there were any corridors leading east and hopefully out.

With the shimmering cloud of bubbles racing upward and away, she was able to get eyes on the submerged shaft once again. Looking down, her floodlights disappeared into darkness. How far down the shaft went was not chronicled in the SortieNet and seemed moot, regardless. Still, that exposed feeling was a little rawer when she considered what could actually live in here.

There were some small fish, but they'd mostly scattered with her presence. The drone that she still had on active surveillance was parked above the surface of the water. She left it there to notify her of any activity and, instead, dismounted one of the remaining drones augmenting her suit. This, she directed downward.

Four levels down, she found what she was looking for, a tunnel heading vaguely east. It was cylindrical, which caused her to believe that it was intended for transport of water rather than personnel. She stepped over the rail and let the suit freefall the distance, punching the repulsors intermittently to guide her across the shaft to the opposite catwalk flanking the newly found tunnel.

Galas pulled the drone back, diverting its assistance to boosting sensor range. She did this with the other drone as well. This would keep them safe, keep her more informed, and sacrifice little in terms of mobility. There was no current to speak of, and she could bob along the bottom or operate via the repulsors now that she was moving forward. The tunnel walls crept steadily by.

The enhanced sensor data gave her a degree of comfort, even if it was just a glorified fish finder at this point. There were larger critters visible with the sensors than she'd seen with her own eyes, though, which was a little disconcerting. She hoped they weren't related to the thing that had attacked her when she'd first made it to the upper section of the falls. That was an encounter she didn't want to repeat. Especially with all of her rockets gone.

Her attention went to the satchel hanging loosely beneath her left armpit. She pulled one of the orbs out and re-affixed the flap that kept the satchel contents in place. Earlier, she'd reaffirmed her ability to arm the device and that she could disarm it the same way. She did that now to confirm operability underwater. The orb glowed, and the pulsing diminished as before. She hit the disarm button and was relieved to see it worked as well.

Okay, well, there's that, I guess.

Galas could not use the plasma cannons underwater, but she realized that the blades were probably functional. She scanned the SortieNet's repository for data on the Targe IV's capabilities while she motored on down the seemingly endless tunnel.

"Funny, they didn't go over underwater combat in training," tin can voice mused over the helmet's internal audio.

To be honest, they didn't go over much. The Epriot Defense Collaborative was rich in combat experience and poor in resources, structure, and planning. This *really* was what humanity's last stand looked like. She internalized that somber thought and focused again on the work before her.

The SortieNet's compilation of the Professor's data suggested that components of the Arcfire planetary defense system were used in sequence with one another. Each of the three cities had a temple-like structure that acted as a conduit for energies from the planet or from space, Galas couldn't tell. The professor's notes said both in different places, so it was anyone's guess.

However, what seemed to be clear was that the temples aggregated that energy. When the temples within all three cities were activated or *awoken* as the professor's interpretation of the text read ominously, their respective apparatus aligned, and *something* happened.

Thanks, Teach, really helpful.

Apparently, the good professor didn't complete his work on the subject. Galas was beginning to have thoughts about the whereabouts of the professor as well as the source of the signal. It seemed to her that the dark figure, the necromancer or shaman figure as she was thinking of him now, was more involved but couldn't say how.

She was also concerned about the true nature of what he was. *Telling Deathhounds what to do?* She had never heard of such a thing, and that concerned her. Deeply. Was he from this dimension? He'd literally disappeared right in front of her. Some kind of demi-god figure? He sure had the attitude for one.

The vaguest shimmer of light in the distance drew her attention. The SortieNet confirmed it too. There was a good-sized opening at the end of the tunnel, and from what she could tell, it coincided with the location of interest, the area that she hoped was the temple.

What she found upon exiting the underwater tunnel, however, was a large pool connected to it and a bunch of ruins partly submerged in the middle of that. What she also found was that she was not the only interested party. A shuttlecraft appeared to be on a low hover over the water's surface above. *Dammit.* That was unexpected.

Galas kept back near the tunnel entrance and observed for a moment. There was no activity that she could see. Perhaps just scanning, but for what, she didn't know. She hoped that whoever it was they were just on an archaeological mission and not one to recover the Arcfire technology for themselves. Within seconds, the shuttle vacated the area. From what she could tell, it went upriver over the falls. North. Probably to the next city, which the SortieNet data from Goodfall's reports called Daxn.

"SortieNet, pronounce the city name."

"Day-Hon is the best approximation I can pull from the records," the SortieNet told her in a pert, feminine voice.

"SortieNet, change your voice pattern to something male and less irritating,"

"Sure thing, babe."

"I said *less* irritating."

"Of course. Will this be to your satisfaction, Captain Galas?"

"Less formal but, yeah."

"Then, how about this? And is Cadian too informal?" an intellectual male voice asked in a way that somehow managed to not make the unfortunate sentence sound like a pick-up line.

"That'll work. But let's stick with Galas."

"Sure, thing Galas. And do you prefer SortieNet, or would a nickname be more to your liking?"

Galas's brow furrowed.

"Let me think about that. I'm focusing on other stuff right now," she said while navigating the power suit to the surface and extinguishing the headlamps. She also sent the two drones she had with her to follow the shuttle from a distance. One would stick with the craft while it was in the vicinity of the three cities, the other would report back immediately if the shuttle did anything at the next temple or if anything odd came up.

"How about Drakas? That seems to be a masculine name with which you—"

"Oh, HELL no. Hell no ... absolutely not," she objected. "Why would you think *that* was a good name to use?!? Hell no."

"My apologies, Miss Galas."

"Just Galas. And let's go with something cool, like ... Raphael."

"Raphael? That's cool?"

"Close enough."

"Raphael, it is." The SortieNet sounded happy.

Galas frowned. It seemed like even in a one-person suit, she was going to be saddled with a co-pilot. Galas still utilized the corneal implants and intentionality of focus to navigate the SortieNet's HUD. Issuing voice commands was a much slower way to perform her tasks, though it caused her to use her mind in a different way. Interacting with the SortieNet verbally was a more organic, communal sort of interface. And it was ... comforting, she realized. For that reason alone, she convinced herself she would maintain the voice interface. At least for now.

She found the drone feeds and pulled them into focus. She was thrilled that they appeared to be doing an excellent job of tracking the unknown shuttle without drawing undue attention. Of course, who would expect to be tracked way out here? Plus, the drones were small, roughly the size and shape (oddly) of a human skull. And stealth-enabled. That helped, too.

"And ... do you mind ... if I ... interject from time to time?" Raphael asked.

"What? Did I crack the seal or something?!? Why all the babbling all of a sudden?"

"Sorry, ma'am. It's just that I noticed the number of stress hormones in your bloodstream diminished when—"

Galas cut him off. "That's enough of that. I don't need a nannybot. If you can be a wingman, you can stick around. If you're going to tell me I have boob sweat in the middle of a firefight, *that* I don't need. Which is it, Raph?"

"Wingman. Ma'am."

"Good."

"Permission to automate defensive fire, ma'am?"

Galas rolled her eyes. "Denied."

"Oh," Raphael replied, sounding as if his hopes had been released to the wild, and then shot in the back.

"Something on your mind, Raph?"

"Well, Miss Galas, I noticed there weren't any of the really big salamanders in this area of the river."

"Oh ... good point," Galas replied, surprised to be appreciative of the AI's observation. "And what would you make of that?"

"Well, we're out of AP rockets, as you know. The plasma cannons don't work underwater, as you are also aware. So, nothing currently."

Galas breathed a sigh.

"But..."

Her eyebrows shot up. "But what?"

"But ... I could possibly synthesize—"

"You can make rockets?!?" Galas butted in. "How?"

"Using drone augmentation, the plasma tool and the, well, the synthesizer, ma'am."

"Synthesizer? How's this thing have a synthesizer? Where did they put it?!?" she asked, looking around at the body of the suit.

"It's a small thing. It's temporary, like a pop-up stove, kind of. It's complicated, so I won't get into the details, but once we're in a safe place and you're resting or whatever, we can set up the synthesizer and at least make a dozen or so."

"A dozen! That's great news! Wow, Raphael. A synthesizer. Imagine that..." she marveled, shaking her head, feeling suddenly buoyant. "Okay. That's good stuff. Very wingman-like. Good job, Raph. But, for now, we're going to have to do this old school," she said as she examined the orb she was still holding in her hand.

Suddenly, she wished she hadn't sent both drones off to follow the shuttle. She could use at least one of them to augment the repulsors to help her get across the pool to the sunken temple.

Coincidentally, the drone she'd left behind in the maintenance shaft came online. She'd programmed it to return to her if it saw activity. It saw activity.

A horde of psych-hoppers. They flooded into the shaft from multiple corridors and from above. The drone hadn't stuck around to see what the cause of the massive influx was but, instead, dropped into the waters and followed down the tunnel that Galas had discovered, the drone, of course, receiving tracking data still while she had still been within close enough range.

It was easy to pick up her trail once it was in the tunnel due to her use of the repulsors. She reeled it in and had it augmented the repulsors. She'd have to figure out what to do with the psych-hopper infestation later. Or find another way back in.

Do they swim? she wondered, a flash of panic reverberating through her mind. A look at the drone's data seemed to suggest that none of the creatures had entered the water behind it. Maybe that was it, maybe they were there to get water. She didn't have time to think about it. She needed to activate this temple or node or whatever it was and move on to the next before any other parties got involved. That shuttle concerned her.

The AstroChron ticked down to 5D:13H:xxM:xxS. Apparently, minutes and seconds were either irrelevant or unknown. She assumed both. Suddenly, the AstroChron data flashed gold, and then all the letters and numbers went red.

"Raph, what was that?!?" she asked nervously.

"The Delvadr have just arrived in system, ma'am. It has been a pleasure working with you."

"Dammit, Raphael. That's not what we say on a mission like this. Our mission goal explicitly states we are to *stop* the invasion from happening. Something we are actively participating in. Do you see the contradiction?"

"Yes, of course. It's just that the odds of success,"

"No. No. No. No. No. We are *not* doing odds. *We* don't *care* about the odds! *We* just *do* or *die trying.* And we *don't* offer *condolences* before we're DONE!!! Got it? Raph?"

Galas could feel the veins pulsing in her temples. Apparently, Raphael, who monitored her vitals constantly, could also sense that the veins were pulsing in her temples and smartly declined to respond.

"Good."

Galas realized, ironically, that the minutes and seconds of the AstroChron were now ticking down with the hours and days. This was one instance where more complete data did little to boost her comfort level.

"Sorry, ma'am," Raphael offered lamely.

Galas just nodded her head, eyes seeking out shapes in the dark recesses of the pool and finding nothing still. She verified that the drone was still online, augmenting her repulsors. She flicked out the plasma blade into her left hand, and purple-white light slashed through the water in blinding flashes shrouded by a chaos of bubbles and glowing steam as she moved the blade around, and then flicked it back into place.

"Well, that should be more than adequate."

"Indeed," Raphael agreed with finality.

CHAPTER 8

COEXISTIUM

Pain pulsed through Overseer Naar's body. It knotted the muscles in his neck into cords. It crowded his mind and gnawed at his vision.

"Make it stop," he hissed through gritted teeth as the newly acquired mech forged on downriver, coming to the swath of forest that had been chewed up and burned away by the Deathhounds' passing the day prior.

"Make it stop," he hissed again, ragged breath panting out in short bursts.

"MAKE IT STOP!!!" he cried out loud, his screams echoing through the empty spaces inside the mech. Slowly, frost crept onto metallic surfaces, and Naar's panting breath came out in plumes of vapor. His eyes squinted with the bizarre change in temperature. Outside the mech, through the shattered canopy, the air had been humid and warm.

"I can make it stop," a voice said calmly from behind him.

Naar spun from the pilot's seat, sawed-off blaster in one hand, and a chewed-up chunk of sharpened steel in the other. But there was no one there.

The voices in his head cried out in alarm, mimicking his thoughts:

What was that?

Who's there?!?

Who could be here?

They've come to kill us!

Finally!

The voices clamored.

"I can make it stop," the voice, the *other* voice, assured him again. But still, there was no one there.

"Show yourself!" Naar snarled, shaking with rage and pain and, what was it... humiliation? The shame of suffering. Of being *made* to suffer.

Silence followed, at least as much silence as could be found within a mech that was in full operation, traveling down a river and quickly approaching shore.

Suddenly the mech lurched as it hit something underwater.

Naar spun back to the pilot's seat, looked again over his shoulder, and then was thrust into the chair by another unseen obstacle in the water. He holstered his weapons and returned to the chair to strap in and pilot the floundering machine.

Cords and wires flowed from the chair and from above like serpents until they nestled into wounds in the overseer's head and hands and body. The mech righted itself and ascended the rising floor of the river, and then the shore beyond it.

Crisp, new peels of anguish coursed through him again as the adrenaline of shock faded away.

The muscles in his jaws grew striated with the strain. Still, the silence remained.

"What do you want?" he growled into the empty space.

"I want what you want?"

Naar's head jerked, but he kept his eyes on the still-smoldering swath of destroyed jungle before him.

"What is that?"

"You know what it is."

"Enough! I won't play your games. Whoever you are," he spat on the floor, bloodshot, jaundiced eyes focused ahead, a strand of fetid saliva hanging from his lips.

The silence hung on for a moment and then was broken by just a whisper.

"Freedom."

The word grated on Naar's mind like a chainsword on duracite. He drove forward but when one of the smaller mechs got too close, even stepped ahead, his large, mechanized hand came down and crushed the smaller mech's cockpit and reactor with a fiery, orange explosion. The smaller mech, headless, fell to the jungle floor and was trampled by the Deathhounds behind it as they followed their overseer. He who had been immortalized with the gift of size and power none had ever seen.

But with that gift came a burden. One that was more than even Naar could bear.

"Do you know how this works, then?" a voice from high up in the treetops asked.

Jinnbo responded, "How what works?" He was focused on the fish gliding in circles just below the surface, hands on the rocks at the water's edge, head back, poised to strike. He lunged, plunging his entire head into the water and coming up with a tail flapping desperately from the side of his snout. He choked it down and then looked up just in time to catch a fruit pit to the forehead.

"Did you not hear me?" the voice from above, presumably the one who'd launched the pit, asked.

"Ouch!" Jinnbo squeaked, rubbing his head and looking up again, but more warily this time. But it was to no avail as another pit struck him squarely on the snout and sent him scurrying for the bushes through howls of protest.

"So, you're just as ignorant as I am, then?" the voice called, questioningly.

"Hardly," Jinnbo shouted from below, but then launched into the air, flapping furiously to gain altitude, and then swooping down on the location of the voice and the pits. He crashed onto the vacant branch with outstretched taloned feet. His head swiveled as he checked for his missing antagonist but found nothing.

An entire fruit whistled at his head, but he ducked just in time. This one had come from somewhere behind him within the next tree over.

"What're you going on about, brother?" Jinnbo asked, his voice syrupy sweet as he scanned the foliage for a sign of his cloned self. His scaled skin blended suddenly to match the foliage around him.

"Why am I here?" the voice called, now from another position higher in the canopy.

"To torment me, I'm sure," Jinnbo said acidly, his voice also echoing from a new position.

"Don't you want to know how? And why?"

A yellow-pink fruit came whistling through the branches and smacked into an invisible wall.

"Ouch. Ugh!!!" Jinnbo growled in surprise, and then frustration at having been found out.

Suddenly, a blur of color flashed, and the sound, not unlike a catfight, ensued, followed by a furious flapping of wings.

Nothing was left near the scene of the invisible chaos but a bright puddle of purple blood dripping from the branch and splattered across the foliage.

"Jinnbo? Dear brother, have you abandoned me?" the voice slid coolly through the morning air of the jungle.

But there was no response.

"Never mind," Jinndu said softly to himself. "I'll find something else to ease my boredom. I wonder where this Galas is. She sounds like she'd be fun to play with..." His voice, at first sweet, finished with a surprisingly menacing twist.

A flapping of wings clattered in the air and then trailed off.

"What have I done? What have I made?" Jinnbo coughed out in a half-sob, half-wheeze. "My offspring, my *me* ... is ... evil?!?"

Another flutter of wings collapsed into a clatter of branches, followed by a pitiful *whump* of leaves in the underbrush below.

"Ooh. Tender..." Jinnbo whimpered. He brought a wingtip around to inspect it more closely as he materialized, adopting his natural orangey-yellow coloring over the palette of greens of the jungle foliage. Purple streaks crisscrossed the wing in question, and there were similarly colored gashes across his face and abdomen. He forged a sulking, hesitant trail through the exploding undergrowth of the jungle floor.

He wasn't sure where to go, but his inner senses told him to go back to the mech, so he started heading south. Maybe Galas found what she was looking for and was heading back downriver? *Oh well*, he thought, settling in for a long walk.

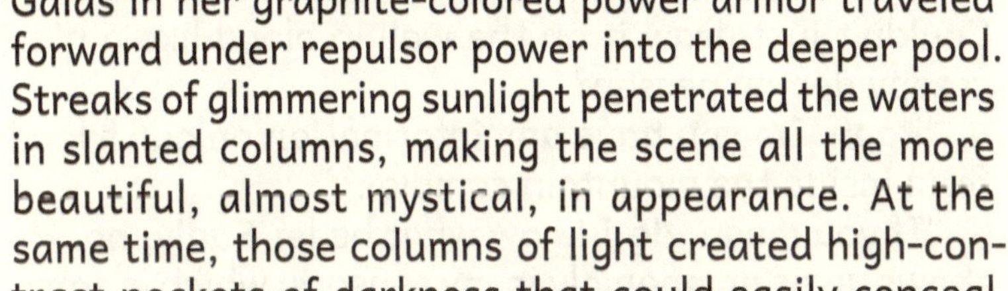

Galas in her graphite-colored power armor traveled forward under repulsor power into the deeper pool. Streaks of glimmering sunlight penetrated the waters in slanted columns, making the scene all the more beautiful, almost mystical, in appearance. At the same time, those columns of light created high-contrast pockets of darkness that could easily conceal the more dangerous creatures Galas knew inhabited these waters. Fairy tales always had monsters. She was certain that they were there, waiting.

Her thumb rested on the arming button of one of the orbs she'd acquired from the shriveled carapaces of the formidable psych-bullies earlier. She pondered that and thought it strange there was no mention of those creatures or of the hoppers in any of the professor's reports. She'd have to look into that later if she had the chance.

In the meantime, her attention was fixed on the sensor data streaming through the SortieNet's HUD. Raphael was already monitoring these feeds intensely in order to notify Galas should one of the huge and exceedingly aggressive fish show up. The attack earlier had happened so suddenly that she doubted she would have much time to react. She was moving slowly but ready to pour on a burst of speed in a hurry.

Galas traveled, submarine-like, in her suit across the pool about three meters below the surface, heading steadily toward the submerged temple structure. It was more like a series of columns arrayed in the now-familiar concentric, broken circle pattern she was seeing everywhere. Most notably from the symbol scrawled in the entrails of the destroyed psych creatures from earlier.

That was a nice touch, she thought sarcastically. Couldn't just draw it on the wall in blood like a nice, creepy demon person?

"Raph. Do you have any information on our friend from inside the mountain complex?"

"If you mean, do I know what he is? Sadly, no. He shows up as an anomaly in my sensors, which is something quite out of the ordinary."

"How out of the ordinary?"

"Well, I've never seen it before. It's like he's only half here," the suit's AI informed her.

"Yeah, that is definitely out of the ordinary. What about the Deathhounds? What do you know about them, and is there any connection?"

"My sensors are incapable of describing a connection between the two, other than they both appear to utilize aspects of the quasi-dimensional element X01101345, or Coexistium-A or just X-ium or X-A for short."

"X-A, that's what we think fuels the Deathhounds, right? Or at least, that's the element we believe acts as the conduit between our realities."

"Yes, that's correct. X-A occurs naturally here. Coexistium-B is identical in makeup but not in appearance. We don't understand how that's possible, but that's what we think the element is that fuels them. That's what we call it when it originates outside of our dimension. That, we think, is the source of the corruptive materials."

"I'm going to ignore all the technical bits and go to the important part. Your assumption is that the dude with the antlers is either *with* the Deathhounds, *in charge* of them, or he's most likely from the same place or dimension or something like that."

"Most likely. Yes," and then, "Galas." Raphael's voice was urgent.

"I see them."

There was movement below as the suit motored forward, looking strikingly like a trolling lure. She was certain. A flash of movement preceded the creatures shooting up from the depths. Galas armed the orb, dropped it, and then, at the last possible moment, shot forward with the repulsors maxed for a quick burst.

She caught the explosion from out of the corner of her eye. A three-meter bubble engulfed the front half of two of the attacking fish and then imploded on itself, leaving just lower halves and a cloud of chum.

Galas's focus was still on the columns only twenty meters ahead when she was struck from below by what felt like a speeding transport. She breached halfway out of the water before being whipped back down and shaken violently.

It took a moment, but the plasma blades sprang to life and the water became a churning mass of light and steam, bubbles and chunks of fish. Galas hung suspended in the cloudy mixture for a second or two, gathering her wits before sheathing the blades and letting the repulsors at her feet push her backward out of the floating murk.

"Raphael?" she asked weakly.

"There are no others that appear interested, ma'am. Are you okay?"

"Thank you. Good..." she answered, short of breath, gingerly stretching her neck side to side to make sure there were no long-term effects from the whiplash she'd received.

"Did you see that?"

"That they had arms and legs? Yes, ma'am. They appear to be another mutation."

"*Another* mutation?"

"Possibly. It's not beyond reason that they, as well as the psych-effective creatures from the tunnel complex, are the product of a mutagen, or possibly some sort of genetic experiment. Or maybe both."

"That could explain why there's no reference to any of these ... *creatures* in the professor's reports," she suggested, still catching her breath from the encounter.

"Yes. Quite possibly."

"So, the shuttle... searching for the Arcfire? Or checking on their pets?" Galas wondered aloud.

"Hard to say, but, if I may, the countdown on the AstroChron ... it appears to be speeding up."

"What?!? Oh, that's not good. That's not good at all," Galas exclaimed, shaking her head, and then regretting it as it throbbed with the movement. "Okay, let's get a move on. Wait, what's it saying? I'm still having a hard time focusing on it."

"It's increased speed by twenty percent and climbing. My estimation is that we have three days, maybe four, since the Delvadr ships will have to slow down an equal amount once they draw near the planet."

She wanted to scream but settled for reaching for one of the orbs in case more of the fish creatures came, but then thought better of that as well. She didn't want to risk using one of the orbs in the temple where it might destroy the node she was trying to activate.

Galas ventured farther into the submerged columns, looking at their peculiar architecture and logging that info into the SortieNet file structure. The columns had wide flutes and trapezoidal bases but other than that were unremarkable, except that in the arrangement and underwater they held a certain mystique.

She continued to make her way between them to the center, where a small structure stood on a raised dais. She could see immediately that the power suit would not fit into the tall, narrow entrance. That was going to be a problem. Now that she was in the maze of columns at the heart of the temple, she was less concerned about the remaining fish mutants. Plus, Raphael was keeping a close eye. That gave her a surprising amount of comfort, she had to concede. But if she had to free dive to enter the temple.

Galas peeled out her remaining drone to examine the interior of the structure. She was able to see that there were no other entrances and no windows. Of course. The room was empty without any furnishings, symbols, markings, or anything of interest.

"Perhaps it is a holographic interface, such as we found in the mountain complex?" Raphael suggested.

Galas nodded. "Yeah, that makes sense, even here in a temple. These guys really had a thing for VRI. Of course, that leaves the big question: Can we get it to work?"

"I'm on it already. The radiation signature that we encountered in the mountain was stronger and more defined. Here it is very weak, possibly due to the temple being submerged in water. Or maybe it's a different system or we're missing something entirely."

"Like what? No, wait. What's that on the floor? Pull back." She spoke to the SortieNet generally now, rather than to its persona, and it felt a little awkward.

Galas scrutinized the drone footage. It was clear that on the floor the concentric broken circle pattern was displayed here as well, only it looked different than before. Here, it appeared that the C-shaped symbols that were nested within each other were all in alignment so that all the openings faced down. Elsewhere, when she'd seen the pattern, the open portion of the C had faced different directions. Galas directed the drone in closer, and it appeared that the C shapes themselves were inset and made of a single piece of material. The material was a dark, gray-gold like Brillian.

She wondered if insets could be manipulated or realigned. Nothing that the drone would be able to do on its own. She knew that it would come down to this, stripping out of the power armor and swimming down into the submerged temple. Galas breathed out a long sigh and surfaced. She looked around and the closest section of shore was forty meters farther on, but it was in a patch of sunlight, at least.

"As good a place as any," she said out loud.

"What is, ma'am?"

"The shoreline there," she said, highlighting it in the battlespace, "I'm going to have to free dive to get inside the temple. I'm hoping that I can manipulate those insets in the floor so that they match one of the symbols that the Necromanc... the antler-guy... I wish he'd given us a name..."

"Sun-Thurr. I believe. I found it referenced in the professor's work. Well, a reference of a reference, anyway," Raphael added.

"Sun-Thurr. If he's referenced by Professor Goodfall—"

"No, he's not specifically referenced by Goodfall. The professor references a manuscript regarding Sun-Thurr. The figure described matches the person you met in the mountain.

"If that's true, he'd be—"

"Very old."

"How is that possible?" Galas asked, shaking her head in disbelief.

"It may be the dimensionality issue. He may age very little in this time-space, or his nature may be altogether different than your own."

"Raphael, how is this Sun-Thurr referenced?"

"As a minor god, ma'am. And *not* a good one. Those standards we saw along the river, with the bodies on them, those may have been warnings, as you had supposed, but they may also have been sacrifices ... lost technology, one culture's interpretation of another. It's hard to say."

Galas's lips pursed, but she said nothing for a long moment.

"Raphael, what would a minor god, whatever that means, want with Antiquity or the Arcfire?"

"The information is incomplete, ma'am. Referenced from inscriptions located in a mountain sanctum within the second city of Daxn. It appears that the professor neither gathered all the information nor was able to translate all of what he had. I'll try to decipher what's here but, we may have to go find out for ourselves. Time permitting, of course."

"Yeah. Let's get this over with."

Galas found a suitable flat spot just beyond the shore and began the process of exiting the Targe IV armor. First the helmet split hemispherically, ear-to-ear. Then the torso section did the same along her sides before protruding forward about a hand's width at the top and considerably more so at the waist-line where she would exit. Then her leg armor split along the inseam with the upper and lower sections folding out to reveal her toned, if pale, legs. Pale for her, anyway.

Her default pigmentation was a medium tan that turned coppery when she was in the sun, which was rarely ever anymore. She stepped clear after what felt like an eternity, waiting for all the sections to unhinge and for the positioning gel to recede. "Raph, seal her up and stay alert."

"I'm not going anywhere, ma'am," she heard him say through her auric implants, which sounded odd after being used to the suit's internal audio. It reminded her how much hardware she was actually carrying around in her head. Good thing the suit's nano suite kept good diagnostics on her biosystems' status. She'd been working solo for so long she hadn't had a chance to get back to FB Dahlen for her routine exams for, well, too many cycles. Actually, the EDC was so depleted at this point, that even if she did go in, they might not have the parts or personnel to fix her.

"Raphael?"

"Yes, Miss Galas."

"Are my interface systems in order?"

"Why are you having trouble hearing me? You should have at least 150 meters of range—"

"No. I just... never mind," she said, suddenly self-conscious. Realizing that worrying about routine maintenance was silly considering that life as she knew it was scheduled to end in less than four days.

"I prioritized the integrity of your implants slightly above boob-sweat, so no worries there," Raphael offered, sounding somewhat smug.

"Thanks. Why don't you take over on the drone and keep an eye out under the surface," she said as she stripped off her pilot's coveralls, and then, thinking about it for a moment, her skivvies too. She figured she'd lose them at the worst possible moment, and they weren't going to offer her any real protection, anyway. She tied her hair back into two short braids tight to her head. The last thing she did was pull her belt and knife sheath off her flight suit. She used her leather bracelet wrap to fasten the sheath to her thigh so it wouldn't flop around while she was swimming.

She looked at her naked body with the belt and knife and shook her head. *Cadian Galas: Jungle*

Warrior, she thought and suddenly hoped that footage of this would never get out if somehow she managed to successfully ignite the Arcfire and save the planet. *I guess that's the least of my worries.*

"Okay, Raph. Wish me luck."

"Oh, good Luck, ma'am."

With that, Galas dove into the cool, clear waters of the temple pool.

Making her way to a column near the temple, she found that she was only waist-deep while standing atop it. The temple entrance, however, was about five meters down. That was going to be tough. She didn't have a rebreather and the suit wouldn't fit. She may have to improvise something, but she could at least try to get down there and take a look.

"Raph. Fly-by, please."

Raphael directed the drone in amongst the columns and into the temple, which was still clear of hostiles.

"Direct some light on the floor with the drone if you can."

"Sure thing."

Galas took a couple of quick, deep breaths and dove in, kicking for the bottom. She could see light emanating from the temple entrance and swam in that direction. Slipping through the entrance, she had just reached the spot on the floor with the inlays when her lungs burned, and that twinge of panic took over. She was about to head back for the surface when she noticed reflected light off the ceiling and diverted upward, reaching through the surface about an arms-length. It felt clear, so she breached the surface and found that there was plenty of headroom. The air tasted stale and damp, but it was air.

She had Raphael pull the drone up into the void to sample the gas mixture. If it was low oxygen, she would be asphyxiating without knowing it. O2 was at 20.4%, which was near ideal and an incredible stroke of luck. She paused there for a moment. The cavity was only about half a meter high, but it extended about three meters. More than enough air up here for her purposes, even at elevated exertion levels. She hyperventilated and then dove back down to the floor.

Up close, she could see that the markings might be able to be manipulated. Currently, they looked like three C's facing downward and nested one within the other. She struggled to remember what the marking should look like from the symbols that Sun-Thurr had scrawled on the floor of the mountain complex. She shuddered again at the memory. But then something else occurred to her. She kicked back up to the air pocket again.

"Raphael. Do you have recorded footage of the encounter with Sun-Thurr in the mountain?" Her voice echoed oddly in the closed-in space.

"Yes, ma'am. All unindexed imagery is held in short-term memory for three days."

"Replay it, please. I'd like to see the symbol he drew again."

"I can generate the symbol for you if you'd like."

"No. I think I want to see it for myself."

The recorded feed showed the so-called minor god, Sun-Thurr in the distance and the strange luminescent wisps escaping from the psych-bully bodies. It showed him scrawling on the floor with the staff, and then it showed the symbol, Galas's hand reaching toward it, and then the feed went to static as if the SortieNet had dropped offline the same time that Galas had lost consciousness. Here was the weird part; when the SortieNet came back online, Sun-Thurr was kneeling directly in front of the suit's helmet camera, what Galas would have seen if she were conscious.

Then the antlered figure reached out one shriveled hand. Long talon-like nails protruded from the fingers, and he traced a symbol on Galas's face shield. The SortieNet feed glitched out again and when it came back online, was when Galas had awoken.

Her blood ran cold. "What the in the hell was that?"

"I'm uncertain. I had not viewed that section of footage before now. I did not know it was there."

"We need to find that place, that sanctum or whatever," Galas said, her voice small, emotionless.

Galas realized she was treading water still, inside the submerged temple.

"Raph, show me the symbol. The one from the floor. Not whatever he did to the visor of the suit."

The pattern came up in the virtual HUD on her corneal implants. The whole symbol was three groups of circles in a vertical line with a bent line between them. Per the data provided, she was at the temple located at the bottom of the symbol. The concentric, broken circles or C-shapes had their openings facing in different directions. The outer ring opened at about the thirty-degree mark, high and right. The middle one around 270 or directly left and the innermost ring about 135 or lower right.

"Raph, you confirmed that the column arrangement in the temple courtyard matches the bottom portion of the symbol, correct?"

"That is correct."

She swam back down but could not find a way to move the symbols. She caught her breath and tried again, but without success, and returned to the bubble.

"Dammit!" she rasped, her voice echoing close. She was beginning to feel claustrophobic with her head nearly bumping the ceiling each time she surfaced.

"Galas, there's something approaching," Raphael warned.

She dove, and there, in the entrance, was a large shadow. At first, she thought it was one of the fishmen and her knife was in her hand in a flash, her heart in her throat expecting to die, but then she realized that she didn't recognize the shape. It moved closer into the light from the drone and Galas's mouth dropped. It was one of the salamanders. It stood upright, and its huge head, with vegetation-like growths radiating wildly outward, stared at her with huge black orbs for eyes. Those eyes were mesmerizing in their alienness. They were intelligent. Scrutinizing as if weighing her in some moral calculation. It was supremely uncomfortable.

Galas had to surface again but pushed back down as quick as she could. The figure still stood there, in the entrance. And then a thought popped into her head: *You, who have come at the appointed time. You have slain the keepers and yet not harmed the children.*

There was a pause. Galas wasn't sure what she was thinking. The words were in her head, but they were not her thoughts.

You have slain the keeper but not harmed the children. You have done so as the plates of heaven are arranged within themselves. You have come for the sky-fire.

Galas shook her head to the affirmative but had to surface again for air.

When she returned below, the creature was gone, but on the floor of the temple sat a large, perfectly polished stone obelisk. It was white and gold and her first thought was that the coloring was a close approximation to that of Skleetrix, Epriot Prime's second moon.

"Galas, are you okay?" Raphael asked, sounding concerned.

She flashed the thumbs-up signal to the drone and then swam down to the stone, picked it up, and then kicked and pulled herself along the floor with one arm. She placed the heavy stone on the center of the floor markings and then surfaced, breathed deep, and dove again.

The silver-gold inlays appeared to float above the floor, but closer examination showed her that this was holography. VRI. Galas reached down and moved her hand over the virtual representation of the outer circle until it came to a stop at the thirty-degree mark. She did the same with the middle and inner circles and watched as the inlays in the floor shifted to match.

Now what?

She slid the stone off the markings and all the virtual figures stayed in position. Galas pushed off the floor, grabbed some more air, and then dove down for the stone. She used it as ballast, to bound in heavy-laden strides across the temple floor and out the entrance. That's when she saw that the columns in the courtyard had rearranged themselves to match the symbol inside.

She was stunned and dropped the rock, but then a subtle vibration shimmered through the water. And then a more emphatic one. The courtyard moved beneath her feet and where there hadn't been a current before, now there most definitely was one.

The water began rushing down around her while the floor felt like it was pressing up from below. It was disorienting until she realized that the entire temple complex was slowly rising. She watched in awe as the mirror-like surface above drew down to meet her. She almost flinched as it crested her head and shoulders, and she found herself giggling while trying to suck in breath and look around to capture the fantastic sight.

Water poured off the temple and courtyard in streams. Everything glistened as the sunlight caught the slick surfaces still dripping with the sudden shift in the environment. And then, as quickly as it started, it was over.

"Ma'am, you should get your suit on, and we should be going. You can tell me what happened on the way."

Galas was still marveling at the experience and the way the temple now rested in the pool with the waterfalls cascading down on one side and the jungle pressing in from every other. Verdant pops of light, the shimmering blue, it was stunning. She could only imagine what the city must have looked like before it was destroyed. That thought jolted her back to the present.

Yes, let's not get destroyed, she thought, picked up the rock artifact. It was considerably heavier now that it was out of the water. She walked over to where she'd stashed Raphael and the suit. It was more than a little awkward strolling naked and wet with an obelisk and a boot knife through an ancient temple.

This was not the image she had in mind when she'd received her brief about this mission from the lieutenant colonel nearly a month prior. She couldn't say she hated it. But then, that could just be the stims talking. She was a bit punch-drunk. Rubbing her eyes and suppressing a yawn, she reached the edge of the temple plaza and the former shore. *One temple down.* She didn't know what that meant, but she was making progress.

CHAPTER 9

SKLEETRIX

Galas ducked in, turned, and then stepped back into the Targe IV suit. It wrapped around her, expanding gel and sealing seams with whirring servos and little poofs of pneumatics before doing one last repositioning of the gel inserts. It was comfortable but a little claustrophobic as it pressed around her rib cage and throat. She swallowed and realized that she had mixed emotions about being surrounded by heavy metal again, even if it was lightweight, ceramo-metal composite.

On the one hand, she was used to the protection, and she appreciated having all of her tools at her disposal. On the other hand, it had felt so liberating to free dive and explore the submerged ruins in the jungle pool below the falls, to feel the water on her skin and the warm jungle breeze on her face. This was something she'd have done in her free time if she'd had the chance. Although, she had probably contracted some sort of parasite, and was suddenly happy to be back in the suit.

"Raph, scan for bugs, please."

"Already done. You're clean. And also, you smell a lot better."

"That's a relief. On both counts," she said, although she wondered what metrics he was using to make that second assessment. For certain, the smell of dried urine had been somewhat off-putting when she'd exited the suit before her swim.

"Ma'am, what happened in the temple ... with the salamander? It looked like it brought you that rock, and that's what you used to activate the node VR interface."

Galas told him the details of how the salamander had spoken to her telepathically. And how it had referred to the "children," which she assumed was how it referred to its own species. She also told him about how the salamander had said that she had come at the appointed time to receive the sky-fire. She refrained from bringing up the part about how she'd named them after Jinnbo because they were disgusting and didn't do much. In hindsight, that seemed an unfair characterization, and then with Jinnbo most-likely dead, well, it was just sad and depressing and made her feel like a really bad person.

"The Arcfire, then," Raphael suggested.

She snapped out of her dismal thoughts and back to the present.

"Yes. That seems to track. He also mentioned something about stacking plates in the sky. I didn't quite get that part. Plates ... or discs maybe? Discs in the sky, stacking or overlapping, could be a conjunction of the moons? Just a guess," she offered, tilting her head and squinting a little.

"No, that's pretty good. We're days away from a lunar co-orbit, with Skleetrix in front, at least briefly," he offered.

"Well, that's interesting, but it doesn't seem to help us much. We still need to activate the next two nodes, and we need to get to the bottom of what's up with our resident demi-god. I don't suppose we should try to head back the way we came. How far is Daxn?"

"About 130 kilometers to the north," Raphael provided.

"Yeah, that's a problem. That'd take days through the jungle. Any thoughts on another way into the mountain?"

"Let's let the drone scan the hillside. There were several corridors connected to that shaft. Also, it's possible that the psych-hoppers are no longer in the shaft at all. If they were coming there for water, or to sleep, or some other reason, we don't know."

"Okay, have the drone check the hillside. What about the other drones, any updates?"

"No. No signal from the other drones, which may be a good thing, but then as I said before, it's quite a ways to Daxn. If the drones went there and back, they'd just be getting back by now."

Within minutes, one of the drones entered the comms envelope and synced with the SortieNet. Raphael pulled the feed immediately, and it popped up on Galas's HUD. The drone footage showed the alien shuttle as it arced into the basin where the second city of Antiquity lay covered by the jungle forest but, rather than following the river to another large pool, it veered left toward a cliff wall with a jutting abutment that again, cascaded with waterfalls.

These falls came from a source within the mountain itself and plummeted into misty plumes near the base. There were more visible structures here than had been evident at the southmost city of Braex. In addition to these stone structures, Galas saw temporary shelters dotting the landscape and a significant cluster of them near the bottom of the cliff wall.

"Dammit. It's an entire operation."

"It appears that way, ma'am."

"Can you tell what they are?"

"Not from this distance. We'll have to get a closer look."

Galas glanced at the AstroChron display, trying to juggle all the variables in her head. It read: 03D12H04M16S.

"Three-and-a-half days," she breathed out. "This is just getting better and better... Raphael, send the drone back for a closer look and to link up with our last drone. Have it download data and upload the new program. Send the third drone to the last city to scout it out. What's that one called?"

"Xiocic."

"Okay, last drone to She-Oh-Chich? Second drone gets a closer look at our new friends at Daxn, locates and scouts the temple there, and then I want it to hunt for the Sanctum from Professor Goodfall's data. All missions fail to high orbit rendezvous at the Daxn temple. Mission success, same. Does that make sense?"

"Yes. What about this new group? Is it possible they would help us?"

"Can't be sure. They could be hostile, they could be Delvadr or Delvadr allies, or they could be indifferent opportunists. They could be trying to sabotage the

Arcfire for all we know. We need intel, and we need a fast way to Daxn. How's that drone doing?"

Instantly, a patchwork of highlighted points was superimposed on a view of the mountainside. They were gray, red, yellow, and one green one, high up above a section of exposed, vertical granite.

"Raph, are you kidding me? Another climb?"

"Looks like that or the submerged tunnel."

Galas wanted to massage her temples but couldn't with the power armor's helmet in the way and her gauntlets on. She was wasting time. There were four options, and all of them sucked.

One: Take the underwater tunnel into a shaft that was possibly filled with hundreds of psych-hoppers, or completely empty and provided the most direct access to the hub and the most direct transit to Daxn. Two: Climb the cliff wall, entering an area that was unknown as to hostiles and also, exposing her to any shuttles flying by either to be spotted or to be shot down, probably the latter. Almost always the latter. Three: Run through the jungle 130 kilometers and arrive in Daxn the day of the invasion, *if* she was lucky. And Four: Swim up the river, against the current, acting much the same as a fishing lure for the hyper-aggressive, mutated fishmen known as the Keepers. It all sucked.

"Raph, how are we doing on rations?"

"A day and a half. Three days if you cut consumption in half, of course."

"Yeah. Do you see anything that I'm not? It's either jungle, river, tunnel, or cliff."

"I can provide odds for each if you'd like."

"Raph, what did I say about odds?"

"That we never do odds."

"Right, cliff it is. Raph, Industrial Orchestra Playlist #3, please. Loud."

Despite neither her previous mech nor her current power armor being designed to climb tall cliffs, she had had good luck thus far. Again, she was utilizing a drone to generate a hyper-detailed pathway. Some she could climb by hand and some she had to utilize the grappling lines to scale. Occasionally she could walk sections like steps, climbing the piles of stacked boulders. Once the path had been generated, she had the drone running a sentinel role to warn her of a shuttle's approach or any other danger.

The spot she was headed for was, of course, at the top of the cliff. It was something like a small shuttle pad. Only large enough for one craft. It barely would have fit her mech had she somehow been able to navigate to that point. A jump mech could have done it, possibly, she thought. Or maybe a low orbit entry with an RVLS—Reduced Velocity Landing System or glide kit. Drakas used to call them slow-droppers, but he was from the northern isles and they had weird names for everything.

She felt a stab of remorse. She hoped he was at peace, but something deep within her suggested otherwise. If she ever got through this, she would hunt down those Deathhounds and destroy them. Every last one.

Galas busied her mind with the climb and the music pounded at her from the suit's immersive audio system, but still, the thoughts came to her: first of Drakas and Betsy, and then Jinnbo. He'd done nothing to deserve to be abandoned on the side of a cliff. There was guilt there, and she knew it was deserved.

And then her mind wandered farther, deeper into the past. She remembered Ensign Matko Dragoii and his wife Sonnra standing in the delivery room. He had survived the Skleetrix counteroffensive after all and been given a medical discharge. The two smiled proudly at her as she held her newborn baby girl. With their help, she'd been able to have a daughter of her own.

She saw the golden river of tumenum foliage as it pierced into the rebuilt village of Kozst, her childhood home. The shop was still there, but she had arranged for an apartment in the new westside when she'd resigned her commission. It would have been too much to see the inside of that old place every day. The memories were still too fresh, even a decade later.

She remembered Seraf, barely three months old, sitting in the same grass near the boulders at village center. The strong scent of lalish rushes on the warm breeze, the tumenum grove, the kids playing tag-rag-seek between their towering trunks.

And then the darker stuff. Mere weeks later, the summer night warm on her sun-kissed skin. She'd heard screams of alarm—warnings. She'd rushed to the street with Seraf still in her arms, still wearing her summer dress, not wasting time to find her sandals. The sky was alive with streaking lights ... and with fire.

What had made her believe that the Delvadr wouldn't be back? Was it wishful thinking or just a longing for some semblance of normalcy, for a life filled with things she could look forward to?

The lunar operation had been a shock to the system for the Delvadr forces. It was only weeks before they abandoned the battlefield, retreating from the system entirely. The Epriots would learn later that it was just part of their bizarre, quasi-scientific religious observances. Things to do with astronomical alignments and supposed energies that flowed through and between the galaxies.

After four years, their return was unexpected, and Galas, along with the rest of humanity, what little was left, had returned to a life that many of them had no prior knowledge of—a life of peace.

It'd taken her a long time to make that decision, scarred by scarcity and loss growing up, it had taken a lot for her to let down her guard. She was still surprised that she did. Of course, she was right not to trust that things would be okay. While the Delvadr lived, they would never be safe.

Galas stared down, remembering the flash of light that dazzled her eyes and left her dumbstruck and temporarily deaf. Remembered looking down at her empty arms. The ash and blood and dirt, her burned and torn summer dress. She'd looked up at the firefly embers drifting up into the glowing clouds of smoke and beyond them, the dark looming shapes of Thune-built Delvadr destroyers hovering in the night sky.

"Miss Galas?" Raphael asked.

Startled into the present, she responded, "Umm ... what?"

"Miss Galas, is something the matter? You've stopped."

"Ohh," she said, looking arouund at the panorama and the hundreds of meters of open-air between her and the valley floor.

"Sorry. Just ... thinking about something. And, no, I don't want to talk about it."

"Fair enough. We're almost there."

Galas looked up and was surprised to see that only two meters farther on was an unnatural, horizontal line that was most likely the perimeter of the landing pad.

She refocused and saw the glowing gold and silver highlights within the SortieNet's augmented reality overlay, the battlespace model. She made quick work of the last few moves and found herself standing atop the broad landing area. Beyond it, an observation room with missing windows that appeared to house the remnants of a huge nest. The drone had provided imagery, but it looked different in real life.

She turned back around to view the long, broad valley following the ridgeline north. The valley extended as far as she could see to the east; the jungle climbing up onto a plateau that just disappeared into the distance. Looking north, she couldn't make out the city from here, but she thought that she could make out the peak above it.

The SortieNet highlighted it as such, so at least she could tell where she was headed. At that point, the ridgeline broke a little bit northeast, which Galas could now match up to the symbol, how the line angled slightly right from the center circle pattern. The symbol was definitely a depiction of the three cities of Antiquity: Xiocic, Daxn, and Braex.

You have come at the appointed time; the salamander had told her. Telepathically, she thought, shaking her head in bewilderment.

What did *that* mean, that there was some sort of prophecy? This was certainly not how she saw this mission going. Another week in this place and she'd probably be running the jungle naked (again) with bat guano smeared on her face and shooting rats with a homemade bow.

Galas realized her eyes were feeling gritty and really heavy ... and gritty. Wait, she'd thought that already. Her arms and legs, too. They felt like they had sandbags tied to them, even in the power suit. That could explain why she kept finding herself losing focus.

"Raph, short-term stim, please."

"At the risk of being perceived as a nannybot—"

"Stim. Please," she interrupted.

"Gladly," he said, sounding a bit too chipper.

"Sarcasm doesn't suit you."

Silence ensued, but Galas immediately felt the kick. She wasn't sure how much sleep she'd gotten in the last day and a half. Other than being knocked out or knocked silly, she hadn't slept intentionally at all. It was definitely grating on her, and her mood was growing darker than usual. Galas definitely had her dark moods. The shit she'd seen and gone through. Lingering too close to that chasm of despair was madness. She focused, pulled up her mental hedges, and just focused on what was ahead of her.

She'd have to get some sleep soon, though. At least a couple of hours. Maybe Raphael could coax the Antiquity systems into running a shuttle? That seemed like too much to ask. Instead, she worked her way through the tangle of branches and feathers and bits of shell and into the back of the observation room.

Typical to all things Antiquity, there were no furnishings or artistry. Just slab-like walls and corridors. This was an unexplored section and so the drone moved ahead and filled in the gaps in the battlespace model. It looked like it would connect to an arterial corridor that could connect to the transport tunnels. So far, no surprises, but she wasn't going to hold her breath.

Reaching the transport tunnels, she found a boarding area and anticipated having to climb down onto the ground level when Raphael broke the silence.

"Miss Galas, I've been negotiating with the Antiquity network over the radiation signal again. I think I *can* call a transport … if one is in a functioning state."

"Well, yeah. That would be preferable to having to jog 130 klicks," Galas snapped, grimacing at her tone as she heard it through the audio.

"Of course."

"Raph, I'm sorry. I'm running on fumes here."

"No need to apologize to me."

"Yes, there is, even if it's only for my own good."

"Well, then, apology accepted," Raphael sounded genuinely pleased. Galas thought that she must be losing her mind. AIs were pretty good at human interaction, but Raphael was better than anything she'd ever dealt with. Maybe it was because she'd been dealing with this particular iteration of the SortieNet for so many years, it could probably anticipate her every thought. That was a little creepy, actually. Still, she didn't know why she'd never used this format. It was so much more … *organic*, for lack of a better word.

"That stim must be wearing off already," she mused loudly when she'd actually not meant to speak at all. *Stims*, she thought, suppressing the urge to take off her gauntlets and scratch the imaginary wool off her tongue. Instead, she attempted to whistle an old

Candor tune her mother used to sing, but it came out thick and clumsy. She abandoned the activity and just stared down at her boots as they peeked out from below her chest armor, one, and then the other, over and over again.

Just then, the lights flickered throughout the tunnelway but partially, not like the first time in the core shaft when it went from pitch black to carnival lights in an instant. Still, a few holograms whisked by—ghosts in red and blue and a myriad of other colors, but more subdued and only, it seemed, in the area associated with the rightmost track.

Within a couple of minutes, a transport showed up. It was faded and dusty, but other than that looked fit for service. Alien-tech or prior race-tech. The fact that it was functional at all was a testimony to how advanced they were.

She expected the squeal of metal on metal to assault her ears as doors swung to either side of a relatively human-sized entry, but it didn't happen. Again, some ancient techno-wizardry at play. Her power armor barely fit through.

Once inside, rather than taking a seat, she just lay on the floor. The shuttle pulsed with cool blue light before the doors sealed up and the transport streaked away with the speed and intensity of the vertical lifts from before.

Galas wasn't aware of falling asleep, but she awoke to a sudden change in speed, and then the transport settling to the ground. She sat up, and her head swam a little.

"Raph, what's up?"

"We've reached the end of the line as far as my ability to negotiate with Braex goes. So far, though the radiation signal is similar, it is weaker here, and I've been unable to interface with the Daxn system."

"How long was I out?"

"About an hour. I had the transport running slower than it normally would. Partly to allow you to sleep longer and partly because I can't be sure that the inertia dampening system is fully functional and whether there aren't any obstacles or damage to the tunnel or track."

"Smart."

"What did you expect?"

"Smug doesn't suit you either."

"Also, it didn't make sense to outrun our drone," he said, not responding to her comment directly, she noticed.

"So, where are we?"

"About halfway out."

"Okay ... any critters?"

"If there were, they stayed well-hidden."

"That's not very reassuring."

Galas scarfed down half of a ration bar and hydrated herself. The stim-induced stale wool taste in her mouth, now reconstituted by the liquid, was off-putting, and she didn't bother to finish the other half. The gritty, jitteriness she felt all over was making her not want to have to use the stims again. She opted to go au natural, at least for now. They had to be affecting her aim, if not her judgment.

"Okay. One foot in front of the other," she said and started jogging, stiffly at first, floodlights bobbing in the distance ahead. *Stabilize*, she commanded via thought, and the bobbing stopped, but now she could hear the tiny servos compensating the beam angle with her gait. This annoyed her, and she recognized that the stims were affecting her more than she'd thought.

She switched the color of the beams from white to red to minimize announcing herself to any creatures that depended on eyesight as much as a human did. Which, upon reflection, was probably an unnecessary precaution in a subterranean environment.

Though Galas was tired, the Targe IV tripled her efforts, transforming her light jog into a ground-eating pace. She'd have pulled back the drone to augment the suit if she'd thought it wise. *Better to move slowly than to run into something without seeing it*, she reasoned.

She had Raphael continue to crack the code of Daxn's network, but when he had little luck, she had him go back to the professor's data.

A few minutes later, he spoke up, "Miss Galas, I've discovered something interesting in the research data."

Galas was down to a slow trot now. Anything to keep her mind off the endless jog was a good thing.

"What'dja find?"

"Well, the professor had not been able to access the Antiquity network like I was able to, at least not in Braex. But it does look like he was able to hack the system locally and use holo-projection."

Galas chewed on this. "So, he couldn't access the functionality of the system, but he could see what was available to be seen?"

"Astute observation."

"Don't be a smart ass. So, how does this help us? Does it mean that even if you can't operate the Antiquity system, we can at least see what the professor saw, like in the Sanctum?"

"Or, if I can hack the local system, we can see all that the Sanctum has to offer. See what the professor *didn't* see."

"That would be good, so long as we can get these nodes working before the Delvadr get here."

"We may not get that chance if we have to activate the node here at Daxn, travel to Xiocic, and then back here to inspect the Sanctum."

"Yeah, I've been worrying about that. Any luck on pulling more clues from the professor's work?" she asked, tripping and catching herself, and then more cautiously resuming her slow jog, which, in the suit, was still upward of thirty klicks per hour. While not blindingly fast, it was still not a speed at which it was wise to be distractable.

"No," Raphael replied.

"I was afraid you were going to say that. So, what? We steal a shuttle?"

"An alien craft that we may or may not have an adequate quantity of appendages to operate? Worth a shot..."

Galas laughed. Wingman. Raphael was definitely turning into a wingman.

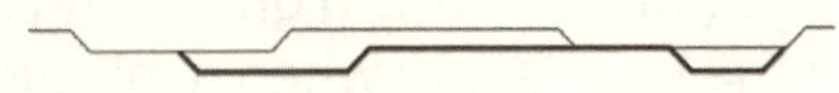

The pock-marked surface of Skleetrix filled the viewscreen in excruciating detail. Sweat populated her brow, but she dared not show any hint of the terror that was gnawing at her insides. She didn't let it enter her voice as she called out coordinates to her co-pilot, Ensign Dragoii, "30.005 by 175.129, forward one-five degrees, decay zero-point-one-one."

"Fade?" Dragoii asked.

"Zero."

"Strong numbers. You sure you haven't done this before? You're not holding out on me, are you?" He looked over at her. "I have money on you screwing this up."

"Money you'll never collect if I do," Galas chided.

"True. But it's the smart money. Prove me wrong," he challenged.

"You willing to double that bet, Dragoii?"

"Sure," he said patronizingly while, she was sure, breathing through the fear erupting in his chest as they drew closer to the surface.

"Then brace for impact. We are good in ... five ... four ... three..."

Galas never got to two. Missiles streamed over the horizon.

"Incoming!" she called out.

"I see them. Deploying countermeasures,"

The gargantuan troop deployment mech hit the lunar surface in a plume of dust and bounced high. This was the hard part that Galas had screwed up so many times in sims. She scanned the HUD, processing angle-of-attack; momentum, fractions of gravity, decay. She was too front-heavy. They were going to bury the nose again when a missile parted the brilliant wall of liquid light and smoke and impacted the mech's shielding. Besides blowing away chunks of ceramic-alloy armor, it actually corrected the mech's over-aggressive angle of approach to something she could work with.

"Oh, you've gotta be kiddin' me. I live and now I'm going to be completely broke!" Her co-pilot moaned, hitting his forehead with his palm.

"Just shut up and do your job, Dragoii. Lotta chances to die out here."

"Un-believable. Just, unf—," expletives poured on as he shook his head. "Did you see that, you silly sonsabitches?!? Yeah, that's right!" He cried at the HUD, though whether he was speaking to the marines strapped to the sides and underbelly of the mech or to the enemy lobbing missiles at them was unclear.

Galas let it go. She was in the zone now. She'd made it farther than ever before in the sims and now the real work started.

The mech, somewhat resembling an ancient box TV set with stubby, muscular ostrich legs, bobbed along the surface of the moon like an umbrella caught in a windstorm and yet, somehow, continued on. Galas flogged it into submission, guiding, chastising, grunting with exertion and mental exhaustion.

The augmented reality of the SortieNet guided her with crimson lines, parallel and ever-inching closer to one another until she could see the wall turrets ahead. And then the horizon exploded into spears of emerald and amber. The SortieNet color-coded enemy and friendly fire since actual laser fire was invisible to the human eye. A blistering array of light displayed on the viewscreen before her shields erupted into splashes of brilliant light.

"Get us out of here Galas!" Dragoii cried.

"She'll take it. Keep your panties on."

"My panties are soiled! I'm gonna need new panties after this."

"Then the shields are in better shape than your... Shit!" she cried as dark shadows loomed over the walls of the base. "Gunships! Look sharp!"

A barrage of missiles descended like locusts on a mech that Galas hadn't noticed was running beside her.

An explosion tore through its body and armor, a tragic yard sale of marine pods and appendages scattered in a hundred directions.

Galas cut over into the mech's previous vector, knowing the gunships would have switched targets and sure enough, a slew of plasma rounds peppered the dusty, pock-marked surface where she'd been only moments before.

"Countermeasures. Now!" she cried and cut back to her previous line. Missiles sliced through the metallic confetti, and whizzed off in drunken spirals, chasing phantom signals into the darkness of space.

Galas blinked and realized the walls were within reach. Gunships flashed overhead on their way to targets that were attainable, leaving the turrets to pick up the dregs. Galas loosed a barrage of plasma and missile fire, and then skittered left again, repeating the process once more before bounding for the wall. The mech exploded off the lunar surface, taking full advantage of the fractional gravity; only this time, she time, she allowed the front to tip over max. Locking on the wall turret closest to the gate, she let loose a hellish torrent, not stopping to watch the carnage.

Screams sounding like excited schoolgirls exploded over her audio—the marines, she thought with thorough satisfaction. The mech continued to tip over until all she could see through the forward viewport was starlight perforating void. The altimeter plunged toward zero and destruction was certain until a flash of geometric shapes rushed up from the bottom of the screen, and the mech was upright and running with the carried momentum.

"You just somersaulted ... a transport mech ... in microgravity!" he panted out. "No one ... has ever ... done that before."

"It was actually a forward flip with a full torso rotation. Hope I didn't scramble our eggs," Galas responded, referring to the scores of pods still connected to the mech. She was sure there were a lot of meals lost on that last bit.

"Smoke. Now!" she cried and then initiated the command without waiting for Dragoii to comply.

"Get off or go home, boys!" She yelled over the intercom to the Marines, who were still waiting for an 'all-clear' and a command to exit the mech and flee its psychotic pilot.

To their credit, they dismounted within seconds, and a new barrage of light illuminated the interior spaces of the base, followed by explosions and defiant screams.

Galas spun the mech on its heels and lit up the gate that was supposed to have been blown by now by the ahead team. The doors blew outward and a row of mechs leaping burning hulks of their compatriots could be seen charging the opening from the other side. Galas beat them through it going the other way and cranked the reactors over max. There were marines out there, and platoons yet to be deployed.

Overseer Naar slowed the mech to a halt. The river flowed around its feet as it stood in the shallows close to shore. The jungle beyond looked like an impenetrable wall of exploding foliage. He was torn. Between loyalty and liberty. The pain echoed in his mind, clamoring, unceasing, demanding attention. It came from everywhere. Every cell in his body was tortured by the demonia, the fracturing of this present reality by the introduction of another, through it, over it, coming out from inside of it.

The voice of the *other* murmured over the voices in his mind, coming from somewhere behind or above, near, but its owner was never visible.

"You know what to do. What must be done. Finish the mission. Destroy the woman."

"But it should have ended with the mech. I have it. I have consumed it. It is part of me," he reasoned, imploring in a strained, gurgling semblance of the local dialect and pounding his chest for emphasis.

"And yet, you have not been sated. The pain consumes you."

There was a long pause, and then the mech turned. The other Deathhounds did not at first notice, struggling more with the current than their larger kin. But then, as they came to the river's shore, they were cautious, not wanting to get ahead of the Overseer, to show that level of disrespect, the kind that had caused the overseer to punish Nub. Nub was brash, overstepped his bounds, and paid for it.

Whatever state of torment he was in at that exact moment, he would endure forever. That was the incentive to follow orders, to obey, to complete the mission. Such was the fate of an insatiate.

Naar bristled under the withheld recompense.

The first voices of concern bubbled hesitantly through the audio, followed by others, more insistent. Soon, an imploring choir assaulted him.

Rockets, lasers, and plasma fire answered them, exploding from the larger Dragoon mech in such massive quantity that it looked as though it was exploding and not just the smaller mechs bunched up against the shoreline. Some scrambled for safety, some stood, too dumbfounded to move. Others stood where they'd remain till rust and rot and the river took them away, utterly vanquished by the surprise betrayal by their leader.

A few petty rockets spiraled off into the sky in response. The Deathhounds, most too honor-bound to actually lock on armaments against their master. Their loyalty, deeper by magnitudes than Naar himself. He felt no pity as the onslaught continued, pouring out his rage and confusion, his bitterness and lostness onto his smaller, weaker brethren. The pack ... was broken. *Much like the promise*, Naar mused darkly.

He turned away. What once had been a Dragoon mech, now a machination of the damned, trudged slowly upriver while corrupted scavengers descended upon the toxic carnage that was once the Deathhounds.

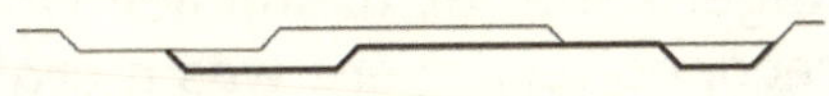

Galas surveyed the temporary shuttle pad. Raphael had performed some AI-wizardry, modifying the Targe IV's shielding to cloak its electronic signature;

essentially matching the low-grade radiation that covered Daxn like a blanket.

Presumably, that radiation was non-toxic and acted as the network superhighway that the middle city of Antiquity had run on. From what he'd relayed to her, it was his estimation that the intruders who'd encamped there had not devised a way to utilize this resource, lest the city would waken and who-knew-what with it.

They appeared to be less interested in the cultural relevance of the ruins and more in its natural resources. Grave robbers, essentially. Not humanoid. More like big praying mantises. Only their heads were small and, actually, in this one way, they were human-like. Their eyes were black, most had beard-like tufts sprouting from the sides of their faces, and on the tops of their heads were a series of ridged plates.

Galas saw no outright militarism amongst their behaviors. They kept no watch. Bodies shuffled from ships to ground machines and back, carting hexagonally shaped containers. This was theft on an industrial scale.

She was unfamiliar with this particular xeno. But then, Epriot had had its hands full for something close to three decades. Who knew how much had been stolen by looters and opportunistic aliens in that time?

A cold boil of anger was growing within her. Righteous anger. She let it simmer while she continued her reconnoiter. There was a craft at the far end of the pad that saw little activity. If she stole it, it might draw attention. Or it might be broken, and that was why it was being left alone.

"Raph. Can you ascertain what's up with that last shuttle?"

"If you mean, can I hack the looters' local network? Already done. They're using a low frequency general network. No encryption. They must think they're the only ones out here. And perhaps they're right."

"Yeah, Raph. Less is more," she chided.

"Of course, ma'am. It's broke."

"Was that so hard?"

"No, ma'am."

"Okay, so what do you think is the best course? Can it be fixed? Should we steal one of the others?"

"Oh, you want me to speak now?"

"Dammit, Raph, what'd I say about sarcasm? And passive-aggressive behavior ... and being smug?"

"I'm afraid that leaves me little to work with in human interaction."

"Fair enough," she conceded.

"If it were up to me, I'd choose the third shuttle from the end. It's getting close to capacity, and the pilot has not yet shown up to perform pre-flight checks. We could probably sneak aboard between the last of the cargo haulers before the pilot arrives. Also, I've been eavesdropping on their conversations. I believe I can approximate the requisite communications to achieve flight authorization. This is not a sophisticated organization."

"Careful, Raph. I've seen some highly violent, not-sophisticated organizations in my time."

"Fair enough," he echoed.

Galas responded with a glance heavenward and a quick prayer for inner peace before carrying on. She saw that the shuttle in question was highlighted in the usual fashion within the AR overlay of the battlespace. A ground transport was just entering the airfield. It was autonomous.

What a stroke of luck.

Galas didn't hesitate but slipped through stacks of cargo and fueling appurtenances to close in on the transport. She then crept in close to its right side, away from the main activity, jogging in a low crouch to match speed. Halfway across the field, the transport broke hard left toward the next shuttle over and Galas stood upright, walking nonchalantly for the remaining ten meters to the shuttle's open rear cargo hold. And then she strolled right in.

One of the mantis-bodied looters was inside the hold. It rotated its head one-eighty, likely to greet its tardy pilot but was met with a ceramic-alloy, power-augmented fist the size of its head. With a sickening *crack*, it greeted death instead.

Galas dragged the slack bulk of its body away from the entrance, stuffing it into a cubby, and leaving it for later disposal. Greenish goo oozed quietly from fractures in its exoskeleton. But, other than that, it gave no complaint.

Galas walked through the hold, hitting a highlighted button at the bulkhead which closed the loading ramp, and then proceeded to what she assumed would be the cockpit, but there was no interface for flight activity.

"What is this, Raph? Is this the cockpit or... I don't know, this could be the lavatory for all I can tell."

"This is, in fact, the lavatory."

"Eewww!" she cried, lip curling in disgust.

Shaking all over, she walked out of the room and followed the highlighted cursors in her AR until she slipped into a small cubby to the side of a corridor, which seemed to go nowhere.

"Why would they need a bathroom that big on a transport shuttle? That's just bizarre." Galas opined.

"I think that it has to do with their pheromones. Some of the mantid species utilize them as a means of communication. Being confined to small spaces like this, if they couldn't bathe thoroughly, after a while, it would seem like everyone was screaming at the top of their lungs all the time."

"Oh. Neat. Is this the cockpit?"

"Indeed. This is the operational interface."

"Okay. What do I do?"

"Nothing. This one's on me," Raphael provided.

A high-pitched squeal that sounded much like over-squelch on a low-frequency radio filled the air. Back-and-forth chatter occurred. There was a pause, and then Raphael broke in, "They have granted us authorization. But it's to fly to the orbital base, not for further terrestrial activity. We will have to, as you say, ditch them."

"I like it. I like it, wingman," Galas said, smiling.

The shuttle lifted off. On the ground, a mantid scuttled toward it, and then tipped over, waving the shuttle off with two left hands before resting its head on the airfield. Galas assumed it was the pilot. Too drunk to function. This was a way-out outpost for these xenos. He'd just done what a lot of people do in their off time on the far outskirts of civilization—get wasted. She probably saved its miserable life. *One for one,* she thought. That had to count for something.

The shuttle cleared the city and gained altitude at an alarming rate.

"Raph? We're going north, right?"

"I'm afraid I am no longer in control of the shuttle. Once it broke the local network, there was another system that took over. This one, much more sophisticated."

"What are you saying, Raph? We're going to space?"

"I'm afraid so, ma'am."

"Dammit!" she yelled, caving in a section of paneling with one armored fist. A diffuse spray of sparks popped and then fizzled pathetically.

CHAPTER 10

GRAND THEFT SHUTTLE

Galas hurriedly scouted for a viewport, but found nothing. At the dead-end corridor containing the pilot's seat, there was a viewscreen, but it wasn't functioning at the moment.

"Raph, can you activate the viewscreen so we can see where we're headed at least?"

"I'm afraid I no longer have access capabilities, ma'am. It would seem that the mantids know they have a hijacked shuttle and intend to confront the situation on their own turf."

"So, we're definitely headed for a transport, if not something heavier."

"From what little I could access from the surface network at Daxn, there appear to be several ships. Which one we're headed to, I am uncertain. But heavier would be an understatement."

"Based on altitude and velocity at the time you lost control, how high up do you think we are?" she asked, scanning the space, then, "Never mind..." She spotted what looked like a control panel at the bulkhead of the cargo bay. She ran over to it and tapped the panel, but nothing happened. Galas pulled off her gauntlet, letting it swing back and lock into its stowed position, and tapped again, but still got no response.

"Raph? Are we locked in?"

"I'm afraid so."

"Oh, *hell* no," she exclaimed and then ran back to the cockpit area, pulled out one of the orbs from the psych-bully's satchel, armed it, and threw it at the bulkhead. It exploded, bending reality and looking much like a water droplet squeezed through a tiny opening, and then quickly sucked back in. What was left was a three-meter circular hole in the bulkhead wall and door.

Lights in the cabin dropped from bright white to dull red, and an emergency beacon started sounding. These signs appeared to be common across space-faring beings, Galas recognized with a small part of her mind not focused on the problem at hand.

"Effective," was all that Raphael could manage before Galas was bolting through the hole into the cargo bay and arming another.

"Do you think that that's the best solu—" was all he got out before another blur in space opened up at the back of the cargo hold and wind and condensation ripped through the cabin, covering surfaces with a sheen of frost. Galas bolted forward and dove through the hole. She tumbled through the air chaotically before settling into a semblance of stable flight, settling into the freefall position.

Her pulse pounding and her stomach in her throat, she was immediately greeted by a yawning view of verdant jungle and altiplano desert peeking through columns of cloud below. It helped her orient, at least.

She knew the mountains ran north-south, and that she'd come from the jungle area to the south. She didn't want to overshoot her destination, though.

"Raph. I'm gonna need a soft spot. Thinking deep water, somewhere near Xiocic. Thoughts?" she yelled over the roar of wind whipping past the suit before realizing she could modulate the audio to drown it out. When the racket faded, it seemed as though she was hanging in space above the surface of the planet, only the billowing clouds sliding away, and the mildly buffeting wind contradicted the feeling. Occasionally, a more enthusiastic movement would threaten to tip her over, so she spread out her arms and legs a little farther to smooth things out and slow her descent. It'd give her a better glide angle as well.

By the types of clouds below her and the visible curvature of Epriot Prime's horizon, she guessed she was somewhere between seven and twelve thousand meters up. It meant she didn't need to pressurize her suit, but it also meant she had less time to work with and less distance she could cover.

"Well, we still have a couple of drones that are MIA," Raphael told her. "I imagine that they're either destroyed, or they followed the shuttle on its way to Xiocic. *If* that was where it was going. We should have a much-improved comms envelope, considering we now have line-of-sight virtually everywhere and thinner atmosphere for the next two and a half minutes until terminus. Chances are good we can make contact and have the drones scout out a deeper pool within our glide path."

Galas scanned the terrain before her. She estimated that they were considerably farther north of

Daxn than she could have even hoped for. They had made good time on their northbound journey before the mothership took over control of the shuttle. That, or the main element of the looter flotilla, was in geo-stationary orbit north of Daxn, to begin with.

It didn't matter. What did matter was that she was now falling toward her destination and needed a way to land without breaking her suit and herself in the process. And she needed to do it as close to Xiocic as she could. *Hopefully, there isn't another mantid encampment at Xiocic*, she thought.

"Raph, do we have a name for these xenos? Are they in the database?"

"I'm afraid not. Our proximity to the warp chan-nels means that we see a lot of xeno activity and don't always have the opportunity to add those encounters to our knowledge base. Plus, as you know, Epriot gov-ernance is at a low ebb at this point in the war with the Delvadr."

"Yeah, tell me about it. Okay, we'll log these in the SortieNet. What's the next letter in the sequence of mantid varieties?"

"That would be the sixth. Zeta."

"Mantid-Zeta. MZ's."

"If we manage to interact with one without killing it, you can ask what they call themselves," the AI offered.

"Good thinking, Raph. If we get close to one of these space vultures *without* me killing it, check me for jungle fever while you're at it. Any luck on those drones? Or do we have to do this the old-fash-ioned way?"

Galas scanned the jungle floor for structures and lakes while trying to guide the power armor's rapid descent in a somewhat northerly direction. The ridge-line was easy enough to follow. She knew Xiocic was at the base of the mountains along the river and the symbol that had been everywhere—provided so generously by Sun-Thurr—made it easy to approximate a location. She was heading that way, the suit having a marginally better glide angle than she would if she were falling on her own due to its lower weight-to-surface area.

"Here we go. Both drones appear to be online. That makes three, including the one still augmenting the suit's systems. I used it to boost the signal to pick up the other two," Raphael offered.

The drone feeds came up on Galas's HUD. She mentally issued the command for them to scout for lakes and pools deep enough to stop the suit's fall without hitting bottom—that hard, anyway. Both drones immediately gained altitude and, between the suit's feed and that of the drones, an enhanced map of the area resolved, the battlespace reaching down to the surface in a cone shape likely representing her glide path. At the north end of it, the surface bubbled with higher resolution data filling in the low-res features of the planet.

The visible extents of Xiocic were automatically tagged and highlighted now that it knew what to look for. Galas was glad to see the vaguest impression of structures appear around what was an expansive complex of river canyons.

The ground was coming up faster now, thin stratus clouds whipped by, and she guessed she had less than sixty seconds before she made a significant crater somewhere on the surface below her. A glance at the battlespace data streaming on the right side of her HUD confirmed it.

"Raph, any luck on our landing? I'm not seeing anything jumping out at me." That was in response to a host of yellow dots beginning to populate the high-res area.

"None. We'd need something roughly twenty-six point seven meters deep to arrest our fall, and there is nothing close to that in the river or in any of the pools. There is a pool at the edge of our glide path. It may be the temple grounds, but it's not a good angle, and the bottom is less than forgiving."

Galas made her decision and recalled the drones. It would be tricky for them to return and attach considering they would be coming at each other from opposite directions, effectively doubling impact velocity.

"Raph, guide the drones back. Have them augment the repulsors. We're going in at the temple pool."

Thirty seconds, she judged. Three drones that might add eleven percent to repulsor power. Entering at an eight- to ten-degree tilt...

Raphael didn't need to be asked to highlight the deepest part of the pool. There was only one section she could make it to. Galas focused on that spot, feeling terrified that it was just too far to make. If she did, she was barely going to clear the edge of the twenty-meter cliff above it. A wide, V-shaped pattern with arcing lines appeared on the HUD and Galas recognized it from her lunar escapades. It was her glide path.

"Distracting. Kill the training wheels," she demanded, and the glide path disappeared.

Fifteen seconds. She was unconsciously holding her breath. The drones blurred in from either side, and the suit thudded as they each connected. The repulsors roared as they pounded on, and she punched through foliage, skipped glancingly off the sloped edge of the cliff, and then hit the water.

Everything went dark. The bone-jarring triple impact of first dirt, then water, and then the bottom of the pool, while effectively scrubbing all her gravity-induced momentum, still left her stunned and floating in a cloud of silt and quickly fleeing bubbles.

The floodlights kicked on, and Galas's first thoughts were of the guardians, the mutated fishmen. She wanted to know whether they were here and, if so, how many. Her second thought was that she was still seeing stars and tasted blood in her mouth. She'd bit her tongue, maybe clean through. It was swelling, and blood gathered in her mouth.

"I count twelve of the creatures. At least those that I can distinguish using the sensors. Whether they're the same thing that we encountered farther south or not, remains to be seen," Raphael provided. At least he was online.

"Twe-oov? Tweh…" she breathed out through her nose in exasperation and growing pain. "Fwed, anomedth … th-woo the thtwaw, pweave," she tried to say before abandoning it entirely and using thought-to-text.

"Of course, ma'am. Administering nanomeds."

Galas took a long but mild pull from the bite tube positioned near her jaw. The taste of blood was overpowering but, within seconds, her tongue tingled and went numb.

Moments later, there was a flurry of activity in the outer edges of her visibility. Dark shapes flitting out of the shadows and darting back in. Flashes of silver in powerful pulses as large fish grew less fearful and more agitated, more aggressive.

Galas pressed her teeth together carefully and fired the repulsors again. She shot toward the surface and fully out of the water. Hovering there momentarily before sinking back into the pool, the surface bubbling like a cauldron due to the firing repulsors. Quickly scanning her surroundings, she shot forward toward the falls and the safety of the shoreline a short distance away.

Her display barely chirped before she was rammed hard from below. Her plasma blades were out before she broke the surface, and she was slashing at the darkness where she knew her attacker would appear. Teeth and a massive mouth exploded into view, and the glowing cloud of steam and bubbles created by the blades quickly turned red and murky with fish gore. She let the suit carry her forward at speed and slammed into the rocks of the shoreline.

She made it out of the water without another attack, but a splash of water and a flip of a large tail told her just barely. Here the falls came crashing over hazy pink walls that towered above her, revealing a cobalt river of sky between them. Much of the pool here was in shadow from those cliffs, but where the sun peeked through, the water was clear enough she was sure she could see the bottom if not for the rippling surface.

She had exited the water only a few meters from the falls themselves and reminded herself not to get complacent just because she was out of the water. She made her way back behind the falls to pause and assess the situation. And to perform any triage. She hadn't had a moment to figure out if the suit was damaged from the fall before being attacked.

"Fwed, wun diag-noth-dic an invendory p-leaz," she said, mildly irritated but also appreciative that the nanos were working quickly. She peeled off two of the drones for recon while she pulled up the feed from her high-altitude, no-arrest descent, freezing the footage around a clear shot of the temple pool.

It looked much the same as the one found in Braex. Only the layout of the columns that she could see underwater was different, maybe. Here they were aligned exactly opposite of the Braex formation, from what she could tell. There was something about the shapes that tickled her memory, but she couldn't quite put her finger on it.

"Systems are functioning normally, ma'am. No more damage than could be expected. I'm utilizing the suit's self-healing circuitry to repair and augment weak points. You appear to be placing considerably more demand on it than the designers anticipated. This is a newer version of the fourth-gen model, so ... still some room for improvement."

"Th-ank you," she worked out.

Just then, a rumbling noise, barely distinguishable from that of the falls, could be heard but was steadily building. Within seconds, a shadow cast down on the pool, sliding in from upstream until a heavy craft could be seen through the gaps in the falls, traveling slowly overhead. This was no exploratory shuttle. This was a gunship or heavy troop transport. The drone feeds confirmed it, too. The gunship hovered slowly over the pool, continuing downstream at an interminably slow pace.

"Looking for us?" Raphael asked, his voice barely more than a whisper, though that was an unnecessary precaution.

Galas kept completely still. She thought the response into text: "Definitely." Also using unnecessary precaution but, given how outgunned they were, she forgave herself the overabundance of caution. She dialed the suit's power output down to the minimum rather than request Raphael to do it and waste precious time. She wanted her profile as small as possible while that ship was around. She had no desire to see what mantid-zeta heavies looked like, even if to log it into the SortieNet. A minute dragged into two before the craft continued out of sight downriver.

"Well, that throws a new wrinkle into things. I wonder how many more of those they've got?"

"I hate to pile on, Miss Galas, but the clock is still counting down to the Delvadr's inevitable arrival. We need to awaken that temple ... to use the professor's term."

Just then, Galas had a terrifying thought. Her hand flew to her side where the satchel had been. It was gone. *Had she lost it when she hit the water?* Or sometime before that? While she was falling? If so, it could be anywhere.

"Raph, the satchel is gone. The artifact. How am I going to activate the node without it?"

Galas dismounted the remaining drone, sending it into the waters to look for the satchel. She piloted the drone herself using augmented reality controls that showed up like faintly glowing compass dials around both of her outstretched hands. She kept it close to the rocks to avoid attracting the over-sized and highly aggressive fish creatures.

She found the satchel almost instantly at the bottom of the pool. Right where she'd impacted just a few minutes before. That meant she was going to have to face the guardians again rather than try to sneak around them to the temple.

Or maybe there was another way?

Galas called in the other two drones.

"Raph, you use the drones to draw out the fish-mutant things. I'll use this one to drag the artifact to the temple and activate the node that way."

"Worth a shot," Raphael surmised, sounding less like an AI vocalized interface and more like the wingman Galas had demanded. "Should I log Fish Mutant Thingy as their formal name in the SortieNet, or would you prefer Guardians as your salamander friend suggested?"

"FiMu's. At least until we can uncover the missing data on what they are. That or Ichy's for Ichthyological Entities. You choose."

"Okay. I like Ichy's," he offered.

"Wrong. It was a test. FiMu's."

"You are uniquely disturbed."

"I try," she quipped, flashing a girlish smile.

And with that, the drones plunged into the water with a splash and instantly dark shapes from below were thrashing to the surface after them. Raphael had no trouble guiding both drones simultaneously. He dodged and slipped between them, even though the FiMus were fast and nimble for their size.

"Galas, a little help?"

Just then, one of the drones burst out of the water, followed quickly by one of the aggressive river monsters. It dove back down, heading in Galas's direction. She strode down toward the edge of the pool, stepping out from behind the falls just as the drone and the fish burst from the water again. A flash of purplish light and the large creature hit the water in two parts. The drone dove back under the waters as Galas returned the plasma blade to its forearm sheath.

Galas returned to her job of remotely salvaging the satchel and dragging it with one of the drone's multitool appendages. It was a slow but steady process but, what seemed like only moments later, Raphael requested her assistance again. Another drone escaped the surface of the pool, followed closely by a flash of dark silver and, again, a slash of the plasma blade rendered the FiMu into separate halves.

Galas, having lived off nutrient bars for days now, found herself wondering what they'd taste like over a fire. She quietly mulled over just how intelligent the fish-mutants were and whether that created a moral dilemma while dragging the satchel closer to the temple. The strength of her argument seemed to be directly proportional to the growing hunger in her stomach. She knew sooner or later it would be a moot point, and she could begin justifying her decision once her belly was full.

Fifteen minutes later, she had made it to the crystal stone pathways that serpentine around and between the columns of the temple courtyard. Angular shafts of light wavered in the clear blue like pennant flags in an afternoon breeze. Raphael again requested help and, twice more, she parted fish as if prepping for market. The drone with the satchel crawled nearer the temple entrance just as one of the drones was swallowed up.

"Slippery bastard!" yelled Raphael over the internal audio of the suit, causing Galas's eyebrows to raise in amusement. "I'm going to lure that one this way. He just ate our drone."

Galas nodded in response as she urged her own drone farther through the temple doors and into the inner sanctuary. Raphael's remaining drone breached the water, but the FiMu did not. Choosing instead to swish down into deeper waters, most likely finding the drone less satisfying than the chase.

Raphael tried again, but to no avail. Galas sighed and stepped into the water before jumping in fully. Many of the fish mutants had grown tired or frustrated and lost interest. This last one, however, had just grown smarter, not wanting to breach as his brethren had, but now that Galas entered the waters again, he disappeared entirely, whether in hiding or lying in wait would remain to be seen. Based on experience, Galas would certainly have wagered on the latter.

"He swallowed it whole, right?"

"Yes."

"Then we can get it in a minute. Let's get woke." Galas hovered in the water where she'd entered the pool, neither floating nor sinking. She manipulated the drone so that the satchel lay in the center of the symbol inside the temple, but nothing happened.

"I guess we're going to have to do it right," she said through a forced smile.

She pulled the satchel to the side of the room and then used the drone's tool arms to extract the large stone, pulling and then pushing it into place. It slipped out of the drone's grip several times before the drone was finally able to get the stone into its optimal location.

As before, holographic shapes lifted off shapes impressed into the stone floor and hovered there. Galas's heart leaped before she realized that the drone would not likely be able to utilize the holographic interface.

"Shit," Galas said, wincing with the disappointing realization of what would follow.

"Agreed," Raphael added.

Five minutes later, she slipped into the waters. Here, the pool was larger than the one in Braex. It was less like a lagoon and more like an appendix to the river itself. The water was colder too. She wasn't sure if it had to do with altitude or the fact that the sun was lower on the horizon and the surrounding cliffs much taller and closer in.

She moved on mentally from the physical discomfort and thought about the fact that there was still at least one of the FiMus down there. She did not relish the idea of meeting it on its own turf, *without* her power armor. Raphael deployed the remaining two drones to keep an eye on things while Galas took long smooth strokes across the waters, the white tops of columns passing underneath her, mostly shrouded in darkness.

She was scared earlier, swimming through the waters at the temple in Braex, but now she was absolutely terrified. Her heart pumped hard and fast, she could feel the water rushing over her goosebumps, her muscles feeling rigid and jittery with the cold, but still, she swam steady and smooth with twenty-five meters to go.

"Galas, the drone is on the move, which means that our creature is aware you're in the water now."

"Got it," she thought into text, keeping her breathing smooth, like her strokes. She reached a column near the entrance of the temple and stood atop it to catch her breath. The wind raising goosebumps across her torso caused her to shiver and sink down into the water for shelter. After intentionally hyperventilating to boost her O2, she slipped off the edge of the column and began kicking for the bottom. She hoped there was an air pocket again, just in case, but didn't want to stay long enough to find out. She wanted to be in and out.

"Galas, the drone beacon is now within the perimeter of the temple courtyard. I'll let you know if it ventures farther in or if there are others."

She didn't respond this time, just kept on kicking for the temple. Once inside, she made her way right to the hologram and manipulated the pattern, having committed it to memory before dismounting from the armor. Her AR overly flashed briefly, confirming completion of the sequence. It only took a second, and the temple structure rumbled.

"It's on the move. Heading toward the temple," Raphael informed her, his pitch rising with urgency.

The grounds were rising. Water currents flowed around, but it was obvious that the temple would not clear the surface before the creature found her. Running out of air, she looked up and saw the hologram mirrored off a small section of water above.

She really should have had the drone confirm the air pocket ahead of time. She raced upward, her hand reaching the smooth marble-like ceiling as she sucked in air as quick as she could get it.

Plunging her head underwater, she remembered the orbs. There were still one or two in the satchel. She kicked off the ceiling and headed straight down when movement outside the door caught her eye.

An ominous, dark shape raced straight for her. She reached in the satchel, armed an orb, and swung it into the creature's path as she kicked off the bottom. The FiMu ripped it from her hand as it swam by. Half a second later, a large shimmering sphere engulfed its body, and Galas sensed the column of water collapse into the void. There were no remains, the whole fish, the drone, and the water surrounding it were just gone.

Galas was still staring at that empty place when the water flowed out of the temple and, in spite of her efforts to the contrary, taking her with it. She slipped out with the current, unable to grasp anything to stop herself until she was finally stranded in the middle of the courtyard, much like a fish from a broken aquarium, but minus at least some of the flopping.

When she was able to stand, she found that there were two more FiMus, but they quickly used their awkward legs and arms to vacate the courtyard and slip into the waters beyond.

Only two drones left, she thought. Not good.

She retrieved the artifact, cleared a compartment to store it, and quickly mounted up, relieved to be in the safety and warmth of the suit. She was beginning to feel like a hermit crab, uncomfortable without the protection of her home. In fact, she found herself missing her mech on a level that she didn't feel entirely comfortable with. Betsy had been her home but, somehow, there was more to it than that. She had been her security. Family.

She breathed in and let it out. It was a pretty pathetic statement, she realized. That her only family was a mechanized warbot. And now she'd lost that, too. She resisted the urge to compartmentalize that uncomfortable feeling and just sat with it for a moment. If the world didn't blow up, there was some soul-searching that she needed to do. Too bad she couldn't do *that* in a mech.

The Targe IV armor's smart-gel reconfigured around the bony parts of her body, locking her in snugly and providing the needed cushion for activity and, inevitably, due to its intended purpose, extreme impact. It also could warm or cool as well as massage muscles to increase circulation and prevent cramping. She used the technology seamlessly with its other functions. Right now, she was using it to warm her body up and perform a medical evaluation. *No flesh-eating diseases or organisms, please.*

Raphael interrupted her thoughts, "Miss Galas," the AstroChron lit up in her HUD, "have you given any thought on how we're going to get back to Daxn and activate the temple in time? Or what to do about our inevitable showdown with Sun-Thurr once we do?"

"When was I going to do that? While I was fighting that fish monster wearing nothing but my skivvies?"

Raphael didn't rise to the bait. "I believe that I may, for whatever reason, have better luck here with the local Xiocic network than I did in Daxn."

"Are you saying you can get the transport system online again?" she asked with excitement.

"Perhaps. But we'll have to get inside to see."

"Yeah, let's do that. Do you think there's another aqueduct like in Braex? Of course, that could mean a whole hive of hoppers, but we'll deal with one problem at a time."

"I did catch something that looked like the outflow tunnel that we utilized before. While the drones were evading the FiMus."

"You saw that while all that was going on? Good for you," she said, mildly impressed. "Lead the way."

Raphael highlighted a path in the battlespace while Galas sent one drone ahead and left the other to follow behind and watch their tail.

"I'm sure you saw that we're out of those orbs. If we run into bullies, we'll be hard-pressed to deal with them."

"Good to know," he said as they entered the tunnel, and the floodlights came up to medium-bright, creating glowing green cones that merged into a dimly luminescent cloud with deepening darkness at its core. She pushed the suit forward through glowing strands of moss. Small shadows flitted about just at the floodlights' extents. Nothing larger than that showed itself, even after she exited the tunnel and came into the submerged portion of the vertical maintenance shaft.

The forward drone had already notified her that the shaft above was vacant and so she didn't bother killing the lights before entering the vertical section and surfacing. Like the previous access shaft, it had ladders and landings all the way up to and beyond the transport level.

Galas found herself wondering at how empty and desolate the cities were. There was nothing here, no signs of the previous inhabitants. It looked as though they had just up and left. Evacuated three entire cities. *What would make them do that?* She didn't have an answer, so she focused on her own dilemma: how to get back to Daxn in time to activate the node and unlock the mystery of the sanctum and what Sun-Thurr had to do with all of this. She had precious little time, and there was still the problem of the mantid looters, the MZs.

She jogged down a set of corridors that led to the transport hub, silently thanking the professor for his research. So far, not a single blip on her HUD appeared, which she was a good thing. The hub turned out to be surprisingly similar to that of Braex, the first city. Similar, but not the same. Wide ramps headed up from several locations, making her wonder if it had multiple levels.

"Raph, any luck?"

"No, not with the transport system, but—"

"But?"

"This is strange. The system seems clamped down, much like Xiocic was, but there's something here, like—"

Suddenly, a flicker of light bounced through the darkness of the wide-open space, like a visible echo, and then disappeared. Another flash rattled through the space only, this time, it terminated near a corridor farther on, down the wall near where Galas stood. It happened again, but with more brightness and a more defined ending point, as if the system were growing impatient with her reticence at following the holographic instructions.

Galas shrugged and jogged along the wall to the last seen light and found another corridor leading up and at a vaguely away. The light flashed again, only this time it clearly shot down the corridor when it was complete. She jogged in that direction, the beams of her headlamps bobbing as she went.

Galas followed the beckoning light for twenty minutes through rooms that looked like meeting chambers and some that looked more like labs, devoid of equipment. After a while, she came to a large circular chamber with snaking depressions in the floor that resembled queues at a theme park.

In the middle of the chamber, the ceiling drooped down toward a raised dais. The arrangement appeared almost as a stalactite and stalagmite growing toward one another, which, in some millennia far in the future, would eventually meet.

The lights clanged off the spaces in the chamber, splintering and refracting, but all converged on the dais. The Antiquity system seemed to be telling her that this was where it wanted her to go. The thought sobered her. Was the Antiquity network still cohesive? Was there an AI at its core, still functioning after all these years?

"So, this is where the breadcrumbs lead? What is it?" Galas asked.

"The Goodfall files indicate nothing concrete. His initial hypothesis, that this was some sort of religious structure, was stricken. I believe the Professor thought that this may have been a technological artifact instead."

"And what does that mean?"

"I don't know. Your guess is as good as mine."

"Doubtful," Galas offered, mildly irritated.

She stepped up onto the dais and immediately was overcome by the sensation of falling and stumbled back. But once she was off the dais, the sensation stopped. She was surprised to find she was still in the same place and hadn't moved an inch. Galas looked around frantically, trying to make heads or tails of the disparate sensations. Warily, she stepped forward and felt the same thing: the feeling of falling in every direction at once. Not exactly down, not exactly forward, just ... motion without movement. She stepped back again, less frantically this time, and it stopped.

"Raph, a little help?!? I think this is a transport, but there must be controls somewhere."

"Let me attempt to access the system again."

There was a silence, but it was a conspicuous one, like what a mother felt after hearing an odd noise from a child's room. Silence with the expectation of something uncertain to follow.

Soon, a holographic console bloomed into the space beside her. This one lacked the garish color palette that Braex, the first city, had displayed. Instead, it was subdued, monochromatic with hints of green, yellow, and orange beneath it. The all-too-familiar tri-circle symbol stood out amongst other shapes that could have been letters or pictograms or solar clusters, for that matter.

Galas waved over the middle part of the symbol. It appeared to stand out in 3D from the others, and then settle back into place, glowing the color of a dried orange peel. She returned to the dais and instead of feeling a tumult of motion when she did, there was a rip and a sudden stop. When she gained a sense of place, she was no longer in the chamber in the northern city of Antiquity. She was somewhere else. Her stomach crept into her throat again as the possibilities of what she'd just done percolated in her mind.

Galas slowly turned about. The room was similar to the one she'd left, but the stone was slightly different, smoother in appearance, with a wide vein of dark crystal that slashed through it at an angle. She looked down and was relieved to see the familiar concentric circle pattern of Daxn on the floor.

Was she back in Daxn?!? A mixed flood of relief and renewed anxiety washed over her. If so... that was... she couldn't formulate the thought fully. Hope rose in her chest but, at the same time, a healthy fear. Now, she just needed to activate the node and investigate the sanctum ... and not get found by the MZs or bullies or hoppers or Sun-Thurr himself. *Easy...*

She pulled up the virtual model of the city ... what had been logged by the professor at least. She found that to be only about fifteen to thirty percent of what was actually here—just the major features and any bits he had personally been interested in. Luckily, the Sanctum was a location of keen interest. It showed up in highlighted gold on her map but was an immense area.

There was a lot she couldn't quite comprehend at first, but the Sanctum didn't look like a church as she'd expected. It looked like a series of buildings strung along a mountainside bordered by a lake ... only underground. *This just keeps getting better.*

Luckily, there were a couple of ways to get there from where she was at.

"Raph, any luck with the local system?"

"I'm afraid not. Daxn seems reluctant to cooperate."

"Yeah. Figured," secretly, she had hoped the Antiquity AI, if that was actually a thing, would now open the floodgates and guide and assist her in her goals. She scolded herself for indulging in vain hopes.

Galas trotted off down the corridor, toward the main thoroughfare that would take her to Daxn's core shaft. She didn't relish what she might find there. Her eyes and limbs were heavy, and she realized just how long she'd been running on adrenaline and stims. The AstroChron pulsed for attention, and she saw it but didn't register what it was saying.

"Ugh. Raphael, work out mix number five, please."

A brief pause followed, and then noise assaulted her ears like the rapid and catastrophic deconstruction of a space station during a meteor shower while ten thousand fighting monks chanted and used feral cats as nun chucks.

"Beautiful. Thank you."

She refocused her attention on the countdown to destruction. It had just crossed the nine-hour mark. *Cutting it very close*, she thought. She should just go to the temple directly, blasting her way in if she had to. But, in her heart, she was certain that entering into a bargain with Sun-Thurr was likely trading anni-hilation for slavery.

Galas peeled out one of the drones to find access to the exterior. She wanted to get eyes on the MZ encampment. She sent another to scout her path to the Sanctum itself.

CHAPTER 11

THE SANCTUM

N aar's skin felt like ants crawled just beneath its surface. His side and neck felt like they were exposed to radioactive isotopes. His tongue was thick and parched, eyes were as if they'd been packed with sand and salt. But other than that, he was just fine. This is what living as an insatiate meant.

Only, he'd fulfilled his mission and should have been free of most of the pain of existence, but he'd been lied to. No surprise there, but some things were unforgivable. He would fulfill his mission in defiance of the so-called demon god, Sun-Thurr, even if it meant opposing him openly.

His new mech was making him cocky, he realized, but then who of his brethren had ever held such power? Who could have stood up to an entire pack of Deathhounds and defeated them single-handedly? Admittedly, some had not fought back, so shocked they were by Naar's betrayal. But still, the point stood. He had it within his power to rectify this travesty of justice. That is, after all, what the system was all about ... justice. He would have his share.

Naar, with his new corrupted Dragoon mech, had made his way back upriver. He found again the pool below the falls. He opted to traverse around it rather than attempting to climb it. That had been the folly of the previous pilot, so desperate she was to escape them.

Still, he had to give her credit. She had scaled a considerable way up the falls before abandoning her mech, he realized now. No mean feat. But now, she was lost in the ether and, with her, his solace.

He would have her, and he would take his time. He'd suffered this long, with agony immeasurable. Hers would be something spectacular. Even her specter, the ghost of the mech, wanted her dead. He would gladly oblige. But only after he, himself, was satisfied.

Now, the overseer stood at the edge of the river. The trail was cold. Night had fallen during his journey and the moons were cresting the ridge of the high mountains above.

"Where is your quarry?" a voice whispered through the vacant recesses of the mech's interior.

The voice, the specter, had been inherited along with the garishly painted Dragoon mech. It was an irritant, but then, everything was. Sometimes, though, the voice made sense.

"Has she gone? Left you ... with your suffering?" But then mostly, it was intolerable.

No response.

"The silent treatment. Are you brooding, Naar?"

"Silence!" Naar spat as he scanned the active array. Tendrils of wire, half-mechanical, half-organic, slithered down from the ceiling of the cockpit, oozed up from the floor, and penetrated Naar's body. He breathed through the familiar pain, bathed in the information it provided. And let it wash over him.

Naar felt the knowledge, tangibly. It was on his tongue and in his lungs and behind his eyes. He let the sensations wash away and only sight and the rush of wind could be felt. His minions. The corrupted scavengers, birds, fish, insects. He was most interested in what the birds would find when some morsel of information flitted through the periphery. A silver flash, a swishing of slick bodies in the dark, the constant companion of hunger, and then the knowledge coalesced into a shape.

The smooth carbon gray surfaces of powered armor. His missing pilot, he was sure. He delved deeper into his minion's mind, that of a fish he realized now. He saw a battle between some larger creature and the pilot. One of those larger creatures could be a useful pet but not worth his time at the present. A power suit, though. *What an interesting turn of events.*

Again, he took in the vast sensory network that was his host. Eyes scanned the night above the canopy of trees, took in the taste of the river, and consumed the decaying organic material of the forest floor.

"Where has she gone? Is she close?"

"Shut up."

"I can tell you how she thinks. I can tell you what she's doing."

Naar stiffened, but he said nothing. Waiting.

"She's looking for something. A signal," the voice said coolly, like the whoosh of air through mechanical ducts, like the snick of cylinders in an airlock hatch.

"I sense no signal. But I do sense something," Naar said aloud, for his own benefit, he assured himself.

Farther upriver. The fliers had seen it. A pool of water, glowing in the silver light of the dual moons. Glowing.

Suddenly the mech spun and burst into the air, echoing subsonic pulses as its hover buckets engaged before it crashed into the waters of the river, wading against the flow, and then burst into the air again. He would see this pool for himself.

Still, he reached out the mech's sensor array and found distant signals far to the north. An oddity in a supposedly uninhabited region of the planet. First the pool, and then he would seek out the nature and source of the signal farther upriver. Even now, he would deploy his scavengers. They would be there by morning.

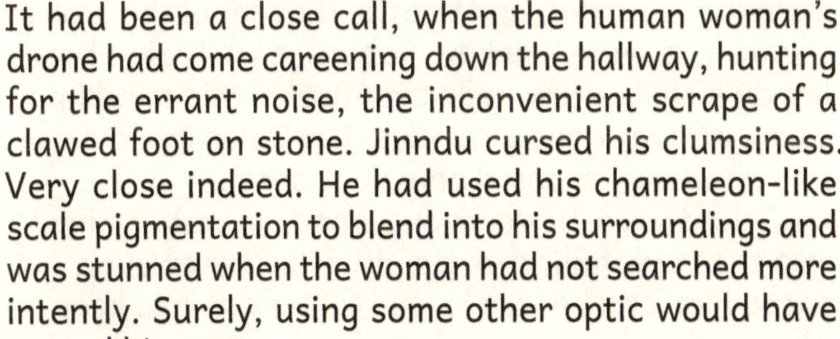

It had been a close call, when the human woman's drone had come careening down the hallway, hunting for the errant noise, the inconvenient scrape of a clawed foot on stone. Jinndu cursed his clumsiness. Very close indeed. He had used his chameleon-like scale pigmentation to blend into his surroundings and was stunned when the woman had not searched more intently. Surely, using some other optic would have sussed him out.

Jinndu may have been an exact replication of his brother/mother, but he was still just a babe in the woods when it came to how things worked. He didn't share Jinnbo's memories, but he did have impressions, intuition, a knowing. He *didn't* know what thermal vision looked like, but he knew it was a thing, and he knew that he had been lucky she hadn't used it. He'd also been lucky to spot the drone flitting across the jungle, and then diving into a cavern that was nearly impossible to spot from below.

That drone had brought him into the impressive interior of the mountain and, ultimately, to his prey, the woman in the power armor. He didn't know why the urge to find the human named Galas was so strong, but it probably had to do with how dearly his beloved other self thought of her. He grinned wickedly.

Creeping down the hallway, he continued to stalk the woman in the power armor. Careful not to make another mistake like before. She returned to the main shaft, and he considered how he would do it—kill her, that was. She was untouchable in her armor. But there were ways. They came to him in snippets of visions.

He saw images of the suit's air supply failing, catastrophic failure of its reactor slowly baking and irradiating the occupant, and then he thought of the drones. The drones were the key. Sabotage. A Trojan horse. Jinndu's smile grew near maniacal as his mind imagined the many delicious ways that Galas could die. It was a shame she could only do it once...

Galas took a lift down and Jinndu launched himself into the void, falling as the lift fell. It, however, outpaced him, and he was forced to work at it to keep up when suddenly it stopped, and he blew past, flapping furiously to slow down and to make his way back up to the Ridgeline tunnel where she'd exited. Perhaps he should have used the lift as well.

He snarled quietly and thought dark thoughts to make himself feel better when sudden movement caught his eye. Creatures he'd never seen before. They looked like bugs but stood upright on long legs and had longer tails. They looked nasty. He thought he'd like one for a pet.

To Jinndu, it appeared they were hunting something. He steered clear and remained invisible, not sure of the creatures' capabilities. But he was curious. So, he picked up a small chunk of rubble and threw it down the corridor Galas had just disappeared into. *This should be interesting,* he thought.

The creatures heard the noise and changed course immediately, moving in the direction of the clatter. Jinndu smiled and followed discreetly when a cacophony of noise echoed from the far end. The deafening sounds of rockets and explosions rumbled, there was a god-awful screeching, and then there was the growing sound of heavy boots pounding back down the corridor, followed by flashes of blinding light as plasma fire blew into the cluster of creatures nearby.

It didn't seem to harm so much as stun the creatures, but within fractions of a second the woman was on them, plasma blades arcing through the diminished light, her helmet-mounted floodlights casting chaotic shafts of light, and then it was over. Nothing but steaming bug parts and silence. A little underwhelming, but Jinndu was still amused.

She truly was a sight to behold. He watched as she turned back the way she'd come and started walking. He waited a couple of beats, and then followed, creeping along the edges of the corridor, interested to see what was waiting at the other end. When something dark and terrible appeared in the distance.

He was confused. Something about the figure was not quite right. It was a tall human-like being, but it was somewhat hard to see. Almost like it was only half there. Jinndu held back, his sense of self-preservation overriding his curiosity for possibly the first time in the whole of his existence.

He watched as the two spoke from a distance, Galas continuing to walk forward even though every fiber of Jinndu's body wanted to run away screaming in the other direction. And then, without warning, the woman collapsed. The dark figure turned around finally and stooped beside her, but only for a moment, and then he looked up and stared directly in Jinndu's direction.

But Jinndu was already gone, flying as furiously as his wings would take him, down the shaft, and then out through the corridor where he'd first followed the drone into the mountain. He squeezed himself through the rocks and emerged outside into the sun and the breeze and to all things good and wholesome and right. Things which he usually found quite boring. Once he'd found somewhere reasonably safe, he breathed for what he thought was the first time since he'd fled the corridor.

His hearts pounded syncopated rhythms in his chest, saliva oozed in pulses between his teeth, and he had to fight the urge to lock up, muscles chattering, ready to pounce or flee again. These were all his natural, instinctual responses, but he'd never experienced them in person. Just in memory.

He entered that tiny space inside his psyche and began the process of pushing outward, making more space for rational thought, squelching the urges honed by eons of predation on a predator's planet. His mind calmed, his eyes un-dilated, and a little bit of the pressure eased all over.

He realized he was absolutely, uncategorically, terrified. Why was he so scared? And then it clicked.

He had thought *he* was evil. Turns out, he was wrong. What he'd just witnessed—the figure in the dark that was only half-there, was *all* evil. Jinndu was just twisted, malevolent, and a likely sociopath. There was a difference.

The Cycarian sucked in a deep breath and willed himself to forget the feeling of overwhelming dread when a faint scuffling noise caught his ear. There was something in the brush below him. His curiosity was piqued, so he tiptoed forward a few paces.

On a rock ledge, just a dozen feet below him, was the most wretched thing he'd ever seen. It looked like an exceptionally large gull, but where it should have been gray and sleek, its feathers were missing in patches, and foaming black and orange goo seemed to be oozing out of open wounds.

Its eyes were bloodshot red, through and through, and there appeared to be small clusters of what looked like machinery breaking through the skin at joints and other places, entirely at random. It was disgusting and pitiful. It was a blight on creation. And what was more, it had a huge lump in its throat as if it had attempted to eat something much too big that had gotten stuck.

The creature flopped pitifully. And then a heavy boulder crushed its head, and Jinndu jumped down to examine the carnage more thoroughly.

What could have possibly brought this magnificently disgusting creature to its demise? Discounting the boulder, of course, it was obvious that the creature wasn't going to make it. Jinndu kicked it with a clawed toe, and the body flapped about chaotically, nearly knocking him off the ledge. He jumped on its neck, slicing and gnawing until the body and its crushed skull were quite severed from one another.

After a minute, the body stopped flopping about, and a small, somewhat spherical object rolled out of its gullet. It was a drone. Jinndu's brow shot up, and he clapped gleefully before snatching it up and whisking it away, flapping out over the jungle canopy.

Captain Vlodir Drakas retarded the Narda super-heavy to forty percent power and kept his senses glued to the defense suite on his HUD. The massive machine was limping along the surface of Skleetrix, the smaller of Epriot Prime's two moons. He was out of countermeasures. Beacons blared and every time he silenced one, a dozen others would take its place. Besides that, he was pretty sure he'd cracked some ribs, and Zudie, Ensign Kerplien-Zuudrik, looked pale and leaned hard on his restraints.

The other three, Mardree, Hondo, and Graff, fared no better, but none complained, and all maintained their stations in the engineering compartment. They'd certainly soaked up their fair share of the action. If not for the Narda's self-healing armor, they'd have leaked all their oxygen out into the heatless void.

Bright green highlights slid up from the lower edges of his HUD, and he saw the rendezvous point was just over a crater ridge ahead. The larger of the two moons, Cyclopedae, just a darkened mass with a razor-thin outline of brilliant white, was setting just beyond. Eight hours from now, it'd be rising in full dusty-orange glory. Hopefully, they'd be long gone by then and not just a hazy metallic smudge hanging over the surface of its ragamuffin kid sister.

More beacons and his attention was drawn from the stark, alien beauty before him and back to the present. Camera five showed a horizontal geyser erupting from the side of the fuselage. They *were* leaking, after all. Great.

Then the SortieNet really started clanging, and he knew missiles were inbound. Must be a gunship slipped through, or maybe enemy reinforcements had arrived. His thoughts went to the three dozen or so wounded marines he was carrying back from the front lines at the Delvadr staging facility. They'd made it so far.

"Force Bedlam, gitty-up. This rounds on me," came a strained female voice over comms, compelling him to clear the area ASAP. Drakas saw that the new girl was coming in fast from behind. Too fast. He peeled out two drones to get eyes on the situation even as he cranked up the reactor and added speed to his own retreat. Just then, the incoming transport leaped into the air, turning and firing a blinding array of plasma and rockets. But he couldn't quite understand what he was watching.

It looked to him as though she was targeting her own missiles, but when the incoming swarm drew close and a wall of explosions shed away half the onslaught, it made sense. Still, it wasn't enough. A second later, the Narda Super-Heavy was engulfed in a wall of gas-fueled fire. She'd managed to shield him and his cargo from the bulk of the damage. Drakas took in a deep, shaky breath and blew it out.

Then came the secondary explosion, the heartbreaker. That meant the new girl's mech, and likely her crew, would *not* be making it back to base with them. He didn't feel the force of the explosion due to how poorly waves propagate in micro atmosphere, but he did feel the pepper of shrapnel and watched as the deconstructed mech's command module blew by, tumbling end over end across the surface of the minor moon, gouging troughs and kicking up huge gouts of powder-like dust.

Drakas saw the enemy gunship icon go from red to gray. Someone had gotten a piece of him, anyway. He spooled down and angled off in the direction of the wreckage. Deploying grappling lines that auto-locked to the module's emergency anchorages, he started dragging. It'd take them a while to get back to the rendezvous point now, even though it was just over the rise. Hopefully, the module's stasis gel deployed properly. It'd preserve the bodies, whether for emergency medical services or for burial.

He hoped the former but wasn't optimistic. The wounded marines on board had no idea how lucky they were ... and to whom they owed their lives. At least the drones had caught the footage. That was some next-level shit for sure. He was glad he had the footage to back up the story.

Galas awoke to the whir of micro-needles and a vague tugging sensation near the right side of her face and back to her temple. That wasn't how you wanted to wake up. Ever. At this point, she was hesitant to let the host of senses throughout the rest of her body check in. Horrified by what she was afraid she'd find out. Then she wondered how much of her was left and was desperate to feel anything from any part of her body. Checking, checking... her corneal implants were turned off. Another not-good sign.

Dammit. *What have I been up to now?*

"She's awake. Ooh, not good. Where's the problem? Oh, pinched tube. Get that... right there. Yeah, pull those up and... okay. Good. That oughta do it."

Before she could protest, Galas faded back out.

Eight days later, she woke with a start, fending off the nightmare feeling of being buried alive in the dark, something fluid flooding her eyes, ears, mouth...

Luminous fuzz greeted her. She licked her lips with a thick tongue. They were dry and chapped. Her eyes felt like beach sand, and her throat elicited a sharp pain every time she tried to swallow. Beyond that was just dull throbbing pain pretty much everywhere.

This was hospital-feel. Then she remembered waking to what she now realized was facial reconstruction. Ugghh. *I was one of the beautiful people,* she thought ironically, but there was a hint of honesty in it, too.

"Good morning, beautiful," a chipper voice greeted her.

"To hell with you, whoever you are."

A warm chuckle responded. "That was quite a show. Started out with a bang and went out in a blaze of glory. The grunts are calling you Maiden Makeway."

"Must have been somebody else. I don't remember anything special. Something about driving a bus and kicking a pinata full of hornets."

"Yeah, that's pretty close."

"I must look a mess, huh? I think they had to put me back together." She broke up a bit and had to blink back some moisture. She still couldn't see exactly, just fuzzy shapes and lights.

"Nah, nah. I think I recognize some toaster parts and surgical tubing, but if you were better looking before, you weren't born on *this* rock. As it is, the line's out the door for possible suitors. Especially after that shit you pulled up there. Anyone who can make a pod-jockey cry must be *pretty* special." He smiled charmingly, but it was mostly lost on Galas.

"You'll have to tell me about it. Like I said, I can't remember much of anything."

Things were beginning to clear up a little, bit by bit. Soon a dark blur coalesced into a smudgy bit of light and dark, and then after a little while longer, the image of a man with dark, wavy hair, warm brown eyes, and chiseled features appeared. Galas didn't recall ever seeing him before and was sure she would have remembered. That was a face you'd like to wake up next to. Oddly, he seemed to know her well enough.

"But first things first. Who are you, and what do I owe you?" Galas asked.

"Huh. You're pretty funny. I'm Drakas. Vlodir Drakas. And it's me who owes you. You and your mech took a half-dozen missiles for me. Well, me, my crew, and about thirty or so wounded marines. Needless to say, you're pretty popular around here right about now. I actually had to bed the nurse on duty just to get in here."

"That doesn't sound so bad." The curve of a mischievous smile touched the corners of her mouth.

"No? You should have seen him."

"Ooh. Ouch." She laughed a little too hard and shrunk into a wincing cough.

"Take it easy. You might bust a seam there." He stood from the chair he'd been sitting in for the last several hours and put a warm hand on her shoulder. "Seriously, look me up when they let you outta here. I don't think you'll be able to buy yourself a drink, pretty much ever now, but I'd like to buy you your first one."

"Your name's Floater?"

"Haha. No, Vlodir. You can just stick with Drakas. Everyone else does," he said resignedly, shaking his head, and then making his way out the door.

"All done," he yelled down the corridor. "Thanks."

"Anything for you, sugar," a surly and decidedly manly voice responded.

Galas's brow shot up, and she instantly regretted the sudden movement. She eased back into her pillow, closing her eyes and attempting to retrace the lines of Drakas' face in her mind as she relaxed and tried to recuperate from whatever she'd put her body through. She guessed a more formal briefing would illuminate some of the details soon enough.

Just then, she remembered Dragoii and the others and was desperate to know how they were.

"Dragoii! Dragoii! Abram? Senche?!?" Her cries grew increasingly desperate, but none of her crew called back.

She heard shuffling footsteps and a low, soft voice responded, "Take it easy, LT. You don't want to get worked up in your current state."

"Where are my men? My crew? Where are they?"

"I'm so sorry. I really hoped your commanding officer would be able to clear that up for you, but he's not here. We notified him you were awake." The man shuffled over to her bedside and checked on some of the equipment.

"I don't care about my commanding officer. I care about my crew. Where are they? I want to see them now!" she snarled.

"Lieutenant Galas, I only know about my patients, and there are none here by those names. Maybe they were here in another ward and released already, or maybe they never came in. I don't know," Petty Officer Manganessi provided. She looked into the empathetic eyes of the bear of a man who was the nurse on duty. Another time, she might have laughed at the disparate pairing of him and the wavy-haired pilot, Drakas, whether real or fictionalized, but then a snippet of an image populated Galas's memory.

In her mind, she saw Dragoii's face. Grim, determined. "That's what's left of Force Bedlam up ahead. They were shredded," she heard his voice, the sadness of it. "Those guys gotta make it back..."

She remembered spooling up the reactor, locking onto the incoming volley of missiles, and thinking that she could just get there in time.

Her eyes dropped. She hoped they were all okay but, based on the extent of what they had to do to her, it was hard to hold out hope.

Galas ran down a darkened corridor in her power armor somewhere deep inside a mountain halfway to a place tagged in her SortieNet's battlefield model space as the Sanctum. Fleeing was a better word. She was tired, sore, hungry, generally pissy, and behind her was another pair of psych-bullies—the oversized, overpowered, and mostly unstoppable minions she'd found scattered around the ancient cities of Antiquity. While she was in the capital city of Daxn, an invasion force, millions-strong, was decelerating into near-orbit and a transdimensional demonic deity was anxiously awaiting his promised tribute.

First, she had to figure out how to get an ancient planetary defense system to work to annihilate the incoming onslaught and avoid the certain genocide of her species. Second, and of near-equal importance, she had to figure out how *not* to have to hand over that technology to the demoniac god who had helped her find it, in order to avoid the certain enslavement of her species. The clock was ticking, and she was running short on ideas.

"I hate to be the bearer of bad news, miss Galas, but—"

"Then don't. Problem solved," she cut in and kept running.

"Except ... I'm picking up life forms ahead," Raphael continued, unfazed.

"Oh, goodie," she said in mock cheerfulness.

"Probably not goodie," said the suit's SortieNet AI and her new wingman. "Sensors suggest it's several dozen of those hoppers."

Suddenly, the walls fell away, and Galas found herself sprinting across an ancient bridge spanning a subterranean river or lake dozens of meters below and the space around her, though dark, was decidedly vast. The SortieNet used the drones to augment sensor functions and a massive cavern materialized in model space, filling in details and dovetailing with the research files provided by the long-dead professor Goodfall.

To Galas it could have been one of a dozen coastal towns carved into the rocky hillside, the road curving along the folds of land, cliffs looming, stone structures placed spectacularly on rises or promontories and especially where bridges spanned yawning voids. Someone could spend lifetimes exploring the cities of the ancients. Apparently, Goodfall had done just that.

A gap in the bridge appeared ahead and suddenly Galas was aware of a din of whirring insect wings. Big insect wings; psych-hoppers. And, yes, there were *a lot* of them judging by the audio coming through Galas's internal audio. Red dots populated her HUD as it rotated through three-dimensional space, flipping, spinning, mapping lines of retreat, places to hide and to fight if needed. It would definitely be needed.

"Raph? Thoughts?"

"Run... fast."

Galas's eyes glowed with the golden light of her corneal implants as more pathways populated the SortieNet virtual battlefield. Raphael laid down the lines. Galas switched the drones' boosting capabilities to powering the suit. She dialed in performance characteristics while sprinting toward the void when a screeching wail of electronica assaulted her ears.

Mix number nine, she recognized. Nice choice. Suitably adrenalized, she poured on the speed. There was probably a stim in there somewhere, too. The time for nannying past, Raphael was tuning *her* performance to keep her alive. The irony wasn't lost, but it was definitely buried under the needs of the moment.

A quick glance and Galas chose the vector highlighted with the highest degree of difficulty on her HUD. There was no way she could clear the gap. But cutting an angle toward the far-left side of the bridge, she launched out into open space, and fired the grappling line at a highlighted section of the crumbling, opposite span. The line retracted immediately so there was a seamless transition from the arc of her fall to the arc of her swing, first beneath, and then past the side of bridge, and back up. She landed neatly back on pavement, turning momentum into speed, and then burst forward even faster. The grappling tool head unlatched as she landed, and the line came whipping back to her.

That little sequence wasn't something they teach in the Targe IV combat sims either, she thought with satisfaction.

The flurry of wings was growing in depth and intensity. The crimson dots of enemy combatants on her HUD looked like a smokescreen fanning out behind her blue one. They were faster while flying and hopping. She needed to get out of the open area fast or she'd be overrun and all they had to do was get close enough to stun her with their signature psychic pulse.

She had no idea what they did after that as they didn't have mouths. She was sure she didn't want to find out. She only had seconds before they were on her.

"Raph, do know what's in that water? How deep it is?"

"No, we focused on the terrain."

"Okay," she replied and turned a hard right, leaping far beyond the edge of the bridge while spinning to her back, firing a few plasma rounds once she had dropped below the hoppers, where she could get direct shots at their underbellies, a gambit that paid off in gooey explosions of bug guts. As she fell, she deployed the grappling line again, whipping her back under the bridge and up, while a flood of insectoid/mammalian bodies rained down from above.

Seeing they'd misjudged their target, they glided toward shore, some of them making it, some not. Meanwhile, Galas retracted the line in an inertial rush that worked to whip herself under and back on top of the bridge on its far side. It was fluid and efficient and surprisingly effective.

"If I may say so, miss Galas, that was not a vector I would have thought to analyze."

"I'll take that as a compliment," she huffed out.

"Do."

There were still a handful of stragglers who hadn't taken the bait or were too far behind to be fully committed to the jump. They reacquired their target and launched, screeching and clicking taloned feet as they hop-flew with renewed fury. Down below, the ones that made it to shore were flooding along its edges back toward the bridge. This fight was far from over. Galas turned and fired, but from this angle, she caught nothing but glancing blows off hard carapace.

Up ahead, a bridge tower and the other half of the horde. Behind her, a dozen hoppers closed fast.

"Raph, do you think that attack is directional? Or just an area of effect sort of thing?"

"I don't have enough data to make an educated guess."

"I think it's directional," she said, huffing with the exertion of the sprinting battle.

"I would advise against testing that hypothesis at the moment."

"Yeah," she veered toward the right side of the bridge to get a look down into the water below, her floodlights careening wildly but spotting none of the darkly glistening bodies she'd expected to see swimming toward shore.

"I don't think they can swim."

"That or they're really good swimmers, but I agree. Judging from the number of combatants visible on my sensors, I'd say you cleared out about a third of them."

That was all Galas needed to hear. She turned and leaped over the edge yet again but, this time, she fell the distance to the water below, scanning depth as she fell, which, thankfully, was plenty deep. Now, the only question was, what lived in *these* waters? She shuddered to think.

Hitting the water, she traded darkness for blinding, blue-green clouds of floodlight-illuminated bubbles before they dissipated, and she had her repulsors propelling the suit forward under the water. She imagined that the psych-hoppers might be inclined to follow the glowing underwater beacon even if they didn't like to swim, so she cut them off. Which, of course, was terrifying.

The suit's array of sensors made it easy to track along the shoreline and make a direct path to the area highlighted in the model and labeled as The Sanctum. It was located at the end of a promontory that dipped into the water, forming a small archipelago of rocky islands. The building itself was on the farthest one, and it appeared it would be easy enough to access from the shore.

Ten minutes at her current speed would have her there. She let out a tentative breath of relief, feeling instantly like all she wanted to do was crawl in bed for a month. The AstroChron pulsed lightly in the upper right corner of her HUD. She didn't want to see it. She already knew what it'd say. An hour? Maybe a little more?

A glance confirmed it. She felt the icy stab of panic in her gut. She still had to make her way to the last temple, perched at the top of the waterfalls with the MZ encampment below. She hoped that wasn't going to present a problem, but experience told her otherwise. But, fingers crossed, she might still be able to engage the Arcfire. What happened after that, she had no idea.

But first, she had to know what she was dealing with as it pertained to 'ol doomy himself, Sun-Thurr. Was there a way to skip the whole giving a demon god a shiny new toy that he could then turn against humanity? That sounded like a very demon-god thing to do. And why couldn't he just do it himself? That seemed like an important thing to know. Maybe something to do with the salamanders? Maybe something to do with Antiquity itself, or the prior race? *Too many questions.*

She actively worked at optimism. Maybe the mantids had already skipped the planet, but they appeared to be very interested in whatever it was they were doing here. In fact, what exactly *were* they doing here? She hadn't run into them inside the mountain, just out in the overgrown city. She shook her head. At least she didn't have the Deathhounds to deal with anymore.

CHAPTER 12

SAPPERS

The jungle echoed with the crashing and snapping of trees far off in the distance. For a moment the earth shook, and then there was silence. Jinnbo, who was curled into the fetal position in a pocket of gnarled roots on the moist jungle floor, sprang to his feet and was reminded of his injured wing and fresh wounds. They ached, but they were healing. His pride, though, at the thought of letting his evil twin brother loose upon the galaxy, stung deeply.

He hadn't known, of course. They didn't teach this stuff in primaries. It was meant as a rite of passage, after all. All your competing desires boiled down to their essence and birthed into reality. And then, a fight to the death to decide who would prevail, good or evil.

The future of the Cycarian race depended on the outcomes. So much of the old text made sense to him now. The duality only hinted at in the scriptures, now fully known. Now, he understood the true purpose of Kanji-Kanthe—The Long Walk. Why some were so different when they came back. He shivered, realizing what they were, an evil alter-ego of the ones who'd left.

Jinnbo swallowed. He knew what he had to do. He had to face his brother ... and vanquish him. The ground grew suddenly dark as if fast-moving clouds had blotted out the sun. Jinnbo looked up and, for a second, struggled to comprehend what he saw. And then he realized he was about to become a gooey mess on the bottom of a huge, mechanized foot.

"Eeep!" was all he managed before the world exploded around him, and he was cantilevered into the sky. He'd had no idea he was resting on a downed tree trunk; it had been so thoroughly camouflaged by the all-consuming forest.

Thrust into the sky and unable to do much more than guide his fall with his crippled wings he landed on the top deck of the most putrid, vile, and disgusting mess of a mech he'd ever seen. Short of the Deathhounds, of course.

He managed to squelch another involuntary noise at the realization that that was exactly what this was. Instead, he grabbed the railing and grimaced in disgust as his lightly furred scales mimicked the toxic ooze over neon-punk paint scheme from the surfaces around him. He matched it perfectly except for purple slashes on his wing, face, and ribs, but those, too, blended with the cacophony of color surrounding him.

The corrupted Dragoon mech squatted down, and then, with a massive clunk and whoosh, burst into the air again. Hover buckets distorted the air as they strained to keep the machine aloft as long as possible before it crashed down again a full kilometer farther on.

Jinnbo realized that the top of this mech bore a striking resemblance to the one he'd inhabited only days ago. He wasn't sure what had changed while he'd been in his birthing chrysalis, but it seemed that things had changed quite drastically indeed. Had the Deathhounds gotten her, his beloved Galas? He needed to know more, and the only way to find out was to follow this mech, wherever it was going.

As for Jinndu, he knew they'd meet again soon. The universe was out of balance until their business had been attended to.

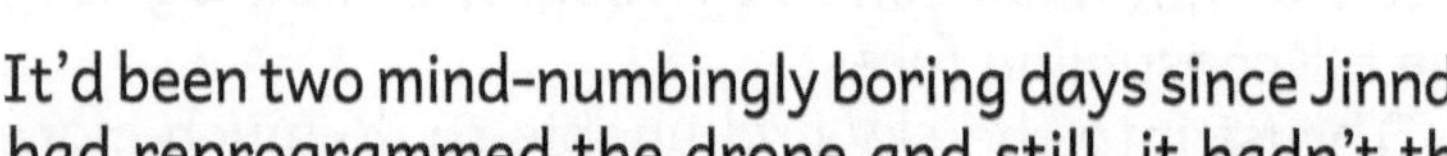

It'd been two mind-numbingly boring days since Jinndu had reprogrammed the drone and still, it hadn't the faintest whiff of a signal to return to its master.

Well, that wasn't true. Yesterday, for the briefest moment, it had sprung into the air and paused as if it had heard something, but then just settled back down onto the ground where it'd been waiting patiently. Then, moments ago, it had taken flight again but was now just doing dejected circles like it was sad or confused or both.

Something had changed. And then he heard it, a *crash* and *whump*. The cracking of whole trees like kindling. Once more, and he was able to locate the source of the racket in the distance. Two contradictory words floated into his mind: Deathhound and Home.

He cursed Jinnbo for his obviously muddled perception of reality that had formed the jumbled construct that was now Jinndu's memory. Still, the drone circled, anxious but aimless, like a confused puppy. Well, he didn't know what it meant, but this was as good a lead as any. He would follow the magnificent metal monstrosity, but he wrinkled his nose at its foul appearance. He would follow at a distance.

Using the fine points of his talons, he input an improvised code into the drone's tactile interface. Jinnbo's hand-me-down genetic memory was shockingly precise in this department. The drone would follow now until a fresh new signal from the human woman's SortieNet was received. At that point, following the big oozy mech would be irrelevant. The real fun would be when the drone was reacquainted with its master.

Jinndu flapped on happily above the jungle canopy, his wings easily holding him aloft in the warm, humid air. The sun's rays, unhindered by the cloudless sky, seemed to darken ever so slightly. But it was still dazzlingly bright and warm and Jinndu couldn't think of anywhere else he'd rather be at that moment.

He was on the hunt. He would kill the human woman for no other reason than she was so important to his weak and simpering contra-self. He would hunt down Jinnbo's body later, just to confirm his suspicion that he was already dead—unable to cope without assistance from others.

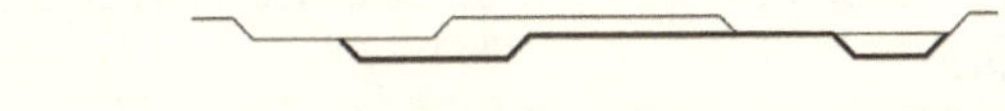

Galas crept up the rocks from the shoreline of what she now understood to be a truly massive subterranean lake. She hadn't seen the extent, but it was modeled fully in the SortieNet battlespace. What was also modeled was a circular stone structure surrounded by columns and with a two-story dome in the middle. This was the Sanctum and, inside, her suit's sensors were picking up two large forms and one that appeared to be only half there. It didn't require a huge mental leap to imagine who the partial form was, but the other two...?

Galas crept closer, concerned about sending a drone that might be spotted and ruin her only lever on the situation, the element of surprise. Tuning her audio circuits, voices grated over the silence in a harsh language she couldn't understand. They sounded angry but were quickly put in check by a more familiar voice. Goosebumps rose on Galas's neck, and she had to resist the urge to sneer in disgust.

It *definitely* was him. He'd left an indelible mark on her psyche with whatever he'd done while she was, she guessed, incapacitated? She realized she was gritting her teeth and had walked nearer to the front entrance without knowing it. She panicked, and it took a monumental force of will to stop herself from con-tinuing further. What was it about this Sun-Thurr?

She realized at that moment that entering the Sanctum would be a losing proposition. She just didn't understand the forces at play or the players, for that matter. She didn't know what he was capable of or who was with him. Then the AstroChron lit up in her HUD as it counted down from 0D:00H:00M:10S ... 09S ... 08S ... 07S...

She was too late. The Delvadr were here, and humanity was lost. She could still activate the Arcfire and do what she could. Invasions of this size would take many waves to get all forces deployed. She could still stop some but had no way of controlling events afterward. They could survive the attack just to be enslaved instead. She didn't like it, but she just saw no way around it.

Then she realized it'd happened again. She stood inside the Sanctum now, and there, facing away with his back to her in typical form, was the demoniac himself, Sun-Thurr. To one side, two of the psych-bullies stood, orbs in hand and staring at her, or at least they appeared to be, since they didn't really have faces to stare with.

"Raph? I may have screwed up," she communicated via thought to text.

"Understatement?" scrolled across her corneal view screen.

"Why'd you let me walk in here if you knew what was going on?"

"I've *been* trying to warn you but, also, I was working on something."

"Were you planning on telling me about it?"

Just then, that rasping voice slid through the silence, filling the room and somehow making it feel even more hollow, "Cadian Galas, my dear. So good to see you again," he said in an almost sweet, sing-song way. The effect was something akin to a child's nursery rhyme whispered into the stillness of a grave-yard mausoleum by an unseen voice.

She didn't respond. The bullies fidgeted nervously with their weapons in hand, clearly expecting negoti-ations to devolve and likely not understanding much of what was being said, anyway.

Sun-Thurr's shoulders rose and then settled as if he were a disappointed parent.

"I expected you'd be saving the world right now, not attempting to study ancient history. Am I really that interesting to you?"

"Yeah, well, it may be that I'm concerned about what you might be planning on doing with humanity once I save them. In our last meeting, you were somewhat less than forthcoming. Do your buddies here know what you did to their brothers?"

He responded with a patronizing chuckle and shake of his head.

"You've no *idea* what you're dealing with."

Galas swallowed, but just then a diminutive line of text scrolled across her vision. "Keep him talking. Something's going to happen. You should strike when it does."

"Vague much?" she returned but received nothing back.

To Sun-Thurr, acidly, "Maybe you can fill me in." She said this while targeting the psych-bullies with her plasma cannons. She was reluctant to target Sun-Thurr himself. His strange powers concerned her, and she didn't want to tip her hand.

As it was, the bullies' attention on her seemed to intensify, though she didn't know what exactly she was picking up on other than body language, which, admittedly, was a dangerous thing to rely on with xenos.

"To the Makrit," he gestured toward the psych-bullies, "and their lessers, I am a benevolent god. I'm sure humankind will feel the same."

Galas assumed lessers meant the psych-hoppers and others like them. Somehow, she was certain that humanity would not be in the mood to accept a new master, no matter how benevolent he claimed to be.

Besides, humanity had always shown a preference for serving gods they couldn't see and murdering those they could. But Galas wasn't about to tell Sun-Thurr that.

"It's time," the text read, and Galas tensed.

Blinding, multi-colored images burst through the room in holographic chaos. Galas made a snap decision, targeting and firing on Sun-Thurr before diving toward the bullies or Makrit acolytes, as she now understood them to be.

Rolling with the momentum, she came up with plasma blades flying. One of the creatures' arms was severed, still clutching an orb, before a leg was severed in one fluid swing that led to an upward abdomen-to-head slash on its partner. Galas was diving away before either body hit the floor and just as an invisible wave of force blew past, sweeping the creatures up and casting their bodies hard into the stone wall with a sickening crunch.

Benevolent god or demonic overlord, Sun-Thurr had seen or sensed the attack coming, evaded, and then replied with his own in the blink of an eye. Still, the kaleidoscopic spray of light cartwheeled through the space, exploding with text and images, casting light and shadow in a schizophrenic fugue. Galas's fight-timing pushed her to dive and roll again and was proven correct as another wave shattered a column she'd been hiding behind just moments before.

"Raph. I can't see him, and he's not showing up in battlespace," Galas hissed in frustration.

"I'm aware. It seems he can manipulate his signature on our sensors. I believe he's using his dimension-shifting ability to evade us."

Just then, a faint gray dot appeared behind hers in the battlespace. Galas's grappling line ripped through the spot just as the gray dot vanished and reappeared meters away to the right. Galas retracted the line, whipping herself away from where she had been standing just as another wave nearly blew out the stone wall beyond.

"Good fun, girl," the dry-husk voice echoed through the chamber, now beginning to swell with swirling dust—the VR lights, looking much like multi-colored ghosts whizzing around the inside of a hurricane. Galas was almost nauseous just watching it. Besides that, she was bone tired, even in her current over-adrenalized state.

"Raph, figure out how to see this guy earlier. And cut-off that VR, I don't think it's helping us at this point."

"I'm afraid I can't. The AI here in Daxn wasn't locked down for security reasons, as I'd expected. It was being repressed by the mantid scavengers. They must have accessed it early on and shut it down."

"Why would they do that?" Galas asked, puzzled, and scanning frantically to see where the next attack would be coming from.

"I think it may have gone insane," replied Raphael.

That was a dumbfounding realization.

"Is that possible?" she asked while sliding through the columns, circling back on her previous position.

"The closer to human abstract reasoning capability that an AI is designed with, I think, the more susceptible it is to human weaknesses. The AI here, if not properly decommissioned, may have literally gone insane from loneliness and boredom."

"You think it was still operating when the predecessors left, like they were expecting to return soon but didn't or couldn't?"

"It's quite a leap, but possibly. Yes."

A swirl of dust nearby barely preceded the appearance of a gray dot on the SortieNet. Galas fired and dove. Sun-Thurr's attack caught her mid-flight, slinging her across the room to careen off a column before hitting the wall. She thought she'd heard a muffled cry just before her senses exploded with light and sound upon impact.

Ears ringing loudly, she struggled to suck in a deep lungful of air to catch her breath. The suit had taken the brunt of the impacts and had softened the blow to her body with its smart gel, but that'd been quite a wallop. Raphael, too, appeared to be scrambling to regain his wits. Nothing but a string of dots was scrolling across her text display and then... [...booting]

Enough was enough. She scanned the battlefield and shot out her grappling line. It connected on a free chunk of the stone wall about the size of her torso. Then she did the same with the other arm. Walking forward, she let the cables rest on the floor, still connected.

There was no sign of the self-professed god of the Makrit — the demoniac, Sun-Thurr. But there was, according to the suit's sensors, the faintest smell of burned fabric over a background of pulverized stone. Burned fabric and organic material... flesh.

Not much of a god, after all, this Sun-Thurr. Powerful? Yes. God? Not so much.

"What'd I miss?" asked Raphael as he came back online. "Did we win?"

"No time to explain. Augment the sensors with the drones and tune them to home in on whatever is happening to the air when Sun-Thurr appears. I saw the dust swirling just as that grayed-out dot appeared in the battlespace model.

"So, we didn't win."

"No! And we're not going to if you keep yammering instead of doing what I've asked."

"I can do both," he said sulkily, and then, "Okay, I've detected a similar anomaly. The air is getting very cold very fast. Location marked in battlespace."

Galas heard the grinding of sand behind her and spun. Nothing was there but swirling dust. Now he was toying with her. She spun around again, expecting to be staring into her imminent demise, but there was nothing there either.

She let out a tight, jittery breath and applied a thermal filter to her visual display. The room turned suddenly blue and violet with just a vaguely reddish-orange mass near a wall at the other end. The Makrit bullies. They were dead, and their bodies were cooling. Somehow, she doubted they were now standing before their god awaiting reward for martyrdom. Or if they were, it wasn't Sun-Thurr.

She scanned the whole area. There was nothing. She turned her back on the main part of the chamber. And after a moment, a deep violet mass coalesced in the center of the room behind her. Galas spun and whipped the grappling lines viciously, retracting the cables at the same time. The two large stone chunks at either end hurtled back toward her, through the swirling dust just as a tall dark form appeared within it. Galas dropped low as the chunks of stone swatted the body through the air overhead, crashing down in a heap a few feet away.

She stood, and then strode cautiously over to the broken and crumpled body and placed an armored boot on its throat and chest. A dull gray, skin-on-bone face stared back at her. Not the face of a god or demon, but of something closer to a man. One of its antler horns was sheared at the base, and the other was broken so that just a foot or so of jagged bone arched away from the skull.

Sun-Thurr's eyes grew round with shock and disbelief.

"You fool! Now, who will protect you?" he coughed out. "You know *not* what awaits you on the other side. Not even the druids could stave them off on our own planet. In our own dimension. But here? Here, I could have kept them at bay! You've ruined us. You've ruined all of us. You deserve what is coming," he spat and, shockingly, in his broken state, actually lifted her boot off his chest with his hands.

Galas enabled the repulsor on her support foot, but in reverse, so it held her in place. Sun-Thurr's eyes grew even more round as he sensed what she'd done. He squirmed frantically under her boot. And then she fired the other repulsor. There was a sickening splat, and she allowed that formerly denied sneer to take its place.

"You know ... you may never get that off your armor," provided Raphael.

Galas just nodded. "One psychotic overlord down. Several million to go. Hopefully, they haven't started their final descent from orbit."

"Do you think that's likely?"

"No. No, I do not. I think that they rolled in hot, squirting out drop pods and transorbital fighter/bombers as they decelerated, and we'll be lucky to survive even if we do destroy their carriers," she stated without emotion. "Now, how do we get outta here?" she asked, twisting her head side to side, making audible cracks as vertebrae slipped back into alignment after the thrashing she'd received.

Right about now, she couldn't wait to get back in a mech and stop playing rag doll with enemies she'd normally be scraping off the bottom of Betsy's feet. That was a gut-punch. No mech. No home. No Jinnbo. She didn't know why she was missing him. She'd never let herself like him all that much. Maybe in his absence, she was realizing that she'd unconsciously come to appreciate the comic relief he provided. That was unexpected...

Raphael interrupted her musings. "Well, we may actually be in luck. Now that we've more fully mapped the area, I think I've spotted a teleport hub at the other end of this complex on the headland."

A point highlighted on the battlespace. "We couldn't have seen that earlier?!?" Galas asked in exasperation.

"There's just one thing..."

Red dots populated the area all around and between the hub and the Sanctum. Galas heard a faint whirring through her audio and knew the horde had caught up to her. She retracted the grappling lines so that one or two meters of cable lay exposed before terminating in the heavy blocks of stone, making two very large, very crude flails. Flails that could be extended and retracted on the fly.

Very effective crowd control, she thought, imagining herself swinging them in huge arcs and crushing hopper bodies in huge swaths. A weak smile crept over her face. The heavy chunks of rock trailed behind her, grating noisily across the floor as she half-stumbled out of the temple structure. Industrial electronica swelled in her audio and then burst loudly through her external speakers. Suddenly, the swarm of red dots moved in her direction.

"Captain Galas, ma'am?"

No response. Galas had her chin over the pull-up bar and was holding. The muscles in her upper back clenched into shredded knots. Her biceps quivered slightly. She lowered herself slowly to halfway, held a five-count, and then even more slowly lowered down to finish the movement. She hung there for a second.

"Captain Galas?" the man asked a little louder, hoping to get her attention.

No response. She shot back up to the top of the bar only, this time, with her legs jackknifed in front of her in a half-pike. And repeated the same movement, sweat beading now on her forehead. Five-count at the top, taking her time down, five-count in the middle. Her arms were quivering noticeably now, and then the rest of the way.

She heard the ensign shift into a parade rest, rolling his eyes, probably at needlessly being forced to wait on a superior officer. She contemplated going up for one more rep but knew she was spent. Last set. She dropped to the floor and turned to look disappointingly at the man who snapped back up to attention, eyes front.

Galas caught her reflection in the mirror and cringed, at least inwardly. She was a sinewy scarecrow, with dark hollows under her eyes, and short-short auburn hair dark with sweat. Every inch of what she saw exuded violence. There was nothing carefree about her demeanor. It was cold and hard and when she let her guard down, bitter.

She didn't know why Drakas put up with her shit, but he did. Glutton for punishment, she guessed. But then, what were blademates for? She wondered to herself, though she knew what she was actually thinking was why does this guy still want to have sex with me? The answer was obvious. He was a guy.

But why me? There's just nothing left here. Nothing feminine. Nothing soft. Nothing to offer but death and hate. She'd gotten good at both over the intervening years since the Delvadr invasion and that final, soul-crushing attempt at loving another human being. The universe had certainly cured her of crying.

The ensign was still standing there. *Probably pissing himself,* she thought, thinking she was dreaming up new and exotic ways to punish him for his slip in protocol. At least he wasn't languishing in self-loathing like she was. She looked at him with his soft, round face and doe eyes with long, natural lashes. He was cute, but not in the way that most girls found attractive. She decided to reserve judgment on what he may or may not be thinking.

"What is it, Ensign?" she said coolly, throwing a towel around her neck and clinging to the ends to rest her fatigued arm muscles. She didn't bother herself to allay his concerns about impending punishment.

Drakas was a few weight racks down, pushing out reps on the bench press like he was seriously trying to get a pump going. She could tell he was eavesdropping on the conversation. He was oddly jealous of any interaction she had with another human of the opposite sex.

If she didn't feel so unlovable, she'd probably get bored with that behavior. She knew this arrangement was, in the end, temporary. She hoped to be better someday, but the universe just wouldn't let up. So, toxic-but-familiar was the option she was running with.

"You have a message, Capt. Galas."

"I check my own messages, Ensign. I don't need a nanny. What happened, Admiral cut off your VR erotica, and you guys decided to finally do your jobs?"

"No, ma'am. Accounts are all intact. It's just that you have an actual physical piece of mail. It came through yesterday," he said, holding up a plas-film envelope. "I was instructed to bring it to you at once, since, well, no one has ever seen you down there and didn't know when you'd ever bother to come looking for it," he offered, still looking ahead nervously.

That was odd. No, it was beyond odd. No one sent her post. She had no one who would send her post. They were all dead, or she hadn't spoken to them in years. How anyone would even find her was beyond her ability to comprehend.

She grabbed the envelope and considered briefly the idea of flirting with the ensign just to get a rise out of Drakas but found that all the spite and rampant insecurity had been drained from her body.

"You're dismissed," she said absently, staring at the address on the front. It was from Sonnra Dragoii. She realized she'd been holding her breath for a considerable amount of time and let out a long exhale. A thousand questions scattered like a disturbed nest of wasps, but she crushed them instantly. There was no going back to that place. That was another life. Another person for all intents and purposes.

Instead of opening the letter, she just slipped it into her back pocket and tried to breathe without looking like she was having to focus on breathing. She darted a preemptive glare in Drakas' direction, and he went back to pretending to work out.

Just then, sirens blared, and the two bolted for the door, heading toward the mech hangar, well-honed battle instincts thankfully bypassing an awkward moment of emotional honesty.

The two barreled down the main corridor, strobes flashing, bodies merged from secondary shafts into the main flow as mech pilots and crew broke for the briefing rooms and maintenance bays.

"MOUNT NOW. NO BRIEF," scrolled across Galas's virtual dashboard.

"No brief?" Drakas panted out, having read the same thing through his own SortieNet interface. "That's bad."

"Ya think?" she yelled back. It was meant to come off jokingly but fell way short. She was *such* a bitch.

Another siren blared over the general alarm and everyone in the corridor dove for the walls, cubbies, pipe stands—anything to brace for impact.

Deep concussive booms rattled through the structure, one after another, and it felt to her like the entire facility was zippered end to end.

"I can't keep track," she exclaimed. "That sounded like armory, operations, central plant—"

The whole space dropped to black and agonizing seconds later were infilled with low red light that pulsed in and out. Everyone was up and moving again but at a tentative jog in case they needed to scramble again.

"What could it be? Aerial bombardment? Drop ships?" Drakas asked.

Galas just shook her head as she racked her brain, trying to make sense of the situation. How was this possible? For them to attack the Spires directly, they'd have to had made their way through several of the outlying outposts...

"Elites!" one of the pilots yelled. *Lieutenant Barsoon,* Galas thought.

"Yeah. He's right. I saw something thru my drone-net. That makes sense," another pilot yelled over the din.

Galas agreed. They were the only thing that could slip through undetected and strike at the heart of the Epriot defenses. *The Spires for Maker's sake!*

Another boom shuddered through the building, and everyone dove for something to hold onto. A wall of smoke and dust burst through a side corridor into the main one, spilling out in multiple directions and making visibility somehow, even worse.

Galas could hear the exchange of laser and plasma fire. *They're in the hangar!* She locked eyes with Drakas, and then as one they pressed off the walls and bolted into the red-gray haze, hustling with hands outstretched, feeling their way as much as anything else until they exited into the hangar and onto a scene of utter mayhem.

A sleek black mech was in the middle of the hangar, sending blistering waves of laser and plasma fire into the contingent of Dragoon and Zulu medium mechs standing lifelessly in their maintenance bays. One closest to the exterior exploded. Beside it was another that had already been obliterated. Galas and Drakas both bolted for their machines. Two more heavy explosions shook the space.

"See you on the other side," she yelled.

"You first, you crazy bitch!" he yelled, flipping her off as he scurried to his mech just two bays further on.

Galas mounted up and was moving before her weapons systems came online. She exited the bay and started the mech running up the A-runway, deeper into enemy mech's blind spot. Out of the corner of her eye, she caught Drakas just getting to his rig. Her weapons went green, and she unleashed a barrage of plasma. It hit the enemy mech in the shoulder but splashed harmlessly across an invisible wall of energy.

"Shields! Dammit," she cursed and started sending a hornet's nest of micro-missiles meant to tear down just that sort of defense.

The enemy mech spun, its weaponry still unloading in a wild splash of light and mechanical carnage as it chased her sprinting form. She kept up the chase, trying to stay just ahead of his ability to rotate. She cut the angle toward the other mech, intending to go right at him to buy time for the other pilots to get to their machines. But, instead, the enemy mech paused, launched a massive burst of missiles toward the back of the hangar, and then bolted for the wide-open hangar door.

This was some sort of hit-and-run thing. Or sneak in, blow shit up, and run away thing she guessed was a better summation. She fumed. The unrelenting barrage she fired at the enemy mech was still chipping away at his shields. In contrast, every shot he took landed on an unprepared adversary. At least five more mechs were laying in smoldering chunks, and who knew if any of the pilots had been injured or killed in the process.

Galas chased the intruder to the end of the hangar and came sliding to a halt as he launched himself out into the empty air, plummeting between the rock pillars of the other spires barely visible in the misty distance. Repulsors kicked on, and he rose into the illuminated gray.

Galas was rockets bingo. At about the same time, her plasma and laser cannons echoed blaring sirens through her SortieNet as they hit temp overload and cooldown measures engaged—steam gushing in obscuring plumes from her shoulders and forearm nacelles.

He was getting away. Galas's Dragoon was not native, with repulsors big enough to fly and especially not big enough to break orbit. But Delvadr Elites were. She turned the mech back to see what the damage was and caught an olive-drab blur of metal rushing past. Drakas launched out of the hangar, and external boosters lit up.

"Drakas! Don't do it. Those guys have built-in booster packs. They can fly circles around you," Galas warned.

"They got Braynam. They got Ceres. Coward sappers!"

"Drakas, you idiot!" she yelled in frustration and ran back to her bay to get her own set of external boosters, but they were a smoldering mess. Everywhere she looked was either charred black or currently burning. People were running around now, grabbing firefighting gear. There was barely a mech in one piece and not a set of boosters that would fit on her Dragoon.

Drakas, you dumb sonofabitch.

She tried to track his signature in her battlespace model, but just as she was able to locate his beacon, it went from blue to gray. Red dots converged on the spot, forming up a contingent of at least seven remaining enemy mechs, and then they all blinked out, presumably initiating stealth mode before exfiltrating to outer orbit.

"Goddammit!" she yelled, slamming the canopy with bare knuckles over and over again until red smears covered the alloy glass and her hand was a hazy fugue of pulsing pain and heat.

It was obvious to her what happened. She didn't have to go back over the sensor data. Late to the action, he had gone off to get his own piece of the glory. She always knew it would end like this, but she had thought she'd be with him when it happened. Like it was supposed to be.

Nothing worked out like it was supposed to. A dull ache swelled in her chest, but not even that was as intense as it was supposed to be. It was just a big

... numbness. Pretty soon, she wouldn't feel a single thing. Well, that would be a temporary problem. Now she had a promise to fulfill.

Her eyes dropped to her chest where she typically had the DDX in its chest rig. She remembered that her vest was stuffed behind her seat. She hadn't had time to don her gear before engaging the enemy. She breathed in a heavy, shuddering breath, and then let it out.

Oh, well. It was always going to be like this. A fleeting concern over her comrades. What shape this was going to leave them in with all the loss of life and machinery, and she was just going to add to that deficit because of some archaic ritual? Where was the honor in that?

Wasn't she just as bound by honor to protect them as she was to witness the passing of her Blademate? Why'd it have to be this difficult? They were supposed to be stuck in some impossible firefight and both go down, guns blazing. Or dismounted, back-to-back, hacking and slashing at the encroaching hordes, so engrossed in the chaos that neither knew who died first, just that they had died together. But this? Him charging off by himself on some ego-fueled mission to avenge their fallen comrades and prove his worth as a soldier? Did the Blademate contract cover valiant stupidity?

Damn you, Drakas. You beautiful, stupid sonofabitch.

Gray smoke was still billowing through the hangar, but now it was mixed with the white of fire retardant and steam. The whole space was a swirling miasma barely distinguishable from the gray mist outside. On top of all of it was the pulsing red strobe of emergency lighting and warning beacons.

It hurt her eyes to look at. Not that it was bright. She just wanted to close her eyes but, when she did, her mind replayed the last images of Drakas flying off into the skies, never to be seen or heard from again. Just a blue dot turned into a gray one.

Her eyes sprang open, and her thoughts drifted to the envelope in her pocket. It couldn't be anything good. But she was thankful to have something else to think about.

She reached into her pocket, and her hand erupted in crunchy fire, causing her to curse and quickly clutch it to her chest.

I broke my hand. What an idiot.

She reached for the envelope with her good hand and brought it out, ripping the edge off with her teeth and shaking the envelope off the folded, natural fiber parchment inside.

Galas unfolded the paper lamely, thankful for the added difficulty that took her mind off the void inside her. One that she knew was really just obscuring the ignited landfill of emotions inside her.

The letter was in Sonnra's hand. It was short.

"Dear Cadian, I'm sure you're busy. That's why I didn't write earlier. I just wanted you to stay focused on the fight and not to be preoccupied by things going on planet-side, but ... I heard some weird news the other day I couldn't, in good conscience, ignore. It was about survivors from the last wave. Matko and I had been looking to adopt, and there was an orphanage in Tuune. Well, some of the kids there were from the last wave. And some of those children were from—"

Galas put down the letter, her hand shaking uncontrollably. What was she saying? There's no way she could be stupid enough to put this to paper. It just wasn't possible. She sat for long minutes, mind spinning a thousand klicks a minute. This is just not possible.

She picked the letter back up.

"...some of those children were from Kozst, which we both were sure was your village. One of the children was Seraf's age. I wouldn't write you about this, but ... I saw her picture. She looks like you. And Matko. Actually, she looks more like his mother's side but..."

Galas stared out the mech's canopy, out into the void between the towering structures of rock barely visible in the mist. There had to be something that could help her make sense of this situation. Something that could put a name to the din of competing emotion that somehow drowned everything out so thoroughly that she could not identify a single one.

She didn't feel sadness at losing Drakas. She didn't feel hatred for the Delvadr or hope she might one day be united with her daughter. She didn't even feel shame for the cold, brittle, and callous person she'd let herself become. She felt all of it and none of it.

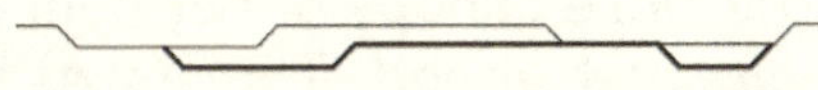

Galas swung the rock chunk at the end of her grappling line through a swath of psych bugs, clearing them from the raised bridge leading to the teleport hub. She'd lost the other one a way back. Her shoulders tensed as she grabbed the still swinging line with both hands and whipped it around and let go down the bridgeway behind, crushing bug after bug in a line of gore. She couldn't keep this up, but the bug horde just kept coming. She had no missiles, only plasma, and her right-hand cannon was wide open, venting steam, useless.

She started sprinting again, sure she would just seize up any moment.

"Right side, Galas." Raphael, too, sounded as though he was growing weary from pointing out new threats if that were even possible.

She looked. Two psych-hoppers had mounted the stone border on the side of the bridge a looked ready to take flight. She sprinted at them, and retracted the machine head of the grappling line, effectively discarding that weapon for the speed she'd need to make it to the finish line.

Drawing close now, she slid on her backside just as they leaped, giving her an unobstructed view of their underbelly. Great shot, but close, much too close. Her plasma cannon lit up the creatures just as Galas felt an invisible impact to her skull. Her face was numb as she slid up onto her feet and kept running.

The battlespace model was a red wave behind her.

"Raph, assist full. Just keep me running," she managed out as she swallowed hard to avoid blowing chunks into the close canopy of her helmet.

The hub was just ahead. There was one hopper. She fired the grappling line and dove, plasma blade forward as she collided with the creature, too stunned to do anything after being impaled, and then jerked directly toward its intended prey.

She couldn't see for the bug juice covering her face shield, but she managed to find the door. Just in time. Pounding and scrabbling claws assaulted her audio inputs. Whatever. She was just happy that there was a door. Maybe it was because she was always going to temples that she didn't think too much about it. None of them had doors. The hub did. That was good. Now, where were the controls?

Galas's flight suit was drenched through and through when she exited the portal and stepped out into the midday sun of the temple courtyard. In fact, it looked more like a ceremonial plaza. She didn't care what it was. She was so tired she could cry. Her arms and legs were lead, and it was everything she could do to just keep moving forward.

Streaks of fire fell from the heavens, all at a very specific angle. Most very, very far away. Some closer. *Drop ships entering the atmosphere*, she realized. Also in the sky, fading in the atmospheric haze, were dark shapes, impossibly huge and outlined on the side closest to the sun, in brilliant white: Thune-made mega carriers. The final push of the Delvadr invasion was in full swing. The noose tightening.

She looked down at the plasma cannon on her right arm. It closed, apparently done overheating. Nice timing. She remembered her grappling line and replaced the broken head. *Anything else? Oh, yeah. Me. No help for that,* she thought through a haze of exhaustion.

She looked up as she dragged one foot, and then the other, forward. Before her, just a few hundred meters below the hillside temple grounds, on the jungle floor, a different sort of chaos ensued. She blinked in confusion.

The mantid ground contingent was still trying to clear the temporary airfield and make good on their escape, but someone or something had other ideas. Galas's jaw dropped open as she recognized the garishly painted Dragoon-class Deathhound mech that was now pulverizing and, in turn, being pulverized by the MZ forces. She looked around for more of the Deathhounds, but there were none to be seen. She scanned the battlespace and came to the same conclusion. That was baffling. Just the one.

Just then, a new feed populated in her HUD. It came from one of her lost drones. Maybe her luck *had* changed. A surprised, foxlike face stared into the camera, and Galas did a double-take. *Oh my god*, she thought, *Jinnbo's alive!*

Tears of joy rather than exhaustion flowed down her face. She had to get to him, but she had to activate the Arcfire, and then she had to put down that son of a bitch who stole Betsy. And then ... after all that, she would sleep. But not before she actually, physically, hugged that troublesome little alien monkey-bat-fox-thing. *Wow, what a weird day!*

Galas stumbled toward the center of the temple, pulling the stone artifact from a storage compartment on her torso as she went. Something caught her attention as she did.

Out over the mayhem, a little above where she stood now, a heavily smoking mantid gunship was moving quickly in her direction. Trailing smoke and bobbing drunkenly, she was sure it was just damaged and looking for a place to put down. Her mind, however, went back to the gunship she'd seen in Xiocic after her HALO jump out of the commandeered shuttle. It'd been looking for her, she was certain.

Given the chaos of the battle below, it seemed unlikely she'd been spotted and that they were actually trying to finish their mission, but xenos were, by definition, alien. They had different minds, different cultures, and values. It was impossible to say. All she knew was she needed to initiate the Arcfire sequence, and every second she waited, more people would die.

The SortieNet started vectoring escape and attack lines. Reinvigorated, kind of, Galas pushed harder toward the temple, leaping tangled knots of tendril-like roots, bashing through smaller trees growing up through the cracks in the stone block of the plaza. The gunship was growing closer, but the temple was just ahead. Just then, something caught her foot, and she went tumbling. Hitting the ground and rolling with the momentum, she came up to her feet empty-handed. What the hell was that? And then her heart sank. "Raph! Where's the artifact?"

"I cannot locate it."

"What do you mean, you can't locate it? You're a supercomputer, for crying out loud."

"I mean, that it is no longer visible in the immediate area."

"Like it's gone or like it's *actually* not visible?" Something crept into the back of Galas's consciousness, a very uncomfortable thought. She knew of two beings who could disappear, one she'd just killed. The other she'd thought was dead up until just a few moments ago.

"Jinnbo? Are you here?" she called, but her voice was drowned in the screeching of metal on rock as the gunship flashed overhead, and then crashed into the courtyard in slow motion as it struggled vainly to maintain control. It plowed through trees and pillars until it finally smashed into the cliff wall at the far end of the courtyard a hundred meters back the way Galas had come. Meters away from the portal hub.

Armored bodies piled out and started firing immediately. Galas, who had been slowly sliding toward the temple entrance, broke into a run. Yelling echoed through the courtyard as the MZ heavies spread out and pressed forward on Galas's position.

"Dammit. Doesn't it ever stop?!?" she breathed as she ducked a blue-white bolt of plasma.

Naar loved this. Carnage. Death. Mayhem. Rockets hurtled from his shoulder nacelles like a stream of angry hornets, a perpetual blaze of plasma fire poured from his cannons, chewing up enemy soldiers, equipment, shuttles, and gunships.

Gunships! He was so happy the enemy bug things had gunships. The power of the Dragoon mech was on full display, and it yielded to his every whim. He and it were entwined like unholy lovers. They were the same, and they rained glorious hell on all comers.

"Enjoying yourself?" a voice asked from the ether.

Naar ignored it. The voices in his head couldn't help themselves.

It's back.

It's come for us.

Kill it. Kill the infidel!

Let it join us. Let us consume his soul.

I'm bored.

Death. Death. Death. Death.

The voices were, as always, a useless torment.

"Don't you think you're forgetting something?" the new voice asked again.

Naar tried even harder, doubling down on the carnage. He knew it wouldn't last, and he meant to get the most out of it. He'd sensed it on the journey back upstream. At first, a small wavering in the flow of corrupted energy. And then that flow diminished more and more as if something slowly choked the feed.

He realized it was because he was acting out of concert with the will of the source. Perhaps the overlords didn't know what he was up to, but their minions, the ones that controlled the flow of the corrupted energy from its source in the other dimension, were beginning to suspect something. The draw was immense for this mech. Surely, someone had noticed.

And what of Sun-Thurr, that pompous salesman? Who did he think he was, commanding Naar to stand down? To accept nothing in return for his efforts. He would make him pay in blood. Now that he had the power of the mech. But he needed to do it quickly. Before they cut off the flow entirely. Perhaps the specter was right. Enough games. Back to business.

Something strange caught Naar's attention. A ruckus up on the hillside. Probably just a damaged shuttle. Or maybe it was something else? He searched his senses. The scavengers, they were everywhere, but the connection was weak. Damn these fools, didn't they know what he'd become? Such a force for chaos, and they would squelch it?

Then there was something. What was it: a shadow, a shiny surface, a form, a figure of a human, a human in power armor? The woman. Through the eyes of his scavengers, he saw her. Naar's mouth literally salivated as maniacal light lit his jaundiced and bloodshot eyes.

"You've found her, haven't you?" the specter asked.

"Yes..." he replied, slowly, savoring the moment. And, with that, the enormous machine turned, hunched down, and launched toward the hillside temple.

CHAPTER 13

POSSESSION

Galas dove into the temple entrance as plasma bolts scorched the walls all around. She rolled and came up ready, slipping to the side to evade any errant shots. She'd made it to the temple, but what good was it without the artifact?

"Dammit! Still nothing?"

"No, I did discern a signal. No visual, but it's a lifeform."

"Is it Jinnbo? That's the only thing that makes sense, but it doesn't make any sense. Why would he take the artifact?"

Then the drone feed locked on to a new threat. Galas watched in horror as Demon Betsy flew through the air in the direction of the temple.

"No! No, they can't come up here! We need to draw them off, so they don't destroy the node. Tune me up. We gotta deal with this head-on."

Galas called in the other drone. She was gonna need all the augmentation she could get. She waited for a pause in the suppressing fire and bolted through the doorway, racing down the open corridor that ran along the left side of the circular stone building. Plasma fire trailed her, but she was moving too fast. Then the ground rumbled as the mech landed on the hillside adjacent to the temple grounds. The MZ's attention turned to the newcomer and Galas raced in that direction, skirting the activity as best she could.

"Raph, keep an eye on that little varmint. He's got a lot of explaining to do."

"Will do, Galas. And, if I may, what's the plan? From here, it looks like you're actually *trying* to kill yourself."

"No. Saving that for later," she said, referencing her pact with the vengeful ghost, Drakas. She continued sprinting forward, as the firefight ensued in earnest between the mantid heavies and the mech, which, in reality, she would not really consider a fight.

Sure, the heavies had some firepower, and even the downed gunship was stepping in, using its high-powered, high-cycle rate door guns. That was until the Dragoon focused firepower on it, and it blew apart, disintegrating it fully and casting most of the fifteen or so heavy infantry about the courtyard like rag dolls. In their armor, they fared okay, but their supporting fire was gone and, in moments, they'd be a memory.

Still, Galas charged forward along the periphery of the main fight. Then her HUD glitched out, and she was left with just her corneal overlay.

"Raph? You there?" she asked as she drew within grappling range of the forty-ton mech.

"Raph!?!"

"I'm here, Galas. There's a glitch with the suit's systems. I'm trying to isolate it but it's almost like a virus."

Galas bounded into the air and fired her grappling line, retracting mid-swing to whip herself up and behind the mech, where she fired again, attempting to swing herself up near the top deck.

Suddenly, the cable stopped, and she swung uselessly into the mech's backside clanging off the slab of armor. She bounced, and then slowly swung back in as the mech rotated on its torso axis to track the movements of the MZs scattering for cover. Thankfully, she was opposite the action as she was unable to do anything at the present. She slammed into the backside of the mech again as if to add emphasis to her futility.

"Raph?"

"Working on it... there. That should be better."

The grappling line retracted again, which then stretched the suit out awkwardly between the two lines. Galas recovered, disconnected the lower anchorage, and retracted that cable even as she allowed the top line to retract again. Walking up the side of the mech as she ascended, she dodged black-orange oozing sores in Betsy's armor, which was the best way she could describe them. It was like the mech was no longer fully machine but, in some way, part creature as well.

"Assessment?" Galas asked as she concentrated on her movement upward on the moving body of the mech.

"As I said, it seems like some sort of virus."

"Where did it come from—the radiation signal from Daxn? Are you going insane like the city's AI?"

"No. But I haven't entirely ascertained the source of the discrepancy either."

"Well, keep trying," she said as she drew near the top of the mech. "The last thing I need is to glitch out again."

The mech lurched to the side and a cluster of rockets burst from its shoulder nacelles. It was awe-inspiring from this angle. Galas had only ever seen it from inside. Of course, it was extremely gratifying from that position but, up here, she felt a goose of adrenaline at the sheer power of it. And this bastard had stolen it from her. Time to rectify that situation.

She ran toward the front edge of the deck and launched herself over in an inverted half twist, shot her line out, and sling-shotted herself into the broken canopy of the pilot's cabin feet first.

She saw the pilot's eyes widen just before impact, then everything went dark. She thought she'd hit her mark but couldn't tell. The blast shield on her helmet visor had deployed, and she was left without sensors and with zero drone footage, since she was using all the drones for augments.

Something hit from the side, and then she was tangled in vines. Or what she thought were vines. Without seeing, she deployed her plasma blades and swiped wildly, cutting the unseen tendrils away.

Out of her sense of combat timing, she rolled right. Luckily, she knew the space intimately, and the ploy worked well enough. She felt the side of the pilot's chair and heard a ricochet of what she was certain was scattergun fire.

She fired a plasma bolt in the direction of the shot, still operating entirely blind. She heard an anguished scream just as she felt and heard another blast from the enemy's gun. It blew her back, but the armor did its job.

She had no choice but to deploy a drone in order to see and, when she did so, she saw living metallic tendrils shooting out from several surfaces and engulfing her suit. The pilot was leaning against the far wall, clutching a wounded shoulder. He too was embroiled with the tentacles but, for him, they seemed to be supporting his weight instead of dragging him down.

Just then, the mech took a barrage of fire from the outside that caused it to slip from its perch on the mountain slope and both parties were thrown into the air as the mech tumbled down the mountain, pilotless.

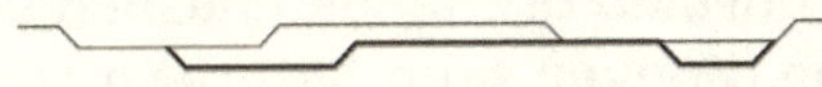

"Good morning, beautiful," a vaguely familiar voice stretched out of the darkness as Galas struggled to regain consciousness.

The voice was close. Intimate. Oddly familiar, but wrong at the same time.

Galas was still blind, or it was dark, she couldn't tell. She heard movement somewhere close by and tendrils tightened around her arms and chest. Suddenly, the world was moving again, and she realized the mech had landed, but gravity was still doing its work. The world slid again, and her stomach was in her throat before a hard impact shook her senses once more. Luckily, the tendrils were doing a great job of keeping her from getting too banged up. She wondered about the pilot.

Galas scanned for the drone feed, but it was garbled as if the signal was poor, or who knew what was going on. She tried to deploy another drone, but it wouldn't release. Then it made sense. That was the virus.

That little monkey sabotaged my drone! Why? Had he actually gone insane? Or was he a double agent all along?

The thought was crazy. She knew she was grasping at straws, but she just couldn't make any sense of it. Sabotaged. By Jinnbo... And now, whoever had taken over Betsy was trying to kill her, or maybe the Deathhound bounty hadn't been fulfilled, and she was still the target. That didn't feel complete. Of all the wrong things about this situation, it had a very, familiar—

Then the garbled drone feed flashed on the image of a man she'd never seen before, a tortured body held aloft by oozing metallic arms stretching from every direction. The pilot. Except, the man's eyes were rolled back in his head. The body shifted forward, new tendrils shooting into his chest and body as the old ones receded behind him, inching him forward, closer and closer. He looked dead but alive and in impossible pain. The mech shifted again, and she heard a deep creaking noise as the whole thing teetered, yawing sickeningly forward, and then back again.

The room was lit in red, and she couldn't tell, but either the cockpit was buried deep into the jungle, or it was actually dark outside. *How long was I unconscious?* Her head hurt like hell, but it was impossible to make an assessment. And besides, she was still a little woozy. But then she saw vapor escape the tortured pilot's nose and lips. *It's cold in here.*

"Drakas? What's going on?" she asked, her own voice sounding timid and weak in her ears. Through the garbled feed, she saw the tendrils twisting and pulling so the man's face turned directly toward her. The face was contorted, twisted. His mouth yawned sickeningly wide, and a voice issued forth, haunting, raspy, and ... impossible to mistake.

"The Deathhound's source is drying up, my love, but there are remnants of its presence still. Too weak to defy me, but still enough that it can be of use. *We're in control now.*"

The man tried to shake his head, but the tendrils tightened. Moisture leaked from his eye, something like a tear but with blood and a tinge of yellow in it. Smaller tendrils crawled up the larger ones and up his chest, sinking into his neck like parasitic worms, and the man stiffened and tried to cry out.

"Drakas. Stop this," she whispered.

"I can't stop this. It's not just up to me. *We* decide."

"We? Who's we?"

"I'm not the only lost soul to haunt this space. Naar had his own demons to contend with."

New voices slithered out of the void.

Kill her.

No! Take our time.

Let her join us.

Make her join us.

I'm bored.

Kill. Us?

The voices came faster and more urgent, clamoring over each other, and the whole mech shook with the chorus, and then it slid again, sickeningly down and sideways, and then lurched to a halt. Still, the voices raged, the tendrils grew tighter, and the man through the drone's image grew closer and closer.

"You should have done right," Drakas told her over the noise, his own voice low and loud, an emphatic hiss.

The tortured pilot's body grew closer still until finally his face was pressed against her helmet in a grotesque parody of a lover's kiss. Then Galas's visor flipped open, and she was face to face, staring into the man's yellow, venous eyes. Tiny tentacles crept in from the sides of his face and stretched, some pressing into the corners of those eyes, yet others straining forward yearningly toward Galas's own only centimeters away.

"She's alive! Drakas," Galas burst out. "My daughter. I found out years after you and I took the vow. But then you died before I could see her. I couldn't do it yet. She's alive," and Galas broke down. "My little girl... I had to see her first... before..." she sobbed.

The tendrils stretched farther and farther and were joined by yet others. They touched Galas's face as she cried weakly, she jerked her head, but the tendrils reached out again, gripping her cheek and turning her back to look straight on as the slow flood of tentacles moved in, gripping her, pushing into the skin of her face, slithering into her hair.

Then an explosion rocked the mech from outside, and the whole thing yawned over onto its side with a groan. She heard voices outside but yelling in a language she didn't understand and in voices that sounded very distinct from human. The MZs! She was still going to die, but maybe not from being consumed by some distorted, demonic machine being controlled by her vindictive, dead ex-lover.

She heard a metallic *thud*, like a metal ball dropping to the sidewall of the pilot's cabin, and then her electronics flickered back online. Her visor slammed down on the tentacles piercing her skin, and they recoiled even as her plasma blades burst to life.

Without a thought, Galas started slashing and blasting. The tendrils. The pilot. Every surface of the inside of the mech glowed from plasma damage. Steaming, smoking tendrils swung wildly through the air.

Galas dragged and pulled herself toward the shattered cockpit windscreen. She jumped clear, twisting midair and blasting away as a tangled wad of tendrils raced after, but then stopped in the face of the barrage. She fell back into the jungle canopy.

"Clear the area."

"Raph! You're back!" Galas cried just as she crashed into a tree, breaking branches on her way down, tumbling end over end, and then weirdly landing on her feet on the squishy jungle floor. She looked around as if unable to believe what had just happened. And then bolted straight away as still more explosions hammered the mech.

"The drone that was sabotaged. While things were getting weird inside the mech, I was able to isolate the corrupted code and eject it, but not before I gave it a program of my own. I'd say we have about forty-five seconds."

"Before?"

"Big boom."

"Nice! I like you, Raphael. You'll never haunt me, will you?"

"No. I'd like you to see your daughter, though."

"Yeah. Me, too," and with that, she started bounding back up the hillside, careful to steer clear of the drama unfolding around the mech as the MZs continued to rain down fire. *They were tenacious, those bugs*, she thought as she fired a grappling line and ripped herself up the hillside, before firing another up a cliff wall that they had presumably tumbled down just minutes before.

Galas saw now that it was indeed dark out. There were still streaks of fire in the sky as subsequent waves of dropships dropped in from the near-orbit carriers. She hoped she wasn't too late, but it was definitely looking that way. She had just rolled over the cliff's edge and onto her back when a massive explosion rocked the area from below. A concussive wave pushing fire, smoke, and chunks of ceramo-metal shrapnel blew past. But, luckily, it was directed overhead by the cliff wall she'd just scaled.

She continued up the hillside in the dark until she reached the temple.

"Raph. Do you have a bead on Jinnbo?"

"I'm not sure. I have two signatures. One is significantly cooler than the other."

She saw in the battlespace, the two dots he was referring to, and walked in that direction, coming to a stop just a few meters away.

"Jinnbo. Is that you?" she asked over her external audio circuits.

His small, foxlike face nodded glumly. He held the artifact in his hands, but it was covered in a syrupy purple liquid. At his feet was a second Cycarian. To Galas, it was indiscernible from the first. She blinked in puzzlement but then shook her head as if to clear her thoughts and focus on the more important thing.

"Jinnbo, I need that artifact. But can you tell me what's going on here?"

He looked at her, tears welling in his eyes, and nodded.

"Maybe in a minute, then?" she asked.

He nodded again and handed the artifact up. Then, seeing the blood on it, quickly wiped it clean with his hands and the thicker fur on his sides and belly before handing it back.

"Thank you. I want to hear about this when I get back," she said, looking down at the impossibly identical creature at his feet. He just nodded again and sat on a large root and looked at the body sadly, with his chin resting on his delicate fists.

Galas waited a moment longer but then remembered what needed to be done and what would happen with every passing second she delayed. She turned and ran into the circular stone building. She didn't know where she was going, but the very layout appeared purpose-built, and she easily found a dais amongst a half-dozen or so raised circles of stone.

"Raph, any idea how this works? Did the professor say anything about this?"

"Not a word. But it seems that there are some new elements here that we haven't seen before." He highlighted them on the wall beyond. More of the circles, but with portions of arcs that crossed or intersected. It was reminiscent of planetary orbits but on a smaller scale. There were other elements, too, lines that were free flowing, which made no sense from Galas's limited knowledge of such things.

"The short answer is no," he said. "I have no idea how the Arcfire works based on what I can see here or from the professor's research."

Galas took off her helmet and gloves and just breathed the air of the ancient place. There was a presence to everything that the ancients made. She hadn't had the time to appreciate it, but it was in every angle, even the minimalist architecture of the monolithic stonework.

She ran her hand along the surface of the raised portion of rock. It was smooth, but not cold. There was nothing that suggested to her how to use the artifact, but she found it obvious that it needed to be placed in the center of the surface before her.

As she did so, the VR holo she'd grown so accustomed to, slid up from the stone itself and hung suspended in the air. A series of concentric circles with tick marks, like dials, hovered where her hands would go if they were outstretched before her.

As she reached out, she sensed power surround her, enveloping the entirety of the temple, the courtyard, warming her, tickling the fine hairs on her neck and face, and the back of her hands. Then, before her, she saw a blue-white column of light rising from three sources, reaching toward each other. They twirled like flames in a windstorm, but slowly.

To her, it was like fire and water and wind and lightning all together, and as the columns touched, a bright corona of light issued from the nexus point. And then the image before her pushed to the background as the sphere of the planet pushed up from below to take its place.

She saw the hulking shapes of the Thune-made Delvadr carriers hovering in the darkness of the void. She saw the rain of tiny specks of fire as the dropships entered Epriot Prime's atmosphere from above.

A cold fury gripped her insides, and as her attention turned first from one carrier to the next, the fire reached out from the nexus of the three flames and consumed it. One by one, the blue twisting column of flame arced out over the planet and caressed each vessel with its light, and then boiled, and then blackened it, and then each ship would bristle with little fires of their own before first imploding, and then bursting out spectacularly like miniature novas.

Galas consumed the carriers and supporting ships and then pecked at the dropships still crashing to the surface and the new wave of ships fleeing the destruction of the fleet. And then, finally, there was nothing left to destroy. Galas stood there motionless, sweating, cold, shaking, spent. Empty.

She wandered out into the cool night air and saw the meteor shower and the boil of what looked like collapsing stars beyond. She remembered that moment when the sky had erupted in fire, and she was left alone, wandering the streets of her burning village, crying over the loss of her only child. And then wandering still farther for days, devoid of feeling, unable or unwilling to eat, just wandering and wondering if life would ever have joy in it again.

She felt wrung out and wholly used up. But, for the first time that she could remember, she at least had one thing: hope.

As she ventured farther out into the courtyard, she didn't see Jinnbo. But then she followed the battlespace model to the edge of the temple mount, and there he was, sitting with his legs hanging over the rock waterfall spilling out from the mountain meters below. He was looking down at the burning carnage of the mantid airfield, the mech, the sky, and then he followed the flaming form of the Delvadr dropship as it struck the forest a little farther beyond. Galas noted it didn't destruct upon impact.

The soldier in her played out a thousand scenarios, lines of evasion, or attack, possibly scavenging a mech from the carnage? Or sabotaging an enemy drone and taking over a fully functioning mech? The idea had merit, but she let it rest for a minute. A couple of minutes, anyway.

There was this small moment in time that was human and Cycarian. It was a brief sliver of time where two souls could connect. Souls born under different suns but sharing, for at least a moment, a similar destiny. And similar pains.

"You wanna tell me about it?" she asked.

Jinnbo nodded, his foxlike face smiling in a way that looked to Galas a little bittersweet. But it was hard to tell with xenos.

Off in the distance, a dropship door opened and what Galas thought was an Elite heavy began, slowly, tentatively creeping forward, out of the flames of the dropship and into the scattered flames of the jungle beyond.

The two looked at each other.

"I'd like to tell you about it, but we still have work to do," Jinnbo offered, his voice melancholic but firm, dutiful.

Galas nodded. "Later, then," she said to him, and then to the suit's AI, "Raph? Do you think you can work your magic on a Delvadr drone?"

"Most definitely, Miss Galas. Just get me one."

Jinnbo looked up at Galas, a little surprised and a little curious. "New friend?"

"No. Old friend, new voice. Without you around, all the quiet was getting to me."

"Oh … really?" he asked, looking up at her again, that curious, child-like persona seeming to creep back into his demeanor somewhat. Galas was thankful for that.

"Just a bit," she said, making a very small space between gauntleted thumb and forefinger and squinting as if to see something between them.

He smiled a toothy smile and stood.

"Well, let's see what we can do about this drone. We'll need a new mech to clean up the rest of this mess," he said, presumably referring to the thousands upon thousands of Delvadr dropships raining from the heavens over the course of the day.

He stretched out his wings. The one that had previously been torn was now patched with what looked like the kind of tape used on mechanical ducts. He saw Galas looking at his handiwork. "I found it on the mantid gunship."

"The one that was violently disassembled by Betsy's demonic alter-ego?" Galas asked.

He nodded vigorously, grimacing slightly, then he flapped a couple of times, winced, and then flapped a little more as if the circulation was working back into all the necessary places. And then he launched himself out into the night. Galas breathed a deep breath. A smile of satisfaction, or maybe pride, played across her face. With a thought, Galas's face shield dropped into place. She stood and launched out into the night air above the jungle.

"You know we can't fly, right?" Raphael asked.

"Yeah, I know. Just find me a soft spot to land."

AFTERWORD

Major Rutker Novak streaked in low over the ridge, his battlespace model a scrolling terrain, gray highlighted dots littering the scene before him. Friendlies, enemies, all dead. He slowed to a crawl and dropped down farther to get a visual on the scene, in order to perform a kind of postmortem on the battlefield.

What he saw was grisly. The carnage was splayed out before him. It was a tooth-and-nail struggle, leaving no one standing. As he crested yet another small rise, he saw the smoking bodies of Novak mechs. Yes, same name. His grandfather had designed the concept, and his dad had fought in them. But that was another story.

Still upright, the mechs were clearly lifeless. They'd fried, as the Long Rifle was known to do. Even from this height and speed, he could see that the baffles were closed. The pilots had carried on fighting so long as their bodies would hold out to the heat build-up in the machine. By the carnage below, these fighters had rained down hell for a long time with stealth mode activated, even though they knew it'd cost them their lives.

Rutker choked down a lump in his throat. The pride he felt for those men, and his father by extension. The sadness he felt for their sons ... and daughters and wives. He rolled Phalanx II trans-orbital fighter right and goosed the throttle, whipping it up to Mach five in seconds. Inertial dampeners maxed out in the process. He still had two more similar scenes to check out, and then something else farther out. Much farther out.

No one knew what happened. Suddenly, the invading fleet had just started to self-destruct. Or at least that's how it appeared except for a bizarre light, like an aurora borealis, that seemed to reach up into the sky, moving from one to the next. No one had ever seen it before. Heavens knew why it'd never happened in previous attacks by the invading fleet. But it had happened this time, and that was all that mattered.

He, himself, had been engrossed in the battle, destroying dropships relentlessly, one after another. Just trying to lessen the strain on the ground troops, but there was only so much he could do. He and what remained of the EDC's aerial contingent. What was able to be rebuilt from the last invasion, anyway. That battle at the Spires had resulted in a near-total loss. He had very few friends left from those days.

He slowed again to view the battlefield, zooming into focus below him. It was very similar to what he'd seen before, only this was a much more one-sided engagement. The enemy forces were deep into the EDC emplacement.

A red dot sprang up onto his HUD just as warning beacons blared through the cockpit. The Phalanx II spiraled as Rutker fired countermeasures just fractions of a second before streaking missiles blew past him, and then exploded in the sky behind. He arced hard toward the dot on the HUD, locked on, fired, and then peeled away, dropping down dangerously close to the deck. The ground was just a blur of green below him.

He turned hard again to circle back around while the red dot faded to gray. He thought he'd caught the form of a Juggernaut heavy-mech when he'd fired, but couldn't be sure.

As he rocketed back around into the battlefield, he cut throttle, and things became clearer. Where the mech had been playing dead before ambushing him was just a flaming pile of indistinguishable wreckage now. His one-two punch of seismic then disruptor charges had overloaded the mech's reactor almost instantly. He wasn't sure what it was about that combo, but it didn't play nice with Delvadr, well, actually, *Thune* tech. The Thune weren't fighters. They just provided the weapons for everyone else to fight with. The Delvadr were huge fans. The Epriots, quite a bit less so.

Seeing nothing but gray dots, Rutker peeled out to the last scene before heading out into the uncharted territory where the arcing fire in the sky had originated. He didn't know what he'd find there, but whoever was responsible for lighting it ... was a hero.

End

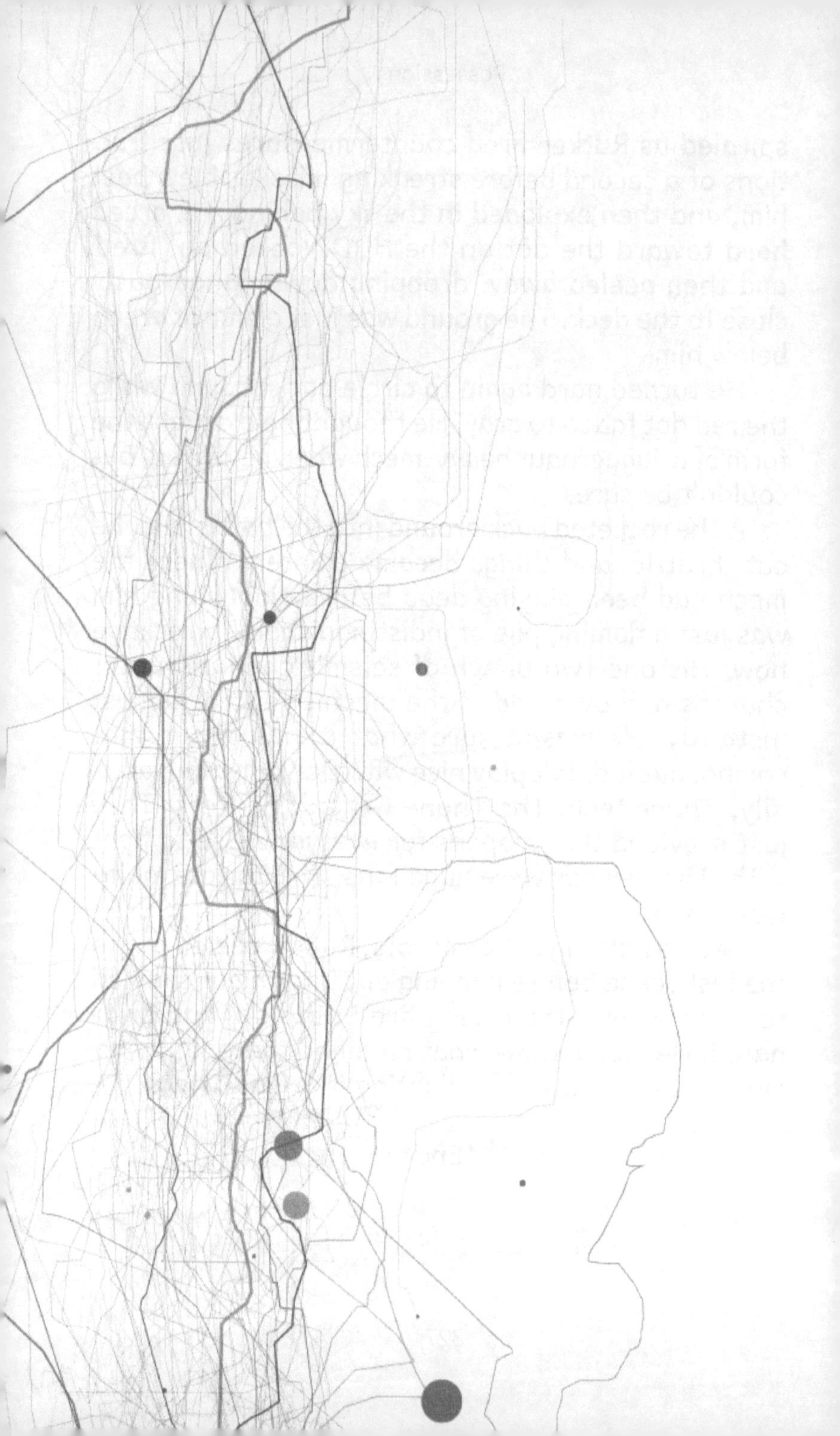

BOOK CLUB QUESTIONS

1. A core theme of Arcfire of Antiquity is vulnerability; the loss of power, security, and/or comfort. Which of these do you think meant the most to Galas, losing Betsy, her mech, or the decision to turn on the audio function of the SortieNet AI which led to the creation of Raphael as we know him?

2. Galas lives with, and even seems to enjoy, the antics of her ex-blademate and boyfriend's ghost, even when those antics present the opportunity for harm or worse. Why do you think she puts up with this behavior?

3. On the theme of vulnerability, which would you find more disconcerting; discovering that Sun-Thurr had monkeyed about in your head while you slept (such as when Galas saw the drone footage of their interaction for the first time) or having to downgrade from the awesome firepower of a 40-ton mech to swimming buck naked through underwater ruins with terrifyingly mutated fish creatures prowling the shadows?

4. Why do you think the prior race left and never returned?

5. In Braex, the city AI had gone insane from boredom and loneliness. Do you think it's possible for an AI to become sentient or go insane? Why?

6. The Deathhounds forfeit their souls in order to evade death. If you had to choose death or a life of forced labor that merely staves off increased suffering, which would you choose?

7. It's a bleak idea, but how different is this Deathhound system of economy from our own existence? Provide an example of why it is or isn't from your own life (or someone you're close to).

8. Galas struggles with guilt over losing her daughter, and probably PTSD. What do you think Galas would say to her if she found her now that she's in her teens?

9. What do you think Galas's daughter, Seraph, would have to say to her if they met accidentally?

10. How would you feel if you discovered that your long-lost parent was a war hero who may have saved the planet but had in some way abandoned you as a child? What would you say to them if you met them on the street?

11. Jinnbo birthed his own evil twin and had to fight him, not just for survival, but so that an evil version of himself would not corrupt his lineage and culture. If you had to battle a version of yourself that embodied your most vile and depraved characteristics, who would win? If you answered, "the bad version," why?

AUTHOR BIO

Eric's base camp is at the foot of the oft-smoldering Sierra Nevada in NorCal where he enjoys surfing, snowboarding & mountain biking with his wife and three adult sons. You can check out excerpts for upcoming projects at his author page: enlard-author.weebly.com.

On his nightstand, The Hitchhiker's Guide to the Galaxy by Douglas Adams, The Martian by Andy Weir, any one of the Muderbot Diaries books by Martha Wells or the Arcane Casebook series by Dan Willis. There's some Stephen King stuff too.

More books from 4 Horsemen Publications

SciFi

Brandon Hill & Terence Pegasus
Between the Devil and the Dark
Wrath & Redemption

C.K. Westbrook
The Shooting
The Collision
The Judgment

Nick Savage
Us Of Legendary Gods
So We Stay Hidden
The West Haven Undead

PC Nottingham
Mummified Moon
Severed Squadron

T.S. Simons
Project Hemisphere
The Space Between
Infinity
Circle of Protection
Sessrúmnir
The 45th Parallel
Orenda

Ty Carlson
The Bench
The Favorite
The Shadowless

Discover more at
4HorsemenPublications.com